# KARLA

Or *The Weight Liftress*

*by*

# BOB ROSS

STEPHEN F. AUSTIN STATE UNIVERSITY PRESS

Stephen F. Austin State University Press
P.O. Box 13007 SFA Station
Nacogdoches, Texas 75962
sfapress@sfasu.edu
www.sfasu.edu/sfapress

Managing Editor: Kimberly Verhines
Editorial Assistants: Katt Noble and Meredith Janning
Distributed by Texas A&M Consortium
www.tamupress.com

ISBN: 978-1-62288-935-8
FIRST EDITION

# CONTENTS

KARLA     5

DUST     62

GERARD     83

SHAME     104

ROOM NINETEEN     174

ABOUT THE AUTHOR     195

# Karla

## One

KARLA ČAPEK WAS JUST A WILD AWKWARD sunburned chit of a little girl when her father—a musician and "a tall dark handsome Slovak son of a bitch," her mother would say when she spoke of him—left his family in Crete, Nebraska, for Australia. Maybe he'd found the better life or maybe he hadn't; they had no way of knowing, since they never heard from him again. He left behind a photograph and his instrument, a so-called "hammered dulcimer." (According to her mom, whenever he went out carrying it, he came home hammered.) Karla's mother worked in a garment factory in the daytime and at a tavern in the evenings, and until she was twelve, Karla had the care of her younger brother Boris. Boris was a musical genius, a prodigy, and he was taken from them at a young age and placed with relatives in New York, where he could study the violin. His absence left Karla to spend summer days alone, and she suffered much from loneliness until she discovered baseball. She played sandlot ball with boys who made up the Junior Legion team; though she never got to play in uniform under the lights, she could catch and throw and run the bases and hit the boys' best pitches. But, at the time when Karla grew up, just before the Vietnam war, girls were not enlisted to play Junior Legion ball. Boys couldn't share the locker room with a girl, somebody said, though there were no lockers at the ballfield in Crete.

Those same boys who couldn't "share the locker room" shared Karla. This started at a party in the woods, where they got her drunk on Pabst Blue Ribbon beer and challenged her to enter their peeing contest. She impressed them all by bending far backwards and peeing over the hood of a car, and afterward they took her aside by turns and used her body without shame, even though she had not yet reached puberty. The boys who performed this rape had names like Anderson and Price and Sanders and were destined to populate the Homecoming court and go on to join fraternities in college. A precedent was set, and it became a condition of her playing baseball that she allow the older boys to use her sexually. She got no pleasure, but she had nobody to protect her and she needed the game. Karla needed physical activity the way a grebe needs water; she could not breathe, she felt, if she could not run. One of the players must have confessed, because one day her mother spoke to her. "The priest says you'd better stop doing what you're doing," she said. "You know what I mean." Karla knew exactly what she meant: no more baseball forever. To illustrate, her mother made Karla buy a ten-pound sack of flour and lug it around on her hip for an entire day.

Already taller than most boys her age, Karla watched her girl peers shoot up around her and start to put on female width and padding. They exchanged knowing looks and whispered about Kotex, and then a couple of them disappeared from school. Karla felt more isolated than ever. Then one day— it seemed to happen overnight—her body transformed into this thing that she barely recognized. It grew, and grew, and grew, and grew, until she imagined her classmates must draw back from her in alarm. She went from a shrill and active beanpole, already taller than some grown women, to a looming luxurious deep-voiced phenomenon with great flopping whopping breasts and hips like the buttresses of a cathedral and, if she wasn't extra careful to be clean, a fragrance rivaling the dog-food cannery on the far side of town. The boys who'd once used her as a sort of sexual sidehorse now laughed at her awkward figure and home-sewn skirts; they gave their attention to girls of more appropriate breeding, and Karla lost her exuberance and pulled back into herself, silent, thoughtful, and, if she only knew it, angry. When, as did happen occasionally, some equally awkward and misfit boy came up to her and offered a mumble of fellowship, her towering need and loneliness would scare him away.

Adolescent girls did not play high-school baseball, so the game that she loved was not an option. Shackled to her schoolbooks during the fall and winter, thighs wedged under desks that never fit, she found a reprieve on the basketball court. As a sport for young women, basketball was "new" after having been suppressed for sixty years. The form it took was six-on-six basketball; each team of six girls was split into two groups, three girls to provide the offense on their half of the court and three to defend the opponents' half. Karla was good at either end, but she got to move more on offense, and she enjoyed knocking prettier girls down. Following her disastrous growth spurt—it was more of an eruption—she was so clumsy that she could barely dribble the ball, but her height and strength and her readiness to do battle made her a presence on the court. She could put the ball in the basket from a distance of three or four feet, and if she missed she usually got her own rebound.

During her junior year, her high school team won a tournament and went to play in the six-on-six finals at Kearney. Karla played hard and scored most of her team's points, but her team was eliminated and no notice was taken of her. It was at this tournament where she fell in love with a pale-haired boy named Michael.

As Karla was a budding athlete, Michael was a boy aesthete. He was there to play his trumpet in the pep band, though he disdained raucous music and people jumping up and screaming. To impress his male peers, he made a bet that he would seduce Karla, and he did so under the diving board in the pool at the motel where the students who made the trip were staying. The witnesses to the bet were at the edge of the pool cheering them on, but Karla's experience had been such that this did not seem strange. She concentrated on trying to keep the much smaller Michael from drowning, and was taken by surprise by her very first orgasm. The watching boys all hooted, and a couple of them jumped in clothes and all to have a turn, but she stayed with her legs wrapped around Michael, lost in his blue eyes.

Begun in circumstances some would call shameful, their love stayed fresh for weeks, then months. Seeing them together supplied their classmates with cheap amusement: the hugely magnificent Karla, still clumsy in her outsized form, walking carefully beside the delicate Michael, holding his pale salamander digits with two fingers. For his part, Michael enjoyed sex restricted only by convenience—to erase the notoriety of the diving-board episode, they now required privacy—and he enjoyed having one more reason to hold his fellow students in contempt. He excelled his peers at all mental activities, puzzles, chess and other board games, mathematics, music, and drawing, and if he was not so very good at any of them, it was not a deficiency that a moonstruck girl would notice. She loved his lofty talk and gentle hands, and his smallish penis that felt like a caress.

She devoted herself to him, coddled his moods and forgave his tantrums; she soothed him and clowned for him and petted his balls when he grew sulky. Because he liked classical music, she listened to records with him, swaying her big handsome head and tapping her feet in all the wrong places. Because he loved chess, she learned the names of all the pieces and their moves, and said "mm" and "mm-hmm" and "oh!" when one of his knights galloped over an opponent's hapless queen. Because he did so well in mathematics, she tried a little harder to learn her algebra and managed to actually learn a little of it, which amazed her as much as her orgasm under the diving board. Michael liked to sit quietly and study, so she spent more time doing her homework; it was a pretext for being near him, and she hardly noticed when her grades went from Cs and Ds to Bs sprinkled with the occasional A. Because he wrote poetry, she tried to read the stuff, and never realized that after two months she'd read more of it than he had.

Karla gave up stealing her mother's beer, drinking in front of the TV and brooding on her misfortunes. Still, when Michael was unavailable she felt glum and lonely, and after the snow melted off the driveways and outdoor basketball courts, she was out pounding the basketball and shooting hoops. Her junior year of school passed into summer, and because she was too grown up for sandlot baseball, she practiced basketball by herself at a playground near her home, sometimes staying out after dark or in the rain.

KEARNEY STATE TEACHER'S COLLEGE WAS an hour's travel from the town where Karla and Michael grew up, but the distance was measured in more than asphalt miles. Affiliated with one of the Midwest's land-grant universities, Kearney State was open to any girl who could get herself there, but working-class students faced an obstacle in that the city of Kearney was known to be a terrible job market. Jobs were scarce, college-age applicants were plentiful, and employers were accustomed to paying miserly wages. Karla understood that if Michael continued his education and she did not, she would be left behind and abandoned. She needed to get into college somehow, and she heard about a female coach at Kearney State who was pushing to expand women's athletic programs. For Karla, a girl with no money, skills, or family connections, an athletic scholarship could be a key to survival, so to see if she could get any useful pointers, Karla made an appointment with her high school's guidance counselor, a man so dense that the only teaching assignment he could handle was Driver's Ed. (He also gave the once-a-year lecture on venereal diseases. The students always found this interesting, though it was woefully short on specifics of how to catch one.)

She found the man sitting at his desk, smoking a cigarette and leafing through a copy of *Field & Stream*. Karla introduced herself and explained who she was and that she hoped to obtain an athletic scholarship. He placed the magazine on his desk protector, still open to the page he'd been studying. "What are your plans after graduation?"

"Plans?" Karla tried to focus on the guidance counselor's shaved head rather than on the large-mouthed bass on the cover of his magazine. When she tried to look him in the eyes, she found them to be locked on her boobs. Somebody had given him a list of questions, and he was asking them.

"You know. Work," the man said, rubbing his jaw. "Have you thought about construction?" He poked at the magazine's spine with his forefinger, pressing it down and letting it spring back up.

"What would I do in construction?" Karla was worried about her period, which was a couple of days late. She and Michael took careful precautions, but you never knew. Those sperms were tricky. "I just told you, I want to go to college."

"A forklift? Lots of women are driving forklifts these days."

"Forklifts are for warehousing," Karla said. "Shipping and receiving. They're not used much in construction. What do you know about women's athletics at Kearney State?"

"Well, if you've got all the answers," the counselor said. His head was pink and glossy at the front, darker where it was shaved close along the sides. He glanced down at his magazine, impatient to get back to his article.

"My boyfriend is getting an academic scholarship to the University," Karla said. "Maybe I'll go there someday, but right now I think I'd have better luck at Kearney State. It would help if I can get on a team. They give scholarships, don't they?"

"What about the military?" the counselor said. "I myself served during the Korean War. I had an important desk in Tokyo, where I spoke to General MacArthur every morning. 'Good morning, General,' I'd say. I always saluted, too. I had a darned good salute in those days. Everybody always complimented me on my salute." He poked the magazine, and the bass on the cover winked at Karla.

"I could always work and take some classes," Karla said, "but to keep up, I need to go full time. My grades aren't good enough for an academic scholarship, but I'm tall and willing to practice hard. I need to find out if they have scholarships for the women's basketball team."

"A women's basketball team at the University! You don't say. What'll they think of next?" He turned his head to glance out the window at a giggle of Junior High girls who were walking by.

"Not the University. Kearney State. They have a women's team at the college here in Crete, but I don't want to go there." The city had a small college on the outskirts, devoted to passing along the East Coast fuckwads whose parents sent them west to get rid of them. They were notorious for crashing their Jaguars and Alpha Romeos, and the local junkyards were a gold mine of expensive wrecks.

"Well, good luck in whatever you decide," the counselor said. He stood up and offered her a sticky handshake. "Let me know if you need a letter of recommendation. I'll have the principal's secretary type one up for you." He sank down into his chair and Karla turned to leave. When she glanced back, the cover photo of the bass obscured his face. It was jumping straight up out of the water, mouth agape to seize a red-and-white-striped lure that looked like nothing to eat that a bass ever saw.

The most trying part of Karla's teenage life was to balance two relationships, one of them with her mother and the other with Michael. Her mother would say of Michael, "That boy is using you. You're going to find out one day that he's as empty as the inside of a blown-up popcorn bag." Karla knew this to not be true—Michael had feelings, he had ideas, he had a heart—but she felt that in defending him she would end up defending herself, which would be a mistake. For his part, Michael spoke of her mother with contempt. "She has the vocabulary of a fifth-grader," he said. "She drinks a lot. She doesn't read or watch the news. She says 'dese' and 'dose' and 'tree' instead of 'three'."

Michael's parents (he still had two of them) were Episcopal, not Catholic, and they could afford to send him to school in fashionable clothing. They did not like Karla, but they tolerated her. They felt their son would soon lose interest in her, and until then she would keep off smaller and sneakier females who might lead him from the upward path to distinction and off into the underbrush of matrimony. If the young couple had shown signs of wanting to get married, there would've been a battle, but Michael passed up this chance to defy his parents (he needed their money) and Karla had other worries. She intended to lift her grade average to an acceptable range, and she intended to perform on the basketball court. Karla understood that her happiness was precarious. When she and Michael were together, she doted on him more than ever. When they were apart, she either studied or practiced, dribbling the ball as if to pound holes in the pavement.

Karla's basketball skills had sharpened over the summer. She could dribble the basketball without bouncing it off her toes, and she could pivot and shoot, using her butt and elbows to clear space for herself. If she decided to go after a rebound, no one else would be likely to get it, and she could use her height to pass the ball out to a better shooter. All in all, she felt she could be a major asset to the team, even though she disliked the girls who were on it.

She had stopped getting taller and was recovering her coordination. The head coach noticed her during the first scrimmage at the beginning of tryouts, after an hour and a half of calisthenics, tests, and laps around the gym. Someone tried a shot and missed, there was a scramble underneath the basket, and *crunch!* went the cartilage; a blonde girl came trotting to the sideline with a bloody nose, and there stood Karla with the ball high above her head. She pivoted, took an awkward step, and hooked it through the basket, and when the coach got his breath back, he blew five sharp blasts on his whistle. "Hey, you!" he yelled. "Forty-four! Get your big ass over here!"

He gave the blonde girl a pat where he shouldn't have and sent her and another girl back in. The two teams continued to play, but he had no eyes for them. Karla stood before him, looking at the floor. The coach scratched his close-cropped gray head and blew his veiny cheeks in and out. "What the hell have you been doing?"

Karla didn't speak because she didn't know what to say. Maybe he'd found out about the ball she had stolen to practice with over the summer. She waited for him to make an accusation.

"You've been practicing," he said in tones of wonder.

"I didn't swipe that basketball," she said. "It must've been Julie."

"I don't know what you're talking about," he said. "Listen, I want you to show me that hook shot again. Take a ball and go over there on the other court."

"Sure," Karla said. She picked up a basketball one-handed and walked over to the far court. The assistant coach in charge of the girls' team, a tall young woman who taught Geometry, came up to him, and together they watched the big girl bounce the ball. She performed self-consciously at first, missing a few times and looking quizzically over at them. After a while she shrugged and began hooking them through. The next time she missed, she collected the rebound and did a baseline reverse layup. She tripped over her own sneakers as if she might fall down; the floor shook, but the ball went in.

"Did you see that?" asked the old coach. "What do you think?"

"She's rough and she's clumsy," the assistant said. "She'll be lucky if she makes it through the first quarter. She'll get herself thrown out of the game."

The coach looked down at the floor, and his ears turned pink. He shook his booze-blotched, gray and craggy head. "That may be, that may be," he said with a crooked smile. "But won't it be one hell of a first quarter, though!"

A boy named Frank Václavik had shoulders a little narrower than a barn door and pimples the size of gooseberries. He could have played on any basketball team in the state except for one small catch: he couldn't read. Frank was ambidextrous, couldn't tell right from left (although he could tell you east, south, west, and north with no trouble) and he was so dyslexic that he could only recognize a STOP sign because it had eight corners. He was forever ineligible due to failing grades, but the boys' coach let him assist the student manager so he could practice with the team. The girls' coach borrowed Frank for an hour each afternoon, and he and Karla banged away at one another, one-on-one, underneath the basket. Frank was unreflectively vengeful, and if she elbowed him he elbowed her in return; if she happened to knock him down, she, too, would soon go sprawling. After the bruises and floor burns had accumulated for a couple of weeks, Karla was ready to soften her style of play. She asked to scrimmage with the girls again.

"Look at my knees," she told the assistant coach. "I'm all over bruises. If he pinches my butt one more time, I'm going to slug him."

Frank went with a cheerful shrug back to carrying towels and water. He grinned at Karla as he was leaving. "Most fun I've had all year," he said.

That winter, Karla's six-on-six team was undefeated. As far as Karla's play went, the very first game was typical. She only made it through two quarters before fouling out, but while she was in, she scored sixteen points and dominated the rebounding, and sent an opposing player to the bench with a sprained wrist. The other team never came out of shock.

Michael watched from the stands; sitting in the pep band with his fellow male non-athletes, he cheered when the other boys cheered and laughed when they laughed. When the concert band was practicing, Michael played first trumpet, and the band director was much taken with him. Two of the arrangements the pep band played were his own.

THERE WERE NO STATE-WIDE track-and-field championships for girls, but Karla set a district record at putting the shot and took third in the discus-throwing competition. Shortly afterward, she was offered an athletic scholarship to Kearney State. No one who had seen her play basketball in the fall was surprised. There was an awards ceremony during graduation week where the scholarships were announced, and the assistant coach came over afterward to speak to her. "You're a terrific girl," she said. "You're going to go places. Are your parents here tonight? I want to congratulate them."

"My mom was planning to come," Karla said, "but the afternoon bartender got the flu. She had to go straight from work and take over."

"Well, she's raised a hard-working daughter," the assistant coach said. "I know you'll be successful at Kearney. I'll expect to hear from you."

Later that same night she and Michael lay in one another's arms, in a motel on the outskirts of Milford, Nebraska, a little town founded by Mennonites where drinking and dancing and movies were prohibited. "Michael," she whispered, her black eyes shining with wonder, "can you believe it? I'll be going to college. I wonder what I'll study. Maybe history, or geography, or navigation. Maybe I'll be a doctor! I'll develop a new technique, taking out tonsils with my tongue. You'll be my patient, and we'll go all around the world, giving demonstrations at famous hospitals. Maybe we'll even get as far as Australia."

Michael stirred. He had fallen asleep. "Australia!" he said. "You don't even know where it is. It's a good thing you're only going to Teachers' College."

"I do, too, know where Australia is," she said. "They have a Teachers' College at the University. Maybe you should enroll in it."

"Certainly not," he said. "I might become a composer or an atomic physicist, but I won't be enrolling in Teachers' College."

"I want to go wherever you go," she said, mouthing his silky hair.

"Go to sleep, then. That's where I'm going."

"I can't. I'm too excited. Michael, make love to me."

"We did that already. Now go to sleep."

"Come on, Michael. One more time. You can do it, buddy."

"All right. But then you have to leave me alone."

KARLA'S FIRST WEEK AT KEARNEY STATE did not go well. Freshman girls were required to live in a dormitory, and dorm life felt like prison life to Karla. The rooms were tiny, and she got stuck with a roommate who gabbed incessantly with other girls but who barely spoke to her. The bathroom was down the hall; the communal shower was wide-open and always cold, and the girls she saw there seemed to be about half her size. Worst of all was the telephone situation. A switchboard operator on the ground floor controlled the telephones, one phone per floor, so that if Karla wanted to phone Michael in Lincoln, she had to make an appointment. If she went out, she had to be back in the dorm by ten o'clock.

Of her twelve years of public education, Karla had spent a good half gazing out the window. She must've learned something because she had been passed through, but she couldn't remember much of it. Consequently terrified, she attacked her studies with a frantic concentration, taking notes and working the exercises, reading and re-reading the assigned text. This set her apart from the other girls, who focused on getting drunk each weekend and, during the week, on packing their weekend schedules with dates. Added to this was her training for the basketball team, which involved drills and exercises she had never heard of, and running, running, running. Karla was tall and strong as expected, but she was no longer a gangly young speedster. The college coach did not show any special liking for her, and the favored style of play was not Karla's knock-them-all-out-of-the-way-and-get-the-ball style. It involved taking up certain positions, knowing when to switch off on both offense and defense. Karla was accustomed to dominating the offense by herself, and could not get used to the idea of playing defense, or switching off, or counting on other girls to do much of anything.

"You have to trust the other players," the coach said. To which Karla's response was, "Who? Them?"

To make it worse, women's basketball was changing. Sometimes they practiced six-on-six, a game at which Karla excelled; at other times they played men's style, five-on-five, where each player had to play at both ends of the court. Karla played well at either end once she arrived beneath the basket, but getting quickly from end to end was a hardship.

## Two

FOR THE FIRST ROUND OF EXAMS, Karla over-prepped and gave herself a ripping migraine. The pain was like nothing she'd experienced; she only got out of bed to put a washcloth between her teeth to prevent them from touching. She kept her eyes squeezed shut against the light, and wept, and suffered. Finally she got her roommate to call her old friend Frank, who had been passed on through high school with a certificate and was now failing remedial courses at Kearney State. Frank managed to send her up some double-strength aspirin. The pills helped a little, and she went to sleep and slept the clock around.

The morning after her migraine, Karla awoke light-headed. Remission from the pain made her feel drunk, but the feeling went beyond that. It was as if her secret self had said, "All right. I quit. We're not beating this poor pony any more," and she had acquiesced to a sort of honeymoon, where she could pay attention to her step on the stairs and the particles of sunlight streaming through the windows. She still had exams to take, but they could wait.

She loaded her breakfast tray with everything available. Institutional scrambled eggs had never smelled so good; apple jelly in packets and steam-table toast made her mouth water and her eyes mist over, and a slightly-green banana and the weak but acrid coffee with bubbles of unrinsed detergent looked like moly and ambrosia. She was late and the tables were mostly empty, so that she could've sat anywhere, but her attention was drawn to a short and sturdily-built girl with straight brown hair, staring hopelessly with gray-green eyes at a textbook with a canvas cover.

"Mind if I sit down?"

The girl looked up. "No. I mean yes, please sit." She closed the book on her finger. "Don't you normally eat with the jocks?"

Karla put down her tray and claimed a seat. "I do," she said. Scholarship athletes had their own table on the other side of the cafeteria. "I feel lazy this morning. I don't want to walk over there."

"There's something about you," the girl said. She studied Karla's face. "You look like you just had sex with a tribe of pygmies and wore them all down to the nubs."

Karla laughed. "No such luck," she said. "I just got over a migraine headache. I never had one before. The pain was amazing, but now I feel so good that it was almost worth it. Like I found somebody's billfold with a million bucks."

"Of course, you would turn it in to Lost and Found."

"Of course, I would. What's that you're studying?"

"It's History. I have a test tomorrow, but all I can remember is that Charlemagne was seven feet tall and could leap in full armor onto the back of his horse, and that William the Conqueror's original name was William the Bastard of Normandy."

"I have a bunch of tests, too. In fact, I'm missing an exam right now."

"You seem strangely unconcerned."

"It's that migraine," Karla said. "It's like a drug or something. I feel like nothing bad could happen to me today. You ought to try one sometime."

"I'd love to," the girl said glumly, "but I can't afford to miss any exams."

Karla took a forkful of eggs. Her mouth filled with saliva, but she suddenly couldn't swallow. She finally spit the eggs into a paper napkin. "I can't either," she said. "But for some reason I just can't seem to worry about it." She tried a sip of the vile coffee. It went down, but only with difficulty. "I thought I was hungry," she said. "Now I can't eat. I don't know what is wrong with me."

"You're strung out," the other girl said. "You're coming down off a high. Did you take anything for your migraine?"

"A friend of mine sent up some pills."

"Give it a little time," the girl said. "You'll be all right. My name is Judy, by the way."

"I'm Karla. I'm here at Kearney State Teachers' College because everyone thinks I'm stupid. Are you a History major?"

"Music and Art," the girl said. "I'm hoping to combine the two. Sort of like Scriabin."

"Scriabin? Is it a rock band?"

"Scriabin was a Russian composer. He died of a cancer on his lip. He saw musical notes as colors. People thought he was crazy."

Karla tried another sip of coffee and spat it back into the cup. "All of a sudden I don't feel good," she said.

"Not pregnant, are you?"

"No," Karla said. "I'm definitely not pregnant."

"I know where you can get an abortion. If you need one."

Judy McDonough came from a town even smaller than Crete, far up in the Nebraska hinterlands next to South Dakota. Her father was a rancher, but her grandfather on her mother's side was an oboist in the Omaha Symphony Orchestra. "My brother is a violinist," Karla volunteered. "He's in New York, studying."

"Is he gay?"

"I suppose he's happy. He doesn't jump around or anything."

"I mean, is he homosexual?"

"'Gay' means 'homosexual'? What do they have to be gay about?"

"I haven't the foggiest idea," Judy said. She glanced up from her textbook and smiled. "You know what? I think we're going to be friends."

The two girls left the cafeteria together and began walking in the direction of the library. It was the first week in October; the bluegrass lawns were green underneath fallen leaves, but flocks of tiny birds were busy in the bushes, squabbling and making quick short anxious flights. The reddish sun warmed the eastern and southern faces of the red-brick buildings. The sky, hazy toward the horizons, was brilliant overhead, blue like swimming pools seen from below the clouds, blue like the irises of Michael's poetic eyes.

Students moved in groups of four or five, hurrying in different directions. For the first time since she'd arrived at that strange place, the faces of her fellow Kearney Staters came alive for Karla. Here was a tall young man looking much like pimply Frank, wearing patched green pants and a cheap but gaudy jacket, rushing along in a great worry with a tattered book under his arm. Over there were three girls looking healthy and wealthy, smart in the fashion sense of the word, probably discussing a fourth girl's clothing, looks, and prospects. At the intersection of two walkways, two young men were engaged in an angry dispute. "They're arguing over which brand of beer gives you the worst hangover," Judy said.

"Everything seems beautiful this morning," Karla said. She glanced down at Judy, and her glance conveyed amazement and understanding. "Do you know, I have been so scared of these people."

Judy smiled. "I should walk with you more often," she said.

The Saturday following her headache, Karla sat with Michael in the lounge at the Student Union. A football game was in progress, and cheering could be heard in the distance. Michael had come down from Lincoln for sex and sympathy; they had done that, and now they were quiet. Michael was studying, and Karla had a book in front of her, but she was mostly gazing around her, at the institutional furniture and the paintings on the walls and the conical copper fireplace that was never lit. The paintings were by present and former art teachers, vivid but not too challenging. "Michael," she said suddenly, "I'm in trouble."

At the University, Michael was expanding his horizons, letting his hair grow long and reading books like Thomas Merton's *Seven-Story Mountain*. His mother had knitted him sweaters in a variety of colors, but the only sweater he would wear was brown and smelled like a sheep. He looked up in alarm. "You mean—?"

His terror did not go unnoticed. "No, I don't *mean*," she said. "I don't fit in at college. I feel like I want to quit."

"You can't quit. What will you do, go back to Crete and work in the bra factory?"

"It would be easier than what I'm doing now. I'm starting to hate basketball. Michael, I want to come to Lincoln and be with you."

"There are no jobs in Lincoln. You'd better stay in Kearney. Maybe after a year you can transfer."

"And what will you be doing in a year? You'll have forgotten me."

Michael closed the book on his finger and looked her in the eyes. "I will never forget you," he said.

"Liar," Karla said. "It's happening already."

Karla did not quit college because she was not a quitting person. She studied and played basketball and screwed Michael on the weekends. On those weekends when he failed to appear, she sometimes went to a movie with Judy McDonough, but there wasn't much to do in Kearney other than drive to Kansas and get drunk on three-two beer. It took more than one pitcher of three-two beer just to get a satisfactory buzz on, and Karla didn't dare put on weight because of her scholarship. She did the driving (in Judy's car) and let Judy do most of the drinking.

THE DIRECTOR OF WOMEN'S ATHLETIC programs at Kearney State was smart, aggressive, and a visionary, but one miracle she could not perform was to drum up competition. Few small colleges anywhere had women's basketball teams, and fewer still had teams that played by the old six-on-six rules. Karla's team had to resort to playing most of their games against high school teams, one of which, from across the Missouri over in Iowa, humiliated them. They played their final game of the year against the University of Nebraska's team. The University's team played by the men's rules, five-on-five, and Karla's team had to adapt. Nevertheless they managed to win a close game, and Karla scored the winning basket over the University's star player. Following the game, the opposing coach came over to congratulate Karla. "You pounded us under the basket," she said, and handed Karla a business card. "Call my secretary with your contact information."

"Really? My boyfriend goes to the University." Karla glanced over at her own coach, who gave her a rueful smile.

"That's great," the University coach said. "I hope he deserves you."

A minute later, Karla found herself walking to the locker room next to the Kearney State coach. "Imagine a women's basketball coach having a secretary," she said.

"Stranger things have occurred," her coach replied. "Maybe a woman will be President someday."

"If it happens, she'll still be making the coffee."

Basketball season was over, but Karla's duties were not. Since she was on the payroll, so to speak, her coach insisted that she train for track-and-field events, even though no formal competition was available. So, that spring, Karla ran around the track and lifted weights with the men. She heaved the shot and threw the discus, and left unofficial marks in the record book that lasted for decades.

Her most memorable achievement during the spring semester was at a kegger following a crane-watching party. One of the football players, a tailback who weighed one-sixty, stiffened his body and allowed Karla to lift him above her head. After she'd put him down, Judy said to her, "You know, that tailback guy weighs twenty pounds more that Michael."

"Oh, I couldn't do that to Michael," Karla said. "Michael would kill me."

She remembered to call the number on the Nebraska coach's business card, and was offered a scholarship to play on the University team. The Kearney State coach practically forced her to accept the offer. Her friend Judy McDonough was transferring to the University too, so she would at least know somebody when she got there. Of course, there was Michael, but he somehow didn't figure in. If she had to depend on Michael, she'd be lonely.

# Three

KARLA SPENT THE FIRST SUMMER of her college life back home with her mother in Crete. Everything and nothing had changed; Crete now seemed like a small town with small-town ideas, and the summer days were stifling and monotonous. The dog-food cannery stank. She worked days at the tavern and re-studied her Kearney homework nights. The corn grew tall and put out tassels. Michael stayed in Lincoln.

Her friend Judy had gotten herself a Lincoln apartment (though it went against the rules for freshmen, which they technically were) and Karla envisioned the three of them living together, since there was plenty of room. Her new coach had other ideas. Scholarship athletes at the U were told what they could eat and where they could live and when to get out of bed in the morning. This discipline paid off in a successful football program, and student athletes did well academically, even though half of them were from places like Steubenville, Ohio, where the main thing they'd learned in high school was that they didn't want to work in a steel mill. The regimentation grated on everyone, but as Karla learned the first week after she moved in, there was a healthy international flavor in the athletes' dorms. She met runners from Somalia, gymnasts from Taiwan, and a Hungarian on the swim team who spoke five languages and majored in mathematics. The female basketballers were either quick and angry as bees or tall and agile as antelopes. Karla knew right away that she wasn't going to fit in, with her deliberate style and her bullish ways under the basket.

She tried explaining her worries to Michael one night as they were studying together in the student union. After she had talked for five minutes, he marked his place and looked up. "What were you saying?"

"Oh, nothing," she replied. "I'm going to be cut from the basketball team, is all. I'm too slow to play five-on-five. Everybody runs right by me."

He went back to his book. "You won't miss it, will you? Last year you were always telling me how your ankles hurt."

"Michael! I'll lose my scholarship, you dodo. I'll have to drop out of school."

"Well. You're not exactly the scholarly type."

"But I'll have to get a job, Michael. I'll probably move back to Crete. I won't see you any more." Tears began to form in the corners of her bright black eyes.

"Oh. That." He reached across and took her hand as if he were picking up a fish. "Listen, don't worry. Something will turn up." He removed his hand from hers to turn the page. Karla frowned and tried to focus on her book. A warning bell rang for the women's curfew, and she began to pack up to leave.

"Aren't you going to walk me to my dorm?"

"Why? Afraid you might be molested?"

Karla sighed. "With you, I'm more afraid that I won't be."

"Won't be what?"

"Never mind." She stood for a moment, backpack in hand. "Michael," she said. "Please look at me."

He looked up. "What?"

"Whatever you do, don't get drafted. You won't survive boot camp."

Basketball practice had begun in earnest, and the pace was vicious. Karla survived the first round of cuts, but the team had to be trimmed to thirteen players, and of the fifteen remaining girls, Karla was the slowest. The coach, a tall spare woman in her thirties whose hair was already iron-gray, was not encouraging, but Karla worked hard and held on, starving herself to lose body fat and running extra miles after practice. She also did an hour of lifting to improve her strength, though the weight rooms, like the jocks' dormitory, were guarded territory.

The Athletic Department had two weight-training rooms deep in the bowels of Memorial Stadium. One was supposed to be for the football team, but Karla trained there whenever she could, not because she liked large grunting men or the smell of their sweat, but because their equipment was up-to-date. She was doing curls one afternoon when she heard a muffled clink and a gasp and looked around to see who was in trouble. A cross-country runner, who like her had sneaked into the wrong weight room, had tried to press too much weight without a spotter. He lay flat on the bench, straining, unable to set the bar back up on the rack.

Karla put down her weights and went over to help. She lifted the bar off him and set it on the mat beside the bench, and reached down to help the man sit up. He mumbled something that sounded more like a curse than a thank-you and buried his hot face in a towel. She was reminded of those boys in Crete who used to laugh until she smacked the baseball over their heads. Then they'd given her looks that bordered on hatred.

Others had arrived at the scene of the small emergency. One of them was Karla's basketball coach; with her was a short and squatty woman whose closest resemblance to a famous person was to the actor Ernest Borgnine. "That bar belongs on the rack," she said to Karla. "Set it back up there." Karla did as she was told, even though, now that the crisis had passed, the bar of weights felt heavy. "Now lift it off and set it on the floor." Karla complied. "Now set it on the rack again." The squatty woman looked Karla up and down, then turned to glance at the basketball coach. "So, this one is yours?"

"Please, ma'am, I was not just goofing around," Karla said. "That runner was going to get his Adam's apple crushed."

"Quiet. You can talk when I'm addressing you," the squatty woman said.

"She's here on a basketball scholarship, at least for the time being," Karla's coach said. "Do you think you can use her?"

"She deadlifted two hundred and thirty pounds, with no warmup and no technique." The squatty woman turned to Karla. "You," she said. "Do you have any soreness? Stomach feel OK? How about your butthole? Cramps or anything?"

"I'm fine." Karla glanced at her coach. "I'm not in trouble, am I? I was only trying to help."

"No trouble." The basketball coach smiled. "You'd better not lift any more today. Do an easy lap around the track and some stretches." Karla's coach turned to the shorter woman. "Well, Ruby, were you going to suggest something?"

"I have five women on my team. Not one of them can do what she just did." Karla caught a sidelong look—they were waiting for her to leave—and, with a glance behind her, lumbered off down the indoor track. As she kicked her legs out forward and lengthened her stride, she felt a little tightness in her thighs but nothing amiss with her butthole. She finished her lap and peeked in at the door of the weight room, where the two coaches were still negotiating. She ran another lap, pounding out the steps. The freedom of the indoor track felt better than the overheated weight room, but it appeared that, if the squatty woman had her way, the weight room was to be her fate.

KARLA'S CAREER AS A COLLEGE basketball player came to an end. She survived the initial cut, and some promising players couldn't take the schedule and dropped out, but the squad was still over the limit. At the end of practice on the last day before the season started, the coach called her over and placed a hand on her shoulder. "Karla," she said, "I'm sorry. I know how badly you wanted to play."

Karla sat down on the bottom row of the bleachers. She held her chin in her hands and stared off across the floor. "Not really," she said.

"But you've worked so hard," the older woman said. "I've never had a player who worked harder than you."

"It's my scholarship." Karla pushed at a spot on the floor with her toe. "Now I'll have to go home."

"Well," said the coach, putting a strand of her iron-colored hair in her mouth and chewing on it. She sat down next to Karla. "First of all, your tuition is paid for the semester. Same is true for your room in the dormitory. A big girl like you has to eat, I know, but I think we can slip you in. If they revoke your cafeteria ticket, come to me and I'll see that something is done. There's no reason for you to leave before the end of the fall semester, and I think we can find you something for the spring semester as well."

"What about next year?" Karla's words came out flat, more like an accusation than a question.

"How are your grades?"

Karla managed a smile. "I'm no Einstein, but I'm passing my courses."

"No chance for an academic scholarship, I suppose," the coach said. "I could red-shirt you, but you're just not quick enough for our style of play, and I can't see that you'll be much quicker in another year. It's not something you can help. And, our funds are limited. Next year there'll be another girl who needs the ride as much as you, who can fit in better. You see what I mean." The coach paused. "There is one possibility," she said.

Here it comes, Karla said to herself. The booby prize.

"Ruby Hoeft keeps asking about you."

"The women's weight coach?"

"That's right. If I send you over, will you talk with her?"

"Sure," Karla said. "What have I got to lose?"

"Well, you won't be needing to lose weight," the coach said. She gave Karla's head an affectionate tousle. "You're not exactly Miss Universe material anyway. I'll tell her you're interested. I warn you, though. Ruby's not fun to work with. It's too bad you're not a scholar."

Karla sat staring at the floor. The basketball coach had turned and was entering the locker room, already thinking about someone else, when Karla ran and caught up to her. "I just wanted to thank you," Karla said, giving the coach a quick embarrassed hug. "You've been extra patient with me."

The coach smiled. "I do wish you well, Karla," she said. "I think you remind me of—Oh, well. Of about a hundred girls, at least."

It was a cold October evening, and the stars shone brightly as Karla walked to her dorm room from the gym. Not Miss Universe material, she said to herself. Hmf, I think I've been insulted. Her back and thighs were sore from the basketball drills, but her heart felt lighter than it had in weeks.

Four

RUBY HOEFT LOOKED UP AT KARLA across a gray metal desk whose top was just visible under a sliding mound of bulletins, pamphlets, and manila envelopes. There was an aluminum clipboard of the folding kind, with papers stuffed inside and clipped to the front. A dark-green telephone with a Rolodex alphabetizer sat among the papers. "I must tell you," Ruby Hoeft said, "that nobody in my program is here for fun. What fellowship there is among my trainees is based on mutual respect and on the shared intimate knowledge of pain. I must further tell you that my operation is not part of the University's athletic program. I report to no one and there is no recourse from my decisions. Any questions so far?"

"Can I keep my athletic scholarship?" Karla glanced around the room. A bookshelf held medical texts and French and Russian dictionaries. A circus poster of a strongwoman decorated one wall.

"Yes, for the time being. You'll be administered as if you were still on the basketball team until your scholarship is replaced by a grant from the federal government. It will be an exact equivalency. It's a matter of bookkeeping and need not concern you."

I'll decide what concerns me, Karla thought. She eyed the woman. "Where does the money come from? What branch of government?"

"It comes from the State Department. Do you know, you're the only one who's asked, other than a couple of my colleagues who are always sniffing around for money."

"My!" Karla said. "The State Department! Is it like the Peace Corps?"

Ruby Hoeft continued. "You will take a battery of tests including X-rays. One of the tests is the C and E evaluation; C and E stands for Computer and Electrode. We hook you up to an analog computer and watch your muscle reactions on the oscilloscope. Mild electrical shocks are applied. There are also psychological tests. Do you like to eat?"

"I like it a lot," Karla said. "My mother is kind of obese. I have to watch my weight."

"And your father?"

"He was tall. That's about all I know. I was five when he left us for Australia."

"Well," Ruby Hoeft said, looking up at her. The woman smiled. "No more worrying about your weight. We'll change your cafeteria assignment. You'll be eating with the men in the football program. You'll be getting plenty of beef, and if you like, you get one glass of beer with your evening meal. How would that suit you?"

"Only one glass?"

The smile disappeared. "Do you have a boyfriend?"

"He's the reason I'm here," Karla said. "If it weren't for Michael, I'd be sewing brassieres alongside my mother. Or I'd be lifting beef carcasses in the dog-food cannery down in Crete."

The shorter woman's glance passed over Karla's body. "There are millions of attractive women who do not conform to the *Vogue* stereotype," she said. "This is a subject about which I have definite views, but I won't bore you with them except to say that I hope you're not the type to let yourself be held back by someone who demands a skinny profile to support his own self-image."

"Michael likes me big," Karla said. "That way, when he bullies me it feels like an accomplishment."

KARLA MISSED SHARING MEALS with Judy McDonough and with Michael, who sometimes sacrificed his own ticket to eat at the girls' dorm. On the other hand, she was amused by the jocks' hoots, brays, farts, and belches. A handful of female athletes ate at their own table, but in a barnful of broad-shouldered males, Karla saw little reason to join a group of women. She recalled her sticky summers as the Junior Legion's practice dummy and took care not to seem too friendly, but she was soon on speaking terms with a number of the men who were as outsized and poorly educated as she was.

In chatting with the male athletes, she learned that they all took pills of one kind or another. Vitamin C tablets, chewable and tasting like oranges, were passed around like breath mints; other vitamins circulated as well. Players who had been injured, or who felt they were likely to be injured, took pain pills. Amphetamines were a standard preparation for exams, and big soft capsules known as yellow-jackets were available. Some needed them as sleep aids; others used them to help control their aggression.

Karla observed that the ones who needed yellow-jackets were also taking small white bitter tablets that had no recreational merit. When she mentioned this, she was shushed and taken aside. "Those are the football program's private business," one of the assistant coaches told her. "There's no rule that says we can't use them, but nobody is supposed to know about it. Don't ask questions because they're a touchy issue with the NCAA."

Private business, Karla thought. It's not as private as you think. She knew the white pills tasted bitter because she got them from Ruby Hoeft.

Some athletes smoked marijuana. Money and drugs changed hands regularly, right there in the cafeteria. Another lively enterprise was the sale of football tickets. After years of mediocrity, the school had developed a winning football program; every enrolled student got a free season ticket, and those tickets could be worth a hundred bucks a game. Certain athletes—elite players on their way to the pros—got extra tickets, supposedly for family members. During the week that preceded each home football game, Econ majors appeared in the jocks' cafeteria and fifty-dollar bills flew like butterflies.

The X-rays that Ruby Hoeft required showed that the growth plates in Karla's leg bones had not solidified; at nineteen, she was still a growing girl. She was kept out of the weight room and made to swim laps until she was ready to drown, and put on a special diet that included two liters of milk a day, any amount of which could be taken in the form of ice cream. She gained weight, most of it going to her arms and shoulders. Karla did not excel academically, but she always did her homework. Much that other students already knew came as a surprise, for instance the Hungarian uprising of 1956. She learned about the Iron Curtain, how Europe had been partitioned after World War II. She wondered if any of her father's relatives had been walled off.

The fall semester passed, and the spring semester arrived. She got all of her credits and managed to get average grades. Ruby Hoeft kept busy with her other weight trainees and mostly let Karla alone, though she did make her repeat the leg X-rays. Michael's parents bought him a new Rambler, and they took advantage of the car's reclining seats. Karla kept up her friendship with Judy McDonough.

BACK IN CRETE ONCE AGAIN for the summer, Karla took up her old daytime job in the tavern where her mother worked nights. The millworkers and cannery hands, who had started calling her "College," followed her with their grins as she hustled steins and boilermakers across the room. Taller than most of them, she laughed away their fumbled propositions. "She's a proud one," they said. "Homely but haughty."

"Look out, College!" they shouted. "You'll break the chandelier!"

They teased her about Michael. "How's the boyfriend? Did you crack his ribs? I saw him yesterday, looked like he was limping."

The summer passed quickly. Karla almost forgot Ruby Hoeft. She ran to stay fit; she ate ice cream and beefsteak, and no one had to remind her to drink beer. When things were slow at the bar, she arm-wrestled anyone who would challenge her. Men liked her, but she was too formidable, so that she did not get many pats and pinches. After work each evening, Karla swam thirty laps at the town pool. Sometimes Michael would come down from Lincoln, and they would go out later for a hamburger and a drive in the country. Most evenings Karla went to the library to read whatever she could find to prepare for the courses she'd be taking in the fall.

The only truly bad thing that happened during the summer was when Frank Václavik, her high-school basketball partner, volunteered for the draft. He'd given up at Kearney State and said the Army beat working in the cannery.

She'd decided on a major: she wanted to specialize in the history of eastern Europe. To earn her living, she could teach History in high school. She hadn't forgotten her idiot guidance counselor and the bass on the cover of his magazine. She could have done his job better herself, but to do it really well would require courses in psychology. That was something she could work toward in the future.

The future! What a concept. Suddenly she had one.

# Five

"ARE YOU TAKING PREDNISONE, by any chance?"

The fall semester had begun, and Karla was visiting the Student Health Service because her menstrual period had gone missing. She hadn't told Michael yet, nor had she discussed it with Ruby Hoeft. Pregnancy seemed unlikely, given their precautions, but she wanted to be sure.

"Prednisone? What is that?" The doctor studied her face, focusing on her chin; Karla rubbed her jaw and looked hard at him, trying to engage his eyes.

"Some of the male athletes take it. We've been trying to get it banned, but the sports-medicine people insist that it's needed to help prevent injuries."

"What's it look like?"

"A little white pill. Bitter taste. Not sour like aspirin. Bitter. Tastes awful. So I'm hearing. I won't touch it."

"I take one of those per day. Coach says it's to build up my muscles."

"No prescription, am I right? You're not supposed to talk about it?" The doctor sighed. He was a dark-haired man, maybe in his thirties; the backs of his hands were furry. He wore a wedding band. "Yes, it'll put muscle on you. Keep taking it and you'll end up looking like King Kong. Are you sexually active?"

*I wouldn't be here if I weren't.* "We use condoms and spermicidal foam. Both."

"That's good," the doctor said. "Because you don't want to get pregnant while you're taking that stuff. Nobody knows what it'll do to a fetus."

"You're saying that I am not pregnant now?"

"It's highly unlikely. I advise you to eighty-six those pills."

"Coach will not agree to that."

"Ruby Hoeft can kiss my elbow. If I had my way, she'd be out of work tomorrow. I'm sure she feels the same about me."

Out on the sidewalk, Karla looked at her reflection in the tinted glass. She rubbed her jaw again. Was there something there? She couldn't see what the doctor had been staring at. The fuzz on her upper lip was darker, but she supposed that that came naturally with age. Her mom had a pretty good mustache for a woman. The golden light of afternoon was beginning to fade, so she headed for the weight room, where she was expected.

She was lifting again, and she was finding that Ruby Hoeft was hard to please. The woman demanded reps and more reps, until Karla's muscles felt like stretched-out rubber bands. It was not the amount of weight— what was demanded was manageable—but the weary repetitions. She found the weight room as boring as Chem lab; worse, because in Chem lab you could cheat on the experiments. She worked out mostly on one of the weight machines, sitting low to the floor and manipulating a pair of chromed cylinders. She made good progress, but she started to suffer from a sense of muscular tightness, which she tried to combat by swimming and by doing yoga stretches that she got from Judy McDonough. She reported this problem to Dr. Hoeft, who was indifferent. "Stay limber if you want. It won't hurt you."

"Last year I could bend and put both palms on the floor. Now I can barely touch my toes."

"And how is this a problem for you? Your toes aren't going anywhere."

Karla would've expected the other female lifters to resemble Ruby Hoeft, but what struck her about them was how like normal college girls they looked. Not one of the five looked fat, or even muscular unless you saw her in the shower. Rather than bulk, they cultivated leanness and efficiency, focusing on the lifts—there were two, the "snatch" and the "clean and jerk"—as complex exercises that had components to be mastered by repetition. After a time, Karla followed their approach and found that focusing on the mechanics made it interesting. As a woman of twenty with a goal in life and a boyfriend, she listened to their anxieties like a visitor from another planet. For their part, they treated her like a grandmother.

What baffled Karla was that there was no competition. Ruby Hoeft's program apparently stood alone; no other school in the Big Eight athletic conference, or seemingly in the whole United States, had a team of female lifters. Nevertheless they trained as if for the Olympics.

THE LEAVES ON THE PIN OAKS had begun to turn red, and the ornamental plums that dotted the campus had taken on a pinkish salmon color, when the first crack in Karla's happiness appeared. Word came that Frank Václavik, barely a week out of combat training, had stepped on a land mine over in Viet Nam. While lying in the hospital at Pleiku, waiting for a medevac flight to Japan, he'd succumbed to an especially vicious form of malaria. The whole town of Crete was in mourning. Frank's parents, a farming couple who spoke Czech at home, were so incapacitated with sorrow that neighbors came together to help them harvest their crops. All Michael had to say about it was "Baby burners deserve to die," which brought

Karla as close as she ever came to slapping him. Michael and Judy marched in the war protests, but Karla would do nothing that might jeopardize her State Department funds. She sent Frank's parents a note saying how much she had liked him; she wondered, briefly, how the world would be different without Frank's shoulders blocking a door somewhere.

The next thing that happened seemed like nothing at the time. Judy McDonough showed up in the jocks' cafeteria carrying a box that held Nebraska-themed Christmas cards. She went from table to table, talking to the athletes (she knew several of them personally) and adding figures and initials to a list. When she came to Karla's table, she said, "Hey! Can I sign you up for a box of Christmas cards? Proceeds will be donated to the Women's Center in support of rape victims."

"Who would I send a card to? My brother Boris? Michael? My mother?"

"It's for a good cause. Long as I'm here, do you want to sell your ticket to the Oklahoma game?"

"Oh. Sure. How much are you paying?"

"It's an easy hundred bucks." Judy opened the box and lifted out the Women's Center cards. Underneath was a stack of tickets and hundred-dollar bills.

Karla glanced at the money. "Okay," she said. "I'll be home for Thanksgiving anyway. We'll be watching the game on television. Why don't you come? My mom would be glad to meet you."

"Not now." Judy slid a folded hundred-dollar bill across the table. "Don't talk about this," she said. "It isn't legal. One ticket." She wrote Karla's name on her list. "Are you sure you don't want to order a box of Christmas cards?"

"No cards. I'll get you your ticket later."

"Not too much later," Judy said. "I'll need time to get rid of them. Don't spend the money until I get my ticket."

Judy frequented the off-campus bars; Karla supposed that was where she would re-sell the tickets. Her friend had gotten wiser in the last couple of years. Karla had gotten older, but as for Judy's brand of wisdom, she hoped she wouldn't need to acquire it.

THANKSGIVING WEEK IN THE JOCKS' cafeteria brought the usual, turkey with cranberry sauce, except that great slabs of ham were also served along with ice cream and cherry (not pumpkin) pie. Karla did not hold back; she expected that Thanksgiving dinner at home in Crete would be turkey fries and sauerkraut, served with mustard at the tavern where her mother worked. Nevertheless, she invited Judy McDonough for the break, two days off plus the weekend. Judy said she'd be glad to come, as her home on a ranch near the town of Turtle Lodge was 250 miles to the northwest and the car she'd been given to drive, a six-cylinder Chevrolet that smelled of cattle feed, was neither fast nor reliable. Besides, she said, the town was isolated and claustrophobic. "I've fucked all those cowboys," she said. "They have as much imagination as a herd of goats."

The two girls cleared out after Wednesday's classes and drove to Crete in Judy's car; Michael had his own vehicle and obligations. They arrived a little after 5 p.m. and pulled up in front of Karla's mother's house. The porch sagged and the clapboards needed paint, and the roses clawing their way up the screens had not been trimmed in years, but Karla felt a little homeward twinge, as if the childhood she remembered had been a happy one. On entering, she inhaled familiar smells, linoleum and baby powder, bacon and coffee. "Mom!" she called out. "Where are you? I've brought company."

Karla's mother appeared from the kitchen, a woman nearly as tall as Karla but heavier and softer. She was holding a Hostess Twinkie in one hand and a bottle of Pabst in the other. "Hi, sweetie," she said. "You might have told me. Who's this? Your roommate?"

"Not my roommate," Karla said. "She's a friend. Mother, this is Judy McDonough. Judy, meet my mom. Her name is Vesna. Vesna Čapek."

"How do you do?" Judy said, and held out her hand to be shaken.

"How'm I doing? Oh, I'm all in a flutter," Karla's mother said, shifting the Twinkie to her beer hand and wiping her fingers on her skirt. "Karla, did you know that Boris is going to be on TV?"

"What? Boris on TV? How is this?"

"It's on the education channel. Some big-shot violinist is giving a master class and Boris is going to be in it. They've already taped it and it's set to play on Sunday afternoon."

Karla stood speechless for a moment. "Wow," she said at last. "Boris on TV! We've got to see that." She turned to Judy. "My younger brother Boris is a genius. They came and took him away from us and flew him to New York, where he could go to music school and learn the violin."

Judy bristled. "They took him? Who took him?"

"I don't know. Rich people. Relatives. Ma, tell her who took Boris."

"It's not as bad as that," Vesna Čapek said. "He lives with my cousin's family. I cry about it once in a while, but I know he'll have a chance at something better. I'm not much good as a mom. Karla's probably told you about my drinking."

"My dad drinks," Judy said. "Do you have pictures?"

"There aren't any recent ones," Karla said. "The last time we saw him he was just a kid. That must've been three or four years ago."

"I study music, too, but I'm no genius," Judy said to Karla's mother. "I can play the piano, but I am absolutely no good on the violin. You must be proud."

"I'm proud of him, but I worry," Karla's mother said. "He was such an anxious boy. He'd cry at anything. What I'm afraid of is, I'm afraid he'll mess up."

"They've got it on tape, ma," Karla said. "They can edit the tape if it's bad. He's not going to mess up."

"Do you girls want a sandwich? There's bread and peanut butter. There's milk and beer in the icebox. I have to go to work in a minute, otherwise I'd fix something."

"We're fine," Karla said. "We'll settle in and figure out what to do next. It's too early for supper anyway."

Karla's mother left for the tavern in her lopsided Studebaker, and Karla took Judy upstairs to see about a room. The house was old and drafty, with tall windows and high ceilings. Boris's room was neat but dusty; the twin-size bed was made up tight but looked as if it hadn't been touched in years. Karla stripped the quilt off the bed—its panel showed a Formula One race car, an aluminum-colored Mercedes with dented fenders and the number sixteen on the hood—and carried it to a window and shook it. "Never mind that," Judy said. "One summer I slept in a bunkhouse that'd had rabbits in it."

"No rabbits here," Karla said. "Only dust bunnies. I'll find you a clean towel."

Karla straightened the towels in the upstairs bathroom and hid the dirty laundry, and made sure the bar of soap in the soap dish didn't have pubic hairs stuck to it. Judy seemed unfazed by the disorder. "You know," she said, "this is like the house I grew up in, except that the upstairs is finished. Ours was nothing but a dusty attic with a pile of books."

"This house is a hundred years old at least. There used to be a barn, but it fell down years ago."

"It was built in one piece, anyway," Judy said. "The one up north is a couple of buildings shoved together. I like old two-story farmhouses. They have character."

"This place has too much character," Karla said. "It might even have a ghost. My mom has seen some pretty strange stuff. Some nights there's noises."

"You didn't tell me you had a ghost," Judy said. "Now I'm envious."

The two girls reclaimed two bedrooms—Karla's room didn't look as abandoned as her brother's—and went back down to the kitchen to prospect for food. Nothing in the refrigerator looked appetizing. "My mom doesn't really eat," Karla said. "I could make us some scrambled eggs."

"Is there a McDonald's in Crete?"

"No, but there's a drive-in. We could get ourselves a couple of burgers and go to the market and buy stuff to cook tomorrow."

"Let's do it," Judy said. "We'll make our own Thanksgiving. Is Michael coming over?"

"Michael who?"

They reached the Hinky-Dinky before it closed and bought the biggest chicken they could find. "A duck would be better," Karla said, and Judy said, "Fuck a duck," and they both got the giggles. They bought canned pumpkin and condensed milk for a pie, two cans of green beans and a big can of little yams, some milk and cereal for breakfast, flour and Crisco to make a pie crust. Before they knew it they had spent thirty dollars. "Ah, well," Karla said. "Easy money goes fast. Do you want to drink beer at the tav? My mom won't card us."

"I've got a better idea," Judy said. "Let's get high."

"High?" Karla tried to not look startled. "Do you mean marijuana?"

"That's exactly what I mean," Judy said. "Have you smoked it?"

"No."

They went back to Karla's mom's house and unloaded the car. At first, Karla felt uneasy, knowing she was in the company of a criminal, but Judy didn't behave like a drug addict, and in a while Karla got used to the idea. After they put the chicken in the half-empty refrigerator and stashed away the milk and Crisco, Judy said, "Do you want to turn on the TV? I like to watch something while I'm getting stoned."

"Oh, we can't do it here," Karla said. "Those East Coast guys at our pay-to-play college all smoke it, so my mom knows what it smells like."

Judy's eyes lit up. "Guys? Are we talking about the male of the species?"

"Wait, now. Hold your horses, babe. Those rich boys are pricks."

They ended up driving the country roads in Judy's car. Every road they took seemed to end at the Blue River; some led to turnarounds, others just quit among crowded yellow weed-stalks. "You'll never guess what these weeds are," Karla said.

"I know what they are," Judy said. "They're ditchweed. Marijuana."

They found a turnaround beside the river, really nothing more than a parking area. "People come out here to screw," Karla said, "but I guess it's too cold for sex. Let's listen to the river." Judy turned off the lights, and they got out. As the car doors closed and the dome light went off, stars above them began popping out like dandelions.

"Wow," Judy said. "Nice."

"There's Old Ryan," Karla said. "He's my favorite. There's his belt and there's his sword." She slapped her neck. "I forgot about the mosquitoes."

"Are you sure it's his sword?"

Soon the sky was carpeted with more stars than anyone could count. By starlight they found their way down the riverbank, on a path slick with spade-shaped leaves. An owl hooted, and its mate answered from across the river. "I used to come here fishing," Karla said. "You catch crayfish and put 'em on your line. Then you can catch a catfish."

"My father likes to fish," Judy said, "so, generally, I don't."

Someone had trimmed a cottonwood log and placed it parallel to the river. The two girls sat looking and listening until the November chill crept in. "OK," Karla said. "I've had enough of these mosquitoes."

"There aren't a lot of them, but they're hungry," Judy said. "It must be horrible in the summertime."

Karla led her friend back up through the jungle. Once in the car, Judy tuned the radio to KOMA. The orange glow of the dial diminished the starlight. "Time to light up," Judy said. "It's not the same as smoking tobacco. Watch how I do it." She depressed the car's lighter and took something from a pack of regular cigarettes. "No ditchweed tonight," Judy said. "This is the real stuff. Expensive but beautifully rolled."

The cigarette lighter popped out, Judy held it to the tip of the joint, and the car filled up with a sharp aroma reminiscent of sage. "Watch, now," Judy said. She sipped at the cigarette and sucked in her breath. "You take it," she squeaked, and held out the joint to Karla. Karla copied her and held in the smoke, suppressing a cough. It made her lungs tickle but had no other effect. She handed back the cigarette, and they took turns smoking it. When it was almost gone, Judy took out a little alligator clip to hold the remnant and continued sipping until there was nothing left but ash and a bit of paper.

"That's it?" Karla asked.

"That's all there is." Judy laughed. "I'll bet you don't feel a thing. Do you?"

"You're right. I don't feel any different." Karla expected to feel drunk, or dizzy, or sleepy, but instead she felt awake and alert. "What's that?" she asked suddenly.

"What's what?"

"I heard a noise in the bushes."

Judy rolled down her window to listen. "I don't hear anything," she said.

"No, there's someone there. Let's get out of here. Somebody's watching us."

Judy laughed. "Okay, okay," she said. "Take it easy, girl. We'll go." She started the car and turned on the lights. When she swung back toward the road, the most sinister-looking raccoon Karla had ever seen ran out of the weeds. "There's your prowler," Judy said. "I doubt if he'll rape you."

"Rape jokes aren't funny. It happens all the time. Men you wouldn't think. So many of them are assholes."

Judy glanced across at her. "Look," she said. "Once you start to put yourself out there, you'll eventually meet some creep who won't give up. That's the way it is at the horse barn, and men are not too different. I can live with human nature. You've got to."

"That's not the way it was at all," Karla said. "I don't want to talk about it."

"Okay, but if you keep having these anxiety attacks, I'm not giving you any more marijuana."

Karla scooted lower in the seat. The cornfield they were passing was not yet picked, and she kept expecting a deer to jump out. Or maybe it would be some other animal. A giraffe? She giggled at the thought of a giraffe jumping out of the corn.

"That's better," Judy said.

"What's better?"

"You."

They drove for a while. Judy made a couple of turns. Karla looked around, but nothing seemed familiar. "Where are we?"

"I don't know," Judy said. "I've kind of forgotten how we got here."

"Let's just drive around in circles all night," Karla said.

"Squares," Judy said. "These roads don't go in circles."

"Let's drive around in squares, then. Or rectangles. We could do rectangles."

"Not triangles, though. Or pentagons. Hexagons would have worked. They could have laid out these roads in hexagons."

"They couldn't. It would have confused the honeybees."

"Why honeybees?"

"Hexagons. Honeycombs. Bees. They don't do squares."

The two girls looked at one another, sputtering with laughter. "We're stoned," Judy said. "We're high. Now do you get it?"

Karla grinned back at her. "I guess so. I certainly get something."

"Do you want to go dancing? Maybe pick up a couple of guys?"

"Oh, gosh," Karla said. "I wouldn't know where to go. Not Milford."

"Why not Milford?"

"They're all Mennonites in Milford. There's no dancing and no movie theater. Nothing else to do. The guys you'd pick up in Milford would be sex maniacs."

They drove until they came out onto a highway. The lights of a town were to their left, and the lights of a larger town were to their right. Judy turned right, and they ended up back in Crete. "Bummer," Judy said.

"What?"

"Nothing," Judy said. "I like your town. Where's that rich-boys' college you keep telling me about? Maybe we can find a frat party."

"I don't want a frat party," Karla said. "Things happen." They drove past Michael's parents' house and the underwear factory where Karla's mother worked. "Let's go home," Karla said. "We'll go for a two-mile run if you're so restless."

"I don't run," Judy said. "I'll take you home, but I'm going to find a party."

"Please, don't go by yourself," Karla said. "Those frat boys have no conscience. They think Nebraska girls are all ugly and available."

"Don't advise me what I should do. I'm not afraid of men."

Judy dropped Karla off at her mother's house and drove away. Karla climbed the steps and went in—the door was never locked—and grabbed two beers from the fridge and went on up to her room. She found her copy of *Paradise Lost* (she was taking an English elective that semester) and read Milton until she felt sleepy. Judy came back in late, still smelling of sage. She didn't stop to say goodnight. Karla knew not to wait up for her mother.

That night she dreamed of Satan, who resembled her father. The lower half of him was hairy and nude, and he had pink and naked balls like an ox. He had one arm clamped around Judy. "What are you doing here?" Karla asked him. "I thought you were in Australia."

"Argentina, not Australia," he said. "You need to go back to sleep. You bother us." With the hand that held her to him, he lifted one of Judy's boobs.

"But I am asleep," Karla said. "And I'll thank you not to do that."

"You see how you are? You bother us." Karla turned over and buried her head in the pillow, but not before she saw Judy reach across to jiggle her father's nuts.


WHEN KARLA WOKE UP THE NEXT morning, her mother and Judy McDonough were busy in the kitchen. The smell of rising bread dough was in the air. "Kolaches!" Karla cried. "Oh, Mom! Thank you, thank you!"

"Ah, well," her mother said with a smile. "I can't cook, but I can bake kolaches."

"Good morning," Judy said. She didn't look any the worse for wear.

"Did you guys happen to make coffee? I would kill for coffee."

"We saved you a cup," her mother said. "It's in that pan on the stove. I didn't want to leave it in the percolator."

"Your mom's coffee makes my head spin," Judy said. "It's lovely after that Student Union crud."

"Her coffee is the best," Karla said. "That's one thing I miss in Lincoln. Nobody makes good coffee like my mom."

Vesna Čapek and Judy McD worked together companionably; Karla and her plus-size mother couldn't share the kitchen without bumping butts and locking horns. "Your mom says we didn't have to buy a chicken," Judy said. "She knows a guy who raises them. We could've got a better one from him."

"I've always hated to clean a chicken," Karla said. "I love fresh eggs, though."

"I've shot grouse and pheasants," Judy said. "My dad makes me clean 'em. It's not so bad."

"Do you have to scald them and pull the feathers off?"

"No."

When the kolache dough was ready to punch down, Karla and Judy stood back and watched the older woman form the soft dough into rounds. She pushed her thumb deep into the center of each round and carefully filled the depression with jam. "You want to smash it pretty thin at the bottom," she said. "You don't want the dough to rise up underneath your jam. I'll give it an hour or so, then we bake. Do you want to put your chicken in before or afterwards?"

"Afterwards," Karla said. "We can eat kolaches while it's cooking. By the time it's done, we won't want any chicken."

Karla's mother made a second pot of coffee so black it was almost sludge, and they drank it with sugar and fresh cream at the kitchen table. "What do you girls do at that college?" her mother asked. "I mean, what's it like, really?"

"I'm always either studying or training," Karla said. "I get to see Michael on the weekends. That's about it."

"I take a different approach," Judy said. "I study enough to get by, but I figure I'm only going to be young once. I'd better meet men while I'm still fresh and juicy."

"Men are men," Karla's mother said. "You don't need to worry about being juicy."

"I dreamed of my father last night," Karla said. "He was in Argentina."

"The only place I want to see him in is hell," Karla's mother said. "Do you want to know how old I was when he left me? I was nineteen, same as you. Two kids already."

"I'm twenty," Karla said. "Judy's twenty-one. In my dream, hell and Argentina were the same."

"I hope he had a nice burn on his you-know," Karla's mother said.

They could smell the kolache dough rising, a fecund sourness. "I have a lifting competition coming up over Christmas break," Karla said. "We compete against a Czechoslovakian team."

Karla's mother sipped her coffee. "I used to understand Czech," she said. "A few of the old people speak it. They use it for cusswords."

"My granddad on my mom's side is Czech," Judy said. "On my dad's side, I don't know. McDonough is Scottish, but that means nothing to my father. His ancestors were in America so long they forgot where they came from."

"Maybe you both can come to my weightlifting competition," Karla said.

"I'll come," Judy said. "I wouldn't miss it."

"I won't," Karla's mother said. "That university, those smart people, they are not for me."

"You don't have to be smart to lift iron, ma. That's what I like about it."

The aroma of the rising kolaches made the two girls impatient, but Karla's mother waited a full hour before she put them in. She baked them for 20 minutes, then basted them with a mixture of egg and sugar water and put them back in the oven. When she took them out the second time, they were perfect, soft and sweet with a little crunch on top, the filling a fruity reward in the center. "My god," Judy gasped after the first too-hot bite. "I'm divorcing my mother and moving in with you."

"I only bake them once a year," Karla's mother said. "Too much trouble, and you have to make your own jam."

"If you ate these for a year," Karla said to Judy, "you'd be shaped like a kolache. Round and soft and doughy on the outside, sweet and sticky in the middle."

They boiled the giblets for dressing and prepared the chicken. They made a delicious dinner of roast chicken and vegetables, but as Karla predicted, they had eaten so many kolaches that they weren't hungry when the chicken was served. After dinner, they all went to the tavern to watch the Nebraska-Oklahoma game; that is, Karla and Judy watched the game in a room packed with shouting men. Karla's mother carried pitchers and ran the cash machine, washed glasses and wiped the bar. They suffered through a bad first half in which the Oklahoma team scored nine points and Nebraska's team scored none. Judy moaned and pounded the table.

"What's the matter?" Karla asked. "It's Oklahoma, but it's still just a game."

"I have a bet down," Judy said. "I had to give up seven points, and now they're behind."

"Did you bet a lot?"

"Put it this way, if I lose I'll have to sell my car."

She remained glum through halftime, but when Nebraska came out hot and won the game twenty-one to nine, she was jubilant. "Hallelujah!" she said, lifting her glass. "There's my Chicago money."

"Chicago money?"

"I'm moving to Chicago. Maybe when this semester winds up after Christmas break. Or maybe I'll wait till spring."

"Jeez," Karla said. "You never told me."

"I'm not telling anybody," Judy said, "in case I decide to skip town without paying my rent."

THEY STAYED IN THE TAVERN AFTER the game; Karla arm-wrestled the men for pitchers, and Judy flirted with some truckers and factory hands, though nothing came of it. The next morning, Judy said she had to make a short trip to Lincoln to collect her winnings and her percentage of the ticket sales. "Percentage?" Karla asked. "What percentage?"

"I don't get paid unless the tickets sold. You didn't think all those hundred-dollar bills were mine, did you?"

Later they wasted a good part of Friday afternoon trying to get Karla's mother's TV to work. Karla called in Michael, who came across town to look at it. He recommended buying a new antenna to replace the old rabbit-ears supplemented by a coat hanger, so they went to the hardware store and found one on sale. Karla spent the rest of the afternoon in the attic, with Judy on the stairs relaying instructions and Michael down in the living room. The best picture they could get was a grainy image that faded in and out. When Karla's mother came home from the bra factory, she told them that the TV was kaput, that sooner or later the image would shrink to a dot. Besides, the sound was terrible, the three-inch speaker either cracked or full of dust.

"Shit," Karla said. "What are we going to do? We can't watch Boris on this thing."

"Buy your mom a new TV?" Judy suggested.

"Can't afford it," Karla said. "She wouldn't accept it anyway."

"The motel in Milford has TV," Michael said. "I'd invite you both to my house, but my dad will be watching a golf tournament."

"Two girls in a motel room," Karla said. "Won't that be something to tell your friends."

"What about the tavern where your mom works?" Judy suggested.

"Same deal at the tavern," Karla said. "They'll be watching golf, or pro football, or boxing, or auto racing, or anything but a violin seminar."

They gave up on the TV and separated. Karla's mother left to go to her second job, and the two girls found themselves at loose ends. "Want to go fishing?" Karla asked. "You can use my mom's rod."

"No, thanks," Judy said. "Let's find that college you keep telling me about. I couldn't sleep for thinking about those poor little rich boys, lonely and far from home."

"I thought you found it the other night," Karla said.

"Well, I didn't. It's surprising how they can hide a college in such a small town."

The red-brick college was situated on the southeast edge of Crete, along a road that led down toward the river. Judy drove past it and turned around and drove back again, slowing down as they passed the dorms and frat houses. "Nothing going on," she said. "No action. Why are they hiding all the men from me?"

"We could go to a movie," Karla said. "We could work a crossword puzzle."

"What's the movie?" Judy said. "Bob Hope and Bing Crosby? Girl, you and Crete are getting on my nerves."

BY SATURDAY, THE WEEKEND HAD become too long. Karla went for a run in the morning, then holed up in her bedroom, studying; Judy borrowed a novel from Michael, *Ada* by Vladimir Nabokov, and curled up on a couch downstairs. They met at supper, a meal of weenies and beans plus leftovers. "You know what," Judy said. "Michael needs to take us dancing."

Karla agreed. "Michael's getting to be kind of a deadbeat. I'll call him up."

Karla knew of a beer hall, situated in a hamlet to the west of Lincoln, whose walls were made of hay bales covered in stucco; people came there from half a dozen towns to drink and dance. Most were men and women of middle age, working through their divorces, but some were old and happy-seeming couples, and a few were still young and footloose. Nobody from the University went there, which was fine with Karla. They picked up Michael in Judy's car and headed north on a blacktop road, past Milford and its sex-crazed Mennonites. "Maybe we should stop here," Judy said. "Maybe I could provide these boys some therapy."

When they pulled into the parking lot and Judy first heard the music, she wrinkled her nose. "It sounds like Lawrence Welk in there," she said. "I count thirty pickup trucks in the parking lot."

Michael agreed. "This place isn't square," he said. "It's cubical."

"Lawrence Welk has actually been here," Karla said. "Most nights it's the Eddie Romance Orchestra. Do you want to dance, or don't you?" Karla paid the cover charge for the three of them, and they all got wrist-stamped and went in. She said, "Michael, when they play polkas, you have to dance with me. You can dance the slow numbers with Judy."

Michael knew how to polka, though he didn't like for his friends to see him do it. Judy could polka also, and the three of them wound up having a blast. Karla danced with Michael, Michael danced with Judy, and, while Michael rested, Karla danced with Judy, taking the man's part and bouncing the smaller girl around the floor. The band finally took a smoke break, and the dancers got a breather. "You know what," Judy said, her gray-green eyes sparkling. "This is way better than sitting at home and playing Clue."

Karla grinned. "Colonel Mustard did it in the library," she said.

"Colonel Mustard and Mrs. Green did it," Judy said. "And they used a wrench."

Michael excused himself and got up to go look for the men's room. Judy leaned toward Karla and lowered her voice. "You should've seen the way he watched us dance together," she said. "I think he wants us to do a threesome."

"You're bad!" Karla laughed. "Why, the poor man would be crushed."

"I'd crush him," Judy said. "I'd squeeze his little naked nuts till they were the size of jelly beans."

Karla stared at her friend. "Stop right there, girl. Don't get any wild ideas about Michael's nuts."

Judy shrugged it off. "I like those basketball players," she admitted. "They're long and strong. But there must be something to be said for a man so small he can bite your nipples and diddle your cunt-hole at the same time."

For their final set, the band played numbers that Karla's mother would have enjoyed: "Stardust," "Perfidia," "Smoke Gets in Your Eyes." Michael and Judy slow-danced; watching them, Karla felt suddenly weary, as if her muscles remembered all the iron she had lifted that semester. She didn't like to interrupt them, but she longed to go home and go to bed. It was going to be a 40-minute drive back to Crete.

The last thing she remembered from that evening was Judy standing before her nude. (They were up in Karla's room. Judy had gone into Boris's bedroom and removed her clothes. Now here she was, complaining about feeling cold.) Karla was struck by the unusual size of Judy's nipples. The brownish aureolae, three times normal size, were each sparsely ringed with a dozen crinkly hairs. "I don't think so," Karla was saying. "No, I really don't think so. I want to go to sleep."

"What's the difference?" Judy said. "A kiss is a still a kiss. A sigh is still a sigh. Don't you and Michael do oral sex? It's amazing."

"No, no, and no," Karla said. "You'd better go back to your room and go to bed."

"This house is cold. I'm freezing," Judy said. "Please let me just slide in with you."

"Promise you won't do anything?"

"I promise."

But sometime during the night, Karla felt Judy's arm clench around her. The smaller girl pressed against her backside, trembling; there was a spasm and release. Karla guessed she was supposed to be asleep, so she pretended. Judy's breasts against her back felt warm, not at all unpleasant. The little town of Crete was at the center of a web of highways, broad and open, stretching away to a world that was vast and full of unanticipated pleasures. She decided that she and Michael would have to find out about oral sex.

KARLA'S MOTHER HAD A FRIEND whose TV worked and who remembered Boris. Michael was flush with cash, having recently had a birthday, so the three young people decided to watch the seminar from the dank little motel outside Milford, where each room's best feature, other than the king-sized bed, was a giant TV which could be turned up loud to cover a noisy assignation. Karla's mother packed them a lunch of cheese-and-pimento sandwiches and sent the two girls on their way. By coincidence, Michael's mother also sent cheese-and-pimento sandwiches; after checking into the motel, they put the sandwiches aside and went in Michael's car to buy a bucket of deep-fried chicken and a container of potato salad. The motel room was tiny, mostly filled by the bed, so that there was no better place than the headboard for the three of them to sit abreast. Karla and Judy piled up pillows on each side and a folded blanket in the middle, and arranged themselves with Michael and the chicken and potato salad between them. "Cheese-and-pimento sandwiches are all right," Karla said, "but they're not food." She chewed and swallowed to clear her speaking apparatus. "I wonder if Boris is scared," she said. "He used to be a nervous little Nellie."

"They taped this weeks ago," Judy said. "He's probably not even watching it today."

The room filled up with silence and chewing noises. Karla got up to tune the TV to the education channel, where a lanky agronomist was wrapping up the prospects for pork bellies. "I brought champagne," Karla said, producing a bottle in a paper bag. "Shall I open it now, or wait until the show is over?"

"Now is always the best time for champagne," Judy said. "A nuclear war could break out any moment."

As the pork-bellies expert gave way to programming announcements, Karla loosened the wire around the cork. She realized that she'd brought no glasses, and got up and went into the bathroom to look for paper cups.

While she was up, Michael shook the bottle and put it back, so that when Karla returned with the cups, it was primed to explode. "What are you grinning about?" Karla said. "You little turd."

"Let it stand a minute," Judy said. "If the cork doesn't blow by itself, it'll be all right."

"If it does blow, Michael gets the wet spot."

"Oh, the wet spot," Judy sighed. "My home away from home."

While a station hack explained the program they were about to see—an up-and-coming young violinist who'd made an international name would be giving a master class, using the facilities at Juilliard—Karla clamped the champagne bottle between her thighs and began to work the cork. It started to creep out of its own accord, then blasted free with a bang; the cork hit the ceiling, but the foam stayed in the bottle. She poured three cups half full of fizz and passed two of them to her friends. "Here's to Boris," she said. "I hope I recognize him."

"Boris the Lost Gypsy Fiddler," Michael said.

"To Boris," Judy said, taking a fizzy gulp. "Karla, when was the last time you saw him?"

"One year they let him fly home for Christmas," Karla said. "Last Christmas he was in Russia."

"So he's brainwashed," Michael said. "I suppose he'll play Tchaikovsky."

"Hist, Michael," Judy said. "Your sarcasms are irrelevant."

The program began with video clips of the star, good-looking and virile, taking bows for the coiffed women of Tel Aviv, of Moscow, of Vienna. He was shown walking the Rue Benjamin Franklin in Paris. These clips gave way to a small live audience in New York City. The camera panned to reveal a simple stage with a chair and two standing microphones. There was a piano in the background.

"He's a Jew," Michael said. "All the famous ones are Jews."

"The man is an Israeli citizen," Judy said. "Michael, are your underwear too tight?"

"Why don't you put your hand in and find out?"

The person who came first to the microphone was Joan Sutherland, the Australian soprano. A tall buxom woman with stage presence, she smiled to acknowledge the audience's applause, turning her head and revealing her profile to the camera. "Look at her jaw!" Michael said. "It's bigger than Karla's."

Karla's hand went to her face, and her eyes darted toward the mirror. Sutherland's hair was auburn, not brunette like Karla's, and her features were Brit, not Slavic. She did have a lower jaw that seemed overdeveloped. "Michael, you perv," Judy said. "If you can't control yourself, I'll have to sit on you." She took away his champagne cup, grabbed his collar, and jerked him lower in the bed; she threw a leg over him, parked her butt on his chest, and plopped a pillow on his face. Michael tried to grab her breasts—this was no accident—but soon he was flailing in earnest. Stifled yells came from underneath the pillow.

"Get off him, Judy," Karla said. "If the two of you are going to brawl, you can both get out."

Judy shifted her derriere and lifted the pillow, and Michael sat up, red-faced. "I'd have kicked you off the bed," he said, coughing, "but I didn't want to hurt you." The two of them glared at one another in a way Karla didn't like.

The famous violinist arrived on camera, and Joan Sutherland and the violinist embraced and kissed; she was half a foot taller. From the confident way the big woman moved, Karla thought she must have money, but she couldn't help staring at the great soprano's jaw, a feature so prominent that she could have plowed snow off driveways. While the couple completed their banter, she glanced at Michael, who was pouring himself a second glass of champagne. His neck was red in patches and his eyes were misty. She was glad he was angry with Judy and not thinking up something to say about her jaw.

The violinist invited the first of four students to take her seat. This was a Japanese girl, thin and tall, with a plain and serious face; she had long straight hair that flowed down past her shoulders, and wore an embroidered silk kimono that glowed electric blue under the camera lights. In flats, she was inches taller than the famous violinist, although his bluish jaw was much the bigger. The Japanese girl's jaw was the tapered arrowpoint of a heart-shaped face. One good punch would have landed her in the hospital.

"Jeez, look at her dress," Karla said. "I wonder what that cost."

Judy said, "You can have the kimono. I'll take her violin." The instrument was a Pietro Guarneri, a few years older than the Declaration of Independence.

The Japanese girl launched a blizzard of bird-notes by Paganini. Before she could finish, the star of the program stopped her in mid-twitter. He said that, even if the expressed emotion was triumphant mastery, it must be felt, and then he asked to borrow her violin. He took it tenderly, raising his eyebrows in acknowledgement, struck a chord, and began to play. Under his hands, Paganini's rondo acquired a more liquid character; whether that was appropriate to the composer's intentions, Karla could not tell. The girl reclaimed her violin and played the rondo from where she'd been interrupted. There was scattered applause, and she bowed three times in the Japanese way, hands clasped around the neck of the precious instrument.

The next student was an overweight young man from Philadelphia, whom a closeup revealed to be sweating heavily. "Greasy," Michael said. Karla jabbed him in the ribs. "Ouch," Michael said. "What did you do that for?"

"If you talk while Boris is playing, I will strangle you," Karla said. "I mean it, Michael."

The Philadelphia fellow, whose jaw was broad and padded with a roll of fat, played an excerpt from Shostakovich's *First Violin Concerto* in a way that made Karla think of high-school geometry. As with the Japanese girl, the Philadelphia man was interrupted, and the famous violinist revealed his deeper understanding. Karla groused, "All he's saying is 'Hey, look, I'm smarter than you, and here's why.'"

"Hush," Judy said. "Now you're the one who talks too much."

The third student, acne-ravaged and cadaverous, towered above the famous tutor. Karla's heart leapt into her throat and parked itself behind her own jaw, which jutted forward a little extra to contain it. "Why, it's Boris! Our little Boris! When did he get so tall?" Her tears started before her brother had time to begin. "Golly, look at him shake! He's going to drop the bow." Boris clutched his instrument the way a drowning swimmer clutches a rope.

It seemed impossible that his white-knuckled hands could play a note, but play they did, a melody by Dvořák, hesitantly at first and then with passion more and more evident both in his music and in his mobile, anxious face. The camera switched to closeup; a bead of liquid trembled at the tip of his long, sharp nose, and Michael erupted. "Ha, ha, ha!" he laughed. "Look out! He's going to sneeze!"

"Not one more peep out of you, mister, or I don't know what!" Karla cried.

Michael turned a surprised glare on her. He opened his mouth. "PEEP!" he shouted. "PEEP, PEEP, PEEP! PEEPEE PEEPEE PEEP PEEP PEEP!"

Karla felt herself swell gigantically. She exploded to her feet, snatched Michael's hand off Judy's leg, dragged him from the bed by the collar and the belt, marched him to the door, and threw him bodily, six or seven feet, to land with a thump on the hood of his bright new Rambler. She stood looking at his back for a moment and slammed the door. "Goddamned little shit!"

"You're going to be sorry you did that," Judy said.

"I don't care. He deserved it."

Already her brother had finished playing and was receiving criticism, his head down as if he expected to be slapped; his gaunt and pitted face was alternately pale and flushed. The man of great fame heaped praise on him, with qualifiers that seemed to strike like rocks. Karla's heart went out to Boris, and her angry tears flowed. "Let him alone, you fool!" she burst out. "You'll kill him with your stupid jealous kindness."

"He played beautifully," Judy said. "Karla, you said he was a genius. Why didn't I believe you?"

"Oh, who knows what's a genius?" Karla said. "All I know is, the day they took him away, that was the worst day of my life. Or one of them."

"He's going to have a rough time in the music business," Judy said. "Where'd he get that mangy-looking violin? It had a strange, sad, creepy sort of voice. Like it wanted to be human."

"He won it in a competition," Karla said. "I guess the judges couldn't afford a new one."

"No, it suits him," Judy said. "It suits that kind of music."

The fourth student was introduced, a girl from Kansas with nothing notable about her jaw or about her playing. Karla and Judy watched the program to its end, hoping Boris would reappear. The camera did show the four aspirants, briefly, but the main focus was on the smooth-talking star, who was masculine and handsome, and on the tall host, Joan Sutherland, who was handsome in spite of her jaw. "Well, that's that," Karla said. She turned off the TV, and suddenly the room was quiet. "Time to make it up with Michael."

But when she pulled open the door, the Rambler was gone.

# Six

MICHAEL LIVED IN COOPERATIVE HOUSING just off campus. Of course there was a phone in the huge old ramshackle residence, but no one there was paid to answer it, and Karla made her two allotted phone calls without getting through to him. He did not call back. On the Tuesday following Thanksgiving, she went over to the place and pounded on the door. One of the occupants, a great big shambling bearded fellow with a pillowcase's worth of bright-red curly hair, came to the door. "He's not here," he told her. Karla knew from his sympathetic tone that the man was lying.

"Where is he, then? You smell like marijuana."

"I think he went to the library."

The cooperative was for men only; women were not allowed, at least not during the daytime, and there was nothing she could do short of homicide. She decided she could play the no-sex game as well as Michael, and she stopped trying to phone him or contact him, but she'd grown too used to his companionship and felt an empty space by her side wherever she went. She would've liked to talk it over with Judy, who was nothing if not experienced when it came to men, but she couldn't find Judy either. She began to think something was up, and it was, because she caught sight of them entering the Music Building hip to hip. This shocked her like a bucket of ice water; blind as a statue, unable to think or talk, she plodded through the weeks remaining until Christmas Break.

The fall academic calendar was divided: thirteen weeks of classes came before Christmas Break, and two more weeks came after. Classes were suspended at noon on Saturday, December 18th, to resume on Monday, January 3rd. The campus shut down for those two and a half weeks, but to accommodate foreign students who could not go home, a wing of the oldest dormitory was kept open. Many of these foreign students were athletes, and the caverns under Memorial Stadium were kept heated so that swimmers could swim, runners could run, and gymnasts could gyrate. The football team was away in Florida, preparing for a bowl game, so both weight rooms were free of access. Karla drove the snowy roads from Crete every day in her mom's lopsided Studebaker, heater at full blast. She dived into Ruby Hoeft's library to try to learn more about women's Olympic-style weightlifting competitions: who held the record in each class, how much she had lifted, when and where the event took place. There'd been female weightlifting events in the Soviet bloc, and in England,

Brazil, and Australia; all the Soviet-bloc results were published in Russian. The team that was coming was Czech, not Russian, but nothing in Hoeft's library spoke of a Czech team. About female Olympic-style lifters from the United States, no information existed.

Karla weighed twice as much as the lightest girl on her team. Weights the others could barely lift she lifted easily; weights she could put up, they stepped carefully around. It was her job as unofficial captain to keep them focused on the upcoming event, but, truth be told, the young women were not unduly concerned with how much iron they could lift. They used Hoeft's discipline as a means to keep their bodies sculpted. Ruby Hoeft they regarded with a touch of pity, since she was unattractive and they were not, and a little of their attitude carried over to Karla. Furthermore, they were natives of Nebraska's capital, confident of their sophistication as compared to a Czech-surnamed peasant girl from Crete.

Christmas approached, with its hangovers and merriment. Karla, with no one to buy a gift for other than Boris and her mom, felt bemused by the swirl of capitalism in its frenzy. If she'd still had Michael to talk to, she could've shared his dismissal of the crassness of it all and bought him an expensive pair of cufflinks. As it was, she needed to distract herself. Unable to sleep, unable to be still, she lifted and lifted and lifted.

She doubled her ration of the tiny white pills and felt herself growing stronger and angrier. She slept four hours a night and woke up in a mood to throw things: an ash tray, an anvil, maybe a cow. She ate four big meals a day, and would've eaten five except that she was afraid to step on the scale. The most worrisome thing was the darkening of the hair on her upper lip; that, and that her underwear no longer fit. To burn off anxiety, she swam—the pool beneath the stadium was open; there was to be a swimming meet in January—and ran laps around the indoor track. The weather turned bitterly cold, and she preferred it so. She saw not a hair of Michael, not in Lincoln, not in Crete, not anywhere, and she missed him. She also missed his Rambler.

Early on the morning of Monday, December 27th, a Soviet airliner of a kind not seen in the United States landed at the Lincoln airport, and the weight team from Czechoslovakia deplaned. Karla stood ready on the frozen tarmac to greet them, having driven up early in the Studebaker, but a bus had been provided to take them to their dorm and they were hustled into it by two impatient men. Karla could tell nothing about the women except that their shoes were ugly. Ruby Hoeft, also present, inclined her head toward the greatcoated men, who had the look of thugs from a black-and-white movie. "They are being minded," she said. "We won't get to talk to them much."

"Did you see anything? Can we beat them?"

"I don't expect us to beat them. We will make a showing, that is all. It will be a valuable learning experience, at least for you and me."

The door between the two weight rooms had been blocked off with plywood; the Czech team had the poorer facility to themselves. From the clanks and grunts coming from within, and from the crashes of iron weights on the mats, Karla understood that the competition would be serious. Her own team did some clanking but not much grunting or crashing. No matter how Ruby Hoeft yelled at them, the girls were well-fed and complacent, having recently received abundant proofs of love. Karla took an extra ration of pills to try to make up the difference. She cursed and clanked and grunted and crashed and made as much noise as possible, but she could not shake the feeling that they were sheep about to be slaughtered.

The meet itself was held on Thursday afternoon. That morning, Karla felt nauseous when she awoke. She started the Studebaker, leaving it to idle and warm up, and went in and sat down to her usual breakfast: three eggs over easy, six slices of crisp bacon, cinnamon toast, oatmeal with raisins, and coffee. "The way you eat, you really should be fat," her mother said. "But it's all going to your arms and shoulders."

"And my legs," Karla said. "I could crush rocks between my thighs."

"Be careful what else you're crushing," her mother said. "While you were out yesterday, the sheriff's deputy brought an envelope for you. You'd better look at it." Her mother heaved herself up and left the kitchen, and came back with a plain brown envelope, printed with Karla's name and tied with a loop of string. When Karla opened it, she found a restraining order.

"Shit!" she said. "It says here that I physically assaulted Michael. I'm to stay at least thirty feet from him and refrain from trying to contact him. What kind of bullshit is that?"

"When did you beat up Michael?"

"I didn't. I just tossed him a couple of feet onto the hood of his car." Karla placed the restraining order on the table beside her plate. "That is downright pissy. They make it sound like I've been threatening his life."

"You've been calling his number."

"I keep trying because I can't get anyone over there to pick up the phone." It was true that she'd been watching Michael's parents' house in her spare time, and it was true that she'd written Call Me in lip gloss on the windshield of his Rambler. The hood still had a dent in it where he'd landed.

That was how the day of the weightlifting competition began.

WHEN KARLA ARRIVED IN THE CATACOMBS beneath Memorial Stadium, she found the other five team members waiting. They forced her into a chair and worked her over, waxing her upper lip, trimming her eyebrows, polishing her nails and fixing her hair. One of them said, "Are those the earrings you plan to wear?" Karla wore two small pearl studs in her lobes; she'd had them since she was a baby.

"I like 'em," Karla growled. "Remove them at your own risk."

"We bought Nebraska ones for you. We're all wearing them." They brought out gold-colored earrings in the shape of the letter N. "Just a touch more eye shadow," said the leader of the tribe. "Looking good here."

Ruby Hoeft made them each go and urinate before they stepped into their singlets. These were special elastic garments Hoeft had bought with her own personal funds; their color was Nebraska scarlet, same as the football team's jerseys, and they clung to each female torso like a coat of paint. The outfits came with opaque cream-colored tights; anyway, Karla hoped hers were opaque. Since Thanksgiving, she'd come to be lax about shaving her legs. Karla's singlet was especially snug, and she couldn't help grinning because putting it on made her think of rolling on a condom.

The two teams sat together for a light meal of crackers, cheese, and sausage. Apple juice was served. Each of Karla's college-pretty teammates had been a cheerleader in high school; lively, full of hope and unapprehensive about the future, they chattered away about everything but the upcoming competition. By contrast, the Czech women's faces were frozen, and they looked silently down at their plates. They were interspersed at table with their trainers, team physician, and the two "minders," and the young women, the trainers and doctor, even the minders who ruled over them, kept their heads pulled in toward their shoulders as if they believed they might be attacked by owls.

One member of their team behaved differently. Older than the rest, she was Karla's size and wore a small cross at her throat; she sat erect, looking around her with eyes coal-black and sparkling, and when one of the minders glanced at her, she glared right back. Her face was a basin of acne pits, her nose had been bashed to one side, and one of her ears was cauliflowered. She caught Karla watching and smiled, revealing a gold tooth. Ruby Hoeft sat next to Karla along with the women's basketball coach. "Sojenica Czorny," Hoeft said under her breath. "She trains in prison."

"What do you know about her?"

"She's famous within the Eastern bloc for speaking out. Her government hates her and makes her life difficult, but she's a world-class competitor."

"She's a monster," Karla said. "She looks like she could lift the moon."

The space below the stadium was always cold. Under the gloomy and distant ceiling, pipes and wires hung from dusty cables; the lighting was at the same time harsh and ineffective, and a giant heat duct sent dry eddies swirling down to chill the lifters. A portable stage had been set up next to the indoor track and reinforced in the center with a double layer of plywood, to form a pad that would be called the "field of play." There was a table for the jury, another table for the scorers and timekeeper, and chairs for three referees, one at each side and one in front. For the audience—Karla hadn't expected one, but a few coat-wearing souls showed up—folding chairs had been set out on the track itself.

The two weight rooms were to be used as warmup areas. The plywood barrier that had separated them was gone, and Karla saw how far Hoeft's operation was outclassed. Each lifter on the Czech team had her own trainer, and they'd come equipped with blankets and a hot-towel oven to keep their muscles warm and limber. Hoeft's friend, the women's basketball coach, served her team as both trainer and physician. Some of Karla's teammates brought stadium blankets, and they shared them, two to a blanket, but nobody had even thought of a hot-towel oven.

Warmup pads had been installed in both weight rooms; women's screams and the crashing of weights echoed from the distant ceiling. Of the Nebraska lifters, Karla was the last to begin her routine. First she lifted the bar by itself, getting her hand placement right, letting her muscles remember the correct technique. Then she added weights, twenty kilograms at a time, doing reps, feeling her body heat up and relax. Once she felt loose and confident, she stopped her workout and went to get a drink of water. As the heaviest, she and Sojenica Czorny would be the final competitors, so there was plenty of time to cool off and tighten up. She would have to warm up again before she went onstage.

Karla stepped out to see if anyone she knew had come to watch. She had let time and place be known, in case either Judy or Michael cared to show; she was not expecting her mother, who'd caught a ride to the bra factory because Karla had taken the Studebaker. Ruby Hoeft, also curious, came alongside. "Supposed to be some important people here," she said. "I don't see them."

"It's a while yet," Karla said. "Their hotel is still serving brunch. Is any of that sausage left? I'm starving. And what if I have to pee again already?"

"Better go do it."

Karla made her way back past the men's locker room and down a narrow hallway under a darkness that expanded upward and out of sight. She found a stall in the women's room, closed the door, wrestled herself out of the singlet, rolled her tights to her knees, and squatted, talking to herself. "Whoever invented this outfit never had to urinate." When she'd finished, she reassembled herself, pulling up her tights and fighting her way back into the singlet. "I am not wearing this again. It's like a swimsuit designed by perverts." She unlatched the door, stepped out of the stall, and was shocked to find she was not alone. One of the Czech team's male minders stood at the sink, examining his rough cheek in the mirror.

Karla balled her fists. "What are you doing here? This is the women's locker room." He gave her a casual glance, said something in his own language, and turned back to the mirror and his mole.

"No, I mean it," Karla said, growing angrier. "You are leaving now. Do you want me to call the campus cops?" She went up to him, grabbed both of his shoulders, turned him toward the doorway, and gave him a shove that would have sent most men sprawling. He spun back to face her and crouched with his hands flat and open. The little eyes in his musclebrowed face were calm and alert.

"Okay, asshole." Karla lowered her forehead and rubbed the tip of her nose with her thumb. "So, you want to fight? I'm not afraid of you."

The man looked past her and straightened. He smoothed his brown suit, said something rude in Czech, and turned aside for a final look in the mirror. Karla heard a toilet flush, and Sojenica Czorny passed by, shooting her a grin and a wink as she did so. Czorny ignored the minder, who fell in step after her, and they left the locker room in single file. Karla unballed her fists and watched them go. "I wonder where he stands while she's having sex." Her forearms tingled, her breath came fast and shallow, and her eyes were open wide. She was primed to lift.

THE MEET WENT AS KARLA EXPECTED. Hoeft's protegees tried hard, showing grit and rising to the occasion. But despite some personal bests in the "snatch" half of the competition, the Czechs won every weight class, including two in which their lifters received a bye. The Czech women remained stoic in victory, smiling only when one of their trainers snapped photographs. They seemed to take pleasure in the lifting itself, a workmanlike task in which their pride was allowed to surface. They rarely made eye contact with anyone but the referees.

Karla's turn to lift came soon enough. In the warmup area of the weight room, she put aside her blanket. The basketball coach slapped her thigh and calf muscles and rubbed her shoulders, then held her face and looked her in the eyes. "Go," she said. "You're the best we've got. Show them what you can do." The Nebraska women lined up to bump fists with her on her way to the door. She paused in the doorway, blinking, certain that the hot stage lights shone through her flimsy singlet. Feeling ridiculous but determined, Karla dusted her hands at the font of chalk, marched to the back of the portable stage, and stepped up onto the field of play.

Roby Hoeft had "declared" eighty-six kilos as Karla's opening amount. The skinny European weights were color-coded, not gray and somber like American ones, but they were no less heavy. Karla multiplied eighty-six times two point two and realized she'd be opening at her own weight.

She bent and spread her hands wide on the bar, adjusting her grip; she raised her head and looked out and up, past the audience to where a young campus cop stood near the back. As her shoulders tensed, a female voice cried out, "Go, Karla! Show 'em your snatch!" This didn't sink in until, halfway through her lift, she realized the voice was Judy's. She lost her focus and searched the audience, and let the weight drop before the buzzer sounded. The early drop resulted in three red cards from the referees. She did an awkward about-face and left the stage. "Well, that was a crock of shit," she said to no one. "I'm going to grab that fat little bitch and rip her head off."

"Not now. No time," Ruby Hoeft said. "Sojenica has declared ninety-two. Unless you want me to raise you six kilos, you have to be back out there inside two minutes."

"Raise me seven," Karla said through her teeth. "God damn it, raise me seven."

"Sure about this? That'll be the most you've ever lifted."

"I'm sure."

Ruby Hoeft hurried off to the scorers' table, and the basketball coach came to rub Karla's shoulders. "Was that somebody you know?" she asked.

"I used to think so," Karla said. "She's a slut and she took my boyfriend. I'm going to kill her."

"Do you want security to speak to her?"

"Speak to her? I'll speak to her, soon as this is over."

By raising her declared amount past Sojenica Czorny's, Ruby Hoeft bought Karla some extra time to listen to the roaring in her ears. Outside the weight room, there was mild applause; Czorny had lifted her opening ninety-two kilos. Karla toweled herself off—the room seemed hot to her now—and got blindly to her feet, ready to go again. The coach behind her gave her a downward smack on both her shoulders. "Focus, Karla! You can do this!"

Karla strode out, chalked up, and made the prescribed march to the bar. Ninety-four kilos might be too much; she didn't stop to compute it. She spread her arms, took her grip, and gave a shout: "Hup!" Then a reedy male voice called out: "Woo-hoo! There's that snatch again, and it's a big one!" Michael. Karla lifted like a robot; the bar of weights went skyward as if on strings. She held it up, shoulders locked, elbows stiff, and when the buzzer sounded, she glared at the referees and threw it to the mat with a mighty crash. She stalked off the stage without a nod, red-carded again.

"Karla, take hold of yourself! You had it! What did you throw it down for?" Ruby Hoeft. If you don't know why, you don't know much, Karla thought. I'll squash that little son of an Anglo-Saxon. I'll put ninety-four kilos of iron up his tight little ass.

"Rub her down, rub her down," the basketball coach said. "She has to go right back out. The Czorny woman just declared ninety-seven kilos."

"Hundred and four," Karla said.

"You said— What?"

"Put me down for a hundred and fucking four. I need time to breathe." Michael and Judy, joined at the hip; all the while she'd been unable to contact them, they'd been screwing and smoking marijuana. Well, she would soon put a stop to that. Once she'd dismembered their bodies and scattered the remains, she'd go happily to prison and train and train and train, and be let out once a year for weightlifting competitions, like Sojenica Czorny.

Time passed. Somebody was beating her on the back and shoulders, somebody else was massaging her calves. She stood up and went out. That bright chrome bar with the colored weights was the only thing. It wouldn't matter if she was heckled by Jesus Christ himself.

Karla hardly knew what she did. She spread her hands. Gave a shout: "Up!" She staggered, she wobbled, the room tilted, the bar went up. The buzzer sounded and she let it drop carefully, as if it were to land among kittens. One by one, she looked each referee in the eye: white card, white card, white card. The small audience caught its breath and exploded.

Karla stalked off the stage. Out of sight of the crowd, she fell to her knees and sobbed. Her teammates gathered around her. "Karla, are you all right? You did it, girl! You're amazing! That was great!" She barely heard them.

"Please get me some water. I'm burning up."

It was Sojenica Czorny's turn to lift. According to Hoeft, Czorny had snatched one-oh-six kilos, but that was done behind the red-tape curtain and couldn't be verified. Karla glanced up as she passed and mentally wished her well. When she heard the audience's applause, she knew the Czech woman had beaten her, even though she'd exceeded her own personal best by—if her math was right—something like seventeen pounds. None of it mattered because she was going to commit a double murder, as soon as she was able to stand up.

There was a ten-minute halftime break before the "clean and jerks" began. Karla spent the break lying on a press bench under a blanket, with a towel covering her face. When the time came for her to warm up in preparation for her next lift, she sat up, threw the blanket off, and said, "I'm going out there."

"You can't," the basketball coach said. "Athletes are not allowed to leave the warmup area during the competition."

"Don't bother," Karla said. "You couldn't stop me any more than you could stop a train." She stood up, straightened her singlet to be sure it covered what needed covering, and headed for the door. Outside the weight room, she passed behind the jury's and scorers' tables and went up the center aisle between the folding chairs.

The pair she sought were near the back. At first, when they saw her face, they giggled like naughty children. But as she drew closer, they huddled together, like Hansel and Gretel nabbed by the wicked witch. Karla envisioned popping Judy's jaw from its hinges, reaching deep inside her throat, and dragging out whatever she found there: larynx, bronchial tubes, heart, lungs, liver. As for Michael, she would grip him by his naked little balls and whirl him the way you would twist the head off a duck. But as she looked down from the height of her rage, the image of her brother Boris came to mind, not the tall skinny violinist but the little boy who liked race cars and kept a poster of Juan Fangio in his room. He was being pulled toward the street by a couple in city clothes while Karla's mother pinned her arms and held her pressed against her fat body like a thumb in dough.

Michael's mouth was open. "Restraining order?" he croaked in a tiny voice. "Thirty feet of distance?" The look on his face was that of a stray dog waiting to be shot.

A male voice behind her said, "Does he really have a restraining order on you, miss?"

"Boris loved kolaches," Karla said. "That's why she doesn't bake them any more." She turned to find the young campus cop standing behind her. "Who are you and what are you doing here?"

"I'm posted here to keep things quiet," he said. "Do you know these hippies?"

"I used to," Karla said. "Lately they disgust me."

"Better not confront them if there's a restraining order," the cop said. "You could go to jail. But—" He pointed to Michael— "I can take this one out in the parking lot and dust him off for you."

"Don't dust him off," Karla said. "He isn't worth the trouble."

"No trouble at all, ma'am," the cop said. "It would be my pleasure. You two, out." Judy and Michael got up in a hurry and scuttled like rats toward the exit. Karla watched them go, seething with crossed impulses. One thing she remarked on, even in her upset state: she had never before seen either of them at a loss for words.

AFTER SHE WAS DISQUALIFIED—because she'd gotten up and left the scene of the competition—Karla watched the remainder of the meet with the audience. When it was over and the Nebraska team had been defeated in every weight class, she stood up to go to the locker room and lose the singlet. But before she got far, two men she hadn't noticed came up to her. One of them was built like a bison, with a big triangular head and curly brown hair; the other was small and fidgety, reminding her of an opossum. Buffalo Shoulders introduced himself as a detective with the Lincoln police department. The opossum was a private attorney.

"Are you Miss Karla Čapek?" Buffalo Shoulders asked.

"You know I am," Karla said. "What can I do for you?"

"This gentleman wishes to ask you some questions." The detective turned aside to let the attorney speak.

"My client, Jason Bigley, says that you gifted him this ticket." Opossum held up a Xerox copy, front and back, of a student ticket to the Oklahoma game. She saw that she'd signed the back of it, a fool's mistake. "Is that indeed the case?"

"It is not the case," Karla said. "I don't know any Jason Bigley."

"Did you lose your ticket, or was it stolen from you?"

"I did not lose it. It was not stolen. I sold it to my ex-girlfriend Judy McDonough."

"Were you given a receipt for this sale?"

"Are you kidding? What's this about, anyway?" Karla turned to Buffalo Shoulders. The attorney put away the Xeroxed ticket in a notebook. Opossum had no more questions. He looked as if he'd anticipated her answer. Sad and cynical but ever hopeful about human nature.

"There's a black market in football tickets," the detective said. "We're trying to take it down. Would you be willing to testify? We can guarantee your safety, to a point."

"I'm accustomed to guaranteeing my own safety," Karla said.

"It would be secret testimony in front of a grand jury." Amid a scattering of important-looking people, many of whom wore overcoats, Buffalo Shoulders wore a Hawaiian shirt, collar open to reveal a rug of curly chest hair. Karla briefly imagined him wedged into a singlet.

"I'd have to think about it," she said. "I'm guessing you know where I live."

"You live in a dormitory. Your mother lives in Crete," the detective said. "I'm from York, myself. We used to beat the shit out of you guys every year in football."

"Some years you did, some years you didn't," Karla said. "If that's all, I have to get dressed."

"You lifted the hell out of it," the detective said. "If you hadn't disqualified yourself for the clean and jerk, you might've won."

"I wouldn't have," Karla said. "But thanks. Sure, I'll testify. Makes no difference what happens to me now. Let the cheating bastards go to jail."

Back in the weight room, the basketball coach was embracing Ruby Hoeft. "Maybe it's for the best," the coach was saying. "Maybe they'll let you have that Fulbright now."

Ruby Hoeft detached herself and blew her nose on a towel. "Karla, you let me down," she said. "I had such hopes for you."

"I couldn't help myself," Karla said. "I keep having these impulses where I want to smash somebody. I think it's those pills."

"Well, you can stop taking them," Ruby Hoeft said. "Go and get yourself showered and dressed. There's someone who wants to meet you."

Karla peeled off the singlet for the last time—and good riddance to you, scarlet garment—and took her time in the shower. When she'd dressed, still wet-haired and rubbing her neck with a towel, she saw Hoeft standing with Sojenica Czorny and one of the younger women from the Czech team. Sojenica Czorny gave her a gold-toothed smile and held out her hand. Karla shook hands with her, briefly testing her grip. "Congrats," she said. "You beat me fair and square."

Czorny said something in Czech. "She is saying you will be champion one day," the younger girl said. "She is wishing you great success."

"Thanks," Karla replied. "Tell her it's an honor to compete against her."

"She is having the gift for you," the Czech girl said. "It is small product from our country." Karla looked at the Czorny woman, who took her hand and placed a glass thimble in her palm. Cobalt blue, painted delicately with miniature flowers, it brought to mind the painted Easter egg that Karla's mother treasured, brought by her own mother from that distant part of the world.

"Gosh!" Karla gasped at the delicacy of the thing. "My mom will love this." She glanced up, feeling teary. "Wait, wait, wait!" she cried as the two Czech women turned to go. Karla ran to her locker and got her purse. In the bottom of the purse was a Christmas gift from her mother, a stocking stuffer that had cost her mom some trouble. It was an uncirculated Kennedy half dollar, fresh from the mint in its blue-and-clear-plastic flatbox.

"Here," Karla said, handing the box to the battered woman. "I hope they let you keep it." Sojenica Czorny glanced at the image of Kennedy inside and clutched the little box to her breast. "Good luck to you," Karla said. "I hope you come back someday."

Karla heard Ruby Hoeft chuckle as the two women walked away. "You know, Sojenica has a glass eye," Hoeft said after the two Czech lifters had turned a corner. "For a second there, I thought she was giving it to you."

## Seven

ON HER WAY BACK TO CRETE from Lincoln, Karla grew hot, then nauseous, so that she had to stop on the shoulder and open the car door to vomit. She did not feel better when she got home, and after she'd stumbled upstairs to the bathroom and puked and shat until she was empty, she took her temperature with the old mercury thermometer. She was running a fever of a hundred and three degrees. Over the weekend she continued to be feverish, and instead of tending bar on New Year's Eve, her mother took her to the hospital's emergency room, where they poked a needle in her vein and hung a bag of fluid above her head. Half a dozen bags later, she was out of the ICU. She hadn't swallowed anything for three days, and explained to the doctor that she hadn't been able to take her prednisone tablets.

"Prednisone?" the doctor said. "Why are you taking prednisone? Do you have an allergy?"

"They're for building muscle mass," she said. "I was in a weightlifting program at the U."

"Who prescribed them? That's medical malpractice," the doctor said. "You should've told me the minute you came in. You're not supposed to quit prednisone cold turkey."

"So do I take them now?"

"Hell, no, you don't take them. Throw those things away. Or grind 'em up and put 'em on your potted plants. I hear they do wonders."

By the time fall classes resumed, she was out of danger but still wobbly on her feet. Seated high up in the amphitheater in Love Library on the first Monday after vacation, suffering through a lecture on Economics, Karla watched a familiar-looking campus cop come to the podium. He said something to the professor, who looked up and said in a clear voice, "Is Miss Karla Čapek in attendance? This gentleman wishes to speak with you privately."

Karla stood and gathered her notes, her heart skipping. When she and the cop were out in the atrium, she asked, "What's happened? Is it my mother?"

"No, no," the young cop said. "They want to see you in the dean's office. I think it's something to do with those two potheads who were heckling you under the stadium. Anyway I've got two more names to pick up, a Michael Brewster and a Judy McDaniel."

"Michael lives off campus in a co-op," Karla said. "I can guarantee you that he won't be out of bed. You'll find Judy in one of the practice rooms at the Music Building. And it's McDonough, not McDaniel."

"You were terrific, by the way," the cop said. "You should've let me drag that little longhair outside and pound him through a crack in the pavement."

"Please, do not pound Michael," Karla said. "He's a nasty soft-handed two-timing twerp, but he's my twerp and I love him."

The dean who wanted to see Karla was not G. Ross Roberts, the big boss; he was the Dean of Student Affairs. His administrative assistant looked up as the cop brought Karla to her desk. "Miss Čapek, is it? Dr. Stevenson is expecting you. Go right in."

Karla had never thought to hear the words *Go right in* spoken in a campus administrator's outer office. The bland look on the dean's face confirmed that there was trouble. A well-tailored skeleton of undiscernable age, of a breed whose fingernails are translucent but whose thoughts are opaque, he had a folder in front of him with her name on it. "Miss Čapek?" he said in a modulated voice. He did not rise to greet her or ask her to sit down.

"That's right." She imagined hoisting him above her head, and reminded herself that, prior to being mummified, he must have had dreams and plans and a mother who loved him.

"It has been brought to my attention by Lieutenant Vernon Crapa of the Lincoln Police Department that the crime of theft of services, a class C misdemeanor, has been committed repeatedly and systematically by you and others on and around this campus. Since this crime was committed on University property, it has been turned over to my office for investigation. Do you wish to comment?"

"What's this all about? Is it that dumb football ticket?" She addressed her question to the man's comb-over. His neck had a patch of psoriasis. "If it's about the ticket, here's the hundred-dollar bill I got for it. I haven't even broken it yet." She rummaged in her purse and brought out her billfold, but the Dean of Student Affairs held up his hand.

"I can't accept money. The bursar's office has no means of accounting for the reimbursement of misappropriated funds."

"Well, if it's not the hundred bucks, then what's the big fuss about? Finals Week is coming up. I've got classes."

The man gave a desiccated sigh. "Miss Čapek, the particular amount is meaningless. What is meaningful is that you received it. Each week during football season, the University loses tens of thousands of dollars in unsold seats. Why? Because students who have no intention of attending games accept tickets and sell them on the black market. The person who bought your ticket should've purchased a regular ticket at the ticket office. This substitution of a student ticket robs the Athletic Department of funds."

"But the games are all sold out. Nobody can get tickets anyway. Why shouldn't we sell our tickets, if the ticket office doesn't have any?"

"It is against the rule as specified in the Student Handbook Code of Conduct, and it contributes to an off-campus criminal enterprise."

"What criminal enterprise? I don't consider myself a criminal."

"I'm sorry, Miss Čapek. According to the Student Handbook, if you're not able to use your athletic ticket, your duty is to notify the Athletic Department and return your ticket for resale. Not to do so is a violation of the Student's Code of Conduct. Theft of services is also a misdemeanor according to the statutes of the State of Nebraska, but the University has elected not to prosecute. Instead, you'll receive a W in all your courses. That means you're withdrawn in good standing. After a period of one semester, you may apply to re-enroll, but you will not receive credit for this semester's courses."

Karla gasped. "You mean I'm expelled? Because of one football ticket? My God, do you understand what you're doing to me?"

"You are disenrolled as of today. You may sell your books and clear out your dorm room. Your tuition will not be refunded."

"But I need college. It's not like I'm one of those rich oafs down in Crete." Karla stared at the top of the thin man's head. He'd already buried his nose in another report. She recalled her high school guidance counselor and his outdoor magazine. This man was a couple of advanced degrees smarter, but he was clearly of the same ilk. "You know what you remind me of?" Karla said. "You remind me of a fish."

As she stumbled from his office, she passed Judy McDonough and the young campus cop. "You," she said to Judy. "You did this. I'm going to wreck your car."

"It's your own fault," Judy replied. "You and your big mouth."

"Don't you big-mouth me," Karla said. "I'll open up your mouth and shove a Student Handbook in it." The young cop raised his eyebrows and tightened his muscles; Karla moved on by. "Give me back my Michael," she said over her shoulder. "Give me back my life."

"He's not yours, but you can have him if you want him," Judy called out after her. "He's twenty and he's already losing his hair."

SEVERAL HOURS LATER, KARLA STOOD on the sidewalk in front of her dormitory, with everything she'd brought to campus piled around her ankles. The shadow of the building covered her, and an icy January wind blew a sheet of paper down 16th Street. She was waiting to see if a taxicab would come by, or if someone would be willing to give her a ride to the bus station. Instead of a cab, Judy McDonough's blue-and-white Chevrolet pulled up to the curb. The window rolled down. "Get in," Judy said. "Pile your stuff in the back. It's freezing."

"I'm not getting in with you."

"Yes, you are. Nobody else will take you. All you'll do is stand on the sidewalk and catch pneumonia."

Judy got out and opened the trunk. Karla's possessions filled the trunk and the back seat. When they had everything stowed away, Karla got into the front seat. Judy got behind the wheel and drove. "Crete?"

"Just take me to the bus station."

"No, I'm taking you to Crete. You'll never get all this crap on the bus."

Karla rode south through downtown Lincoln for the last time. O Street was bleak but crowded with five o'clock traffic. The red-brick buildings had frost halfway up their windows. Every car was followed by a plume of steam.

"Why are you doing this?" Karla asked.

"I wanted to talk to you," Judy said. "I'm leaving for Chicago."

"Now? Why?"

"Certain people are displeased with me," Judy said. "It's better if I go."

"Does this have to do with those Oklahoma tickets?" Judy was silent. "If I got you in trouble, I'm sorry," Karla said. "I didn't know what I was doing. That detective asked about my ticket, and I told him."

"There's no way you could've known," Judy said. "I didn't know what I was doing when I fucked Michael."

"Michael." Karla exhaled through her nose. "Did he sell you his Oklahoma ticket, too?"

"Michael has turned state's evidence, so to speak," Judy said. "They're allowing him to finish the semester. He'll transfer his credits to Moose Head, Minnesota. Some name like that."

"Morehead State College," Karla said. "They have a school of music, and it's close to Canada in case he needs to run away." They rode in silence. "When is he leaving?"

"Give it up, Karla," Judy said. "The man has no more heart than a gumball machine."

"Never been in love, have you." Judy shook her head. "Pity."

"I don't think so."

"Something I've been wanting to ask you," Karla said, her lip trembling. "Where did you go that night in Crete, after you dropped me off at my house and went out for a couple of hours?"

"Don't ask dumb questions," Judy said. "You know where I went." She was silent for a mile or two, but her mouth opened twice as if she were going to speak. Finally she said, "I don't know why I do stuff like that. You were my one true friend."

They drove past picked cornfields, all the empty rows pointing north. Karla said, "What's the name of that town you come from? Turtle Lodge? I think I'll go there. That way, I can be sure I'll never see you."

"Suit yourself," Judy said. "It's a hellhole."

More cornfields, more silence. Karla said, "I guess it's been good to know you. But it's over. I don't know you any more."

"Me, too," Judy said. "Me, too. Same everything. Me, too."

Karla had already called and told her mother the news. Though her shift at the tavern should have started, Vesna Čapek was waiting at the door with a can of Pabst Blue Ribbon in her hand. "Come in, honey," she said as the Chevrolet drove away. "Let me help you move your stuff. Was that your friend?"

"She's not my friend, ma."

"I always told you Michael was a shit." Karla's mother sighed. "Well, live and learn."

"Live and learn," Karla said.

"Except by the time you learn something, it's too late."

"I hope you've got beer in the fridge." They gathered Karla's belongings and brought them inside.

# Dust

## One

HERE'S CLEANUP HITTER KARLA ČAPEK, stepping out of the warmup circle with bases loaded. The plastic fern applauds. She strides to the batter's box, past Praying Hands, The Last Supper, Angel at the Door of the Tomb, and a horse and buggy crossing a covered bridge (no covered bridges in Dunlap County, Nebraska). The pictures have glass, to keep the residents' fingers off and give her one more item to wipe down. She steps to the plate and takes her stance, lifts the bat just off her shoulder. The pitcher shows her a steely smile; she answers with a sneer. Here comes a fat slider, high and outside at first but curving down and inward toward the plate. Her forearms tense, her irises dilate. Whock! Her dustmop shakes the wall. Far and away, the ball descends; as the celebrating runners circle the bases, she arrives at the end of the hallway. Room Nineteen. Five residents have had Nineteen since she started here, and all of them left feet first except for Edward Stevens.

Time to play Musical Furniture. She whangs Edward's floor lamp with the dustmop, dongg! Then the metal legs of the green chair (Edward is in the chair, but she has to dust, doesn't she?) dink! dink! dink! dink! Now the dust bunnies under the bed, whank! whank! whank! whank! Next a wreck with the tray table, chinkle-clingg, and a grand cymbal smash into the heating unit, chlammmm! under the window at the far end of the room.

This nursing home was built on the northeast edge of town, so there's a view of Turtle Lodge Butte out the window. The butte has the shape of an upside-down flowerpot, with a radio tower stuck on top. Karla stands looking at it for a moment. "Summer league's almost over," she says. "One more week and then the tournaments. Softball, too." She props her dustmop against the wall and turns and sits down on the heating unit, and leans forward to let cold air blow up her back. The heating unit squeaks. "One quick puff," she says to herself; she unbuttons the top button of her scrubs and slides a pack of Marlboros out of her bra. "That's a Major Violation, Miss Čapek," she says in a supervisory sort of voice. "I'm going to have to write you up for that." She lights a cigarette from the book of matches tucked into the cellophane and inhales. "Thanky Jeezus, thanky thanky," she says. "God bless nicotine."

Karla sneaks a second puff and stubs the cigarette, and twists her head around to look out the window. The crabapple tree's shadow is creeping toward the sidewalk; a robin under the tree is pulling at a worm, but the worm doesn't want to meet the family. The worm's attitude makes her think of her old boyfriend Michael, who likewise wanted nothing to do with anyone's family. In Karla's case, that would have been her mother, since everyone else left. The sprinkler cycles through its pattern, chattering.

"Hey, Edward, did I tell you about this ex of mine, little Michael? He bought one of those suction things to try and make his weenie bigger. Michael was half my size and twice as smart as me. I liked his cute little weenie the way it was." Still looking out the window behind her, she crumbles the cigarette and drops the shreds into the heating unit. "Nothing to report today, Edward. Nothing happens to me any more."

There's a dry cough like a statue clearing its throat. A hollow voice says, "That's a Major Violation, Miss Čapek. I'm going to have to write you up for that," and Karla stands straight up and knocks over her dustmop.

"I too was once disappointed in love. It was with a pair of twins, actually."

There's a reason why Karla presses her hand to her chest, a reason why her eyes dart all around the room. Nobody's there but Edward, and he's blind and unresponsive. Each day, someone lifts him and puts him in his chair. Someone feeds him and changes his sheets and puts him back in bed. Then they water the plant—every room has a potted plant—and leave.

"Who said that? Edward, what the hell? Can you talk?" She sneaks a quick look under the bed. Checking for the prankster.

"It was during baseball season."

This old guy, Edward Stevens, is from the Rez. He's here at the nursing home in Turtle Lodge, rather than in South Dakota, because his son, who doesn't go by the name of Stevens, feels obligated. That doesn't mean he ever comes to visit. An Indian woman came once, claimed in a raspy voice to be his daughter, but they wouldn't let her in because she'd cursed at them.

"Hold on, now," Karla says. "Give me just one second to shift the gears. Edward, you antiquated turd factory, have you been fooling us? Everybody here thinks you're a vegetable."

"I am not a vegetable, and I am not a turd factory. I am a ninety-seven-year-old human being with things to say."

Karla collapses back onto the heating unit, and it squeaks. "All right. If you want to say things, say them. It's getting close to lunch; they'll need me in the kitchen."

"We boys from Willow rode the train to Turtle Lodge to play town-team ball. Our coach was the school janitor, Tom He Catches Them. We used to call him Chases-Dirt-With-A-Stick. All of us were half Indian except for our shortstop, Billy Doolin. There was a camp outside Willow at that time, and several of the railroad men had Indian wives. This Catches, though, he was a full-blood. One of the old ones."

"When was this? How old were you?"

"This was the Dirty Thirties, the years before the war. I was in the prime of life. Been married, had two sons, but what I loved was baseball."

"Indians love baseball? I did not know this."

"We invented it. One year our Willow team only lost two games. People came for miles just to yell and throw pop bottles. There'd be a fight if the score was too uneven, so we tried not to run it up. Our guys liked to hit, though. Sometimes Catches couldn't hold us back."

"What position did you play?" Karla is skeptical in two ways. First, Abner Doubleday invented baseball. Second, it could be that her mind is playing tricks. Edward Stevens DOES NOT SPEAK. It says so on his chart. Big red letters.

"I was an outfielder, left or center. I threw them out at home plate from the fence. If I could've thrown a curve ball, I might've been a big-league pitcher."

Karla sighs. If this is a hallucination, it isn't going away. "OK, you played ball. What's baseball got to do with love's disappointments? You were starting to tell me you were in love with a pair of twins."

"Disappointments? Twins? Let's see—" Edward cranks up a cough like he's got gravel in his lungs; his milky eyes bulge, his tongue comes out, his old prune face turns blue. He slobbers. Karla waits for him to finish and asks if her smoking bothers him, and he answers, no, in fact— She catches the whine of a deprived tobacco addict, and some imp of rebellion gets into her. She lights another cigarette and walks over to his chair and holds it to his old cold lips, that are purple like a rose that's drying up. Outside, it's blazing, a hundred and two degrees. Turtle Lodge is in the middle of a drouth. Every afternoon, clouds build up. Then they glide right over.

Edward clamps onto that cigarette and gets in one good drag before she can snatch it away. She takes a puff herself and snuffs it. "Baseball has to do with those girls—" wheeze, hack, drool— "because that is how I met them. Their father was a religious crank who built his own church out in the sandhills. He must've had a soft spot for baseball, because he let his girls come to the games. Thanks. I can't tell you."

"You're welcome. When they catch us, you can help me find another job. That Hazlett can sniff out tobacco smoke farther than Hank Aaron can hit a home run."

"It was a hot August day. No wind. The dust we raised hung in the air. Bottom of the seventh, score tied. Our team at bat—"

Karla finds the room's washstand mirror and winks at herself. The speck on the mirror that moves turns out to be a spider. "Doesn't the home team bat last?"

"The sun had gone behind the stands. In a few minutes, the field would be in shadow. Their pitcher threw a good fastball, and in poor light our hitters wouldn't see it. So, it was now or never. Runners on first and second—"

"You stepped to the batter's box. The pitcher showed you a steely smile." Old people in nursing homes are always mocked. It's wrong, but the staff all do it.

"The first pitch was a curve, low and outside. Ball one." Cough cough cough. "The second was a fast ball, down the pipe. I swung and fouled it off, back out of play. One ball, one strike. Our runners were leading off to try to rattle the pitcher. I called time out and asked the umpire to wipe the dust off the ball.

"The next pitch was high and outside, a pickoff at second. The runners got back all right. Two balls, one strike. Now Tom Catches gave the steal sign. The pitch was low, another fast ball, and I swung at it to give the catcher something to think about. Both runners went, the throw was quick but the third baseman dropped the ball. Runners safe on second and third; two balls, two strikes."

"I think you'd better hit this next one."

"One curve, one wasted pitch, two fast balls. I figured it was time for the curve again, and since a couple of pitches had been low I looked for something higher. I thought he might try to throw inside, so I crowded the plate. The ball came just where I expected it, and I hit a sharp grounder between the shortstop and second base. The ball made a wild hop over the center fielder's head. The throw in to second went wide when it came; another run scored, and I took an extra base. Then our catcher came up to bat and bounced the first pitch off the left field fence. I beat the throw home from second, and that was the game; we won it, five to two. Neither team got a hit after that."

"Whew! Great baseball story, Edward. But, what happened to those twins?" Karla glances out the window. The robin that was under the crab tree has taken her worm and flown. Now Jack Keogh is out there with his back to the sun, picking up a scrap of paper from the curb. Jack Keogh is a resident; whoever turned him loose should be watching him, but there's nobody in sight.

Unless he poops on the floor, Jack Keogh is not Karla's problem.

"Well," Edward says, "instead of a fight, there was a party after the game. Somebody got hold of a jar of liquor, and the Turtle Lodge team invited us Willow boys. Tom Catches tried to stop us, but we dodged him.

"Some white girls were at the party. The pretty ones came to flirt with us Indians and see if they could get a riot started, but two girls were there who weren't like the others. They hung back in their homemade dresses, taking everything in, as if they'd never seen a party before."

"Were they beautiful?" Edward Stevens frowns. "Average looking, then?"

"Who cared about that? They were nice girls. They were white. They didn't have a bad figure. Figures, I should say. I went over and talked to them, and they invited me to come out and see them at their ranch."

"Didn't you say you had a wife and two kids?"

"My wife left and my sons were living with my sister. I didn't think twice about going to see those girls."

"So," Karla says, pointing the finger, "you used to play baseball and chase those homely women instead of taking care of your two sons."

Karla's finger-pointing is useless because Edward doesn't see. "I spent Saturday night in Turtle Lodge and started walking as the sun came up. I must've got to their place at about eleven o'clock on Sunday. That was my first mistake, to come while their father was preaching. He thought I was there to be saved. I listened to the last of his sermon—it was only me and Baldwin McDonough's first wife, the one who died—and stayed to dinner."

Edward's speaking of dinner makes Karla think the head nurse might be looking for her. "Edward, how long will this take? I'm supposed to help prepare the evening meal. When a person my size is missing, people notice."

"It happened in the course of a year, summer around to winter and back up through spring."

"Long story, in other words. That means I haven't got the time. They'll be washing down the dinner trays and chopping lettuce."

"Trays can wait," Edward says. "I might not talk again."

"Tell me the first part and quit when you get to a stopping place. I'll try and get back to you, but I need this job. I can't just disappear."

Edward starts to describe the chicken they served. It was tough. Karla tells him, hold it, if you go on ten minutes about how tough the chicken was, you're never going to get your chicken. Summarize, Edward. Summarize.

"That's not how we do it. Besides, it's the little things. They lived in a sod house with a blanket divider, yet the woman, the girls' mother, brought tea in little cups that came from England. There was a shelf of books, ruined because the rain had leaked in: Dickens, Swift, Shakespeare. But the girls, you want to hear about the girls, to find out if anything went on. You want the monkey business.

"After dinner, for the first and only time, the three of us went for a walk together. Just across the fence was a beautiful wet meadow, which the preacher would've farmed to blowsand if he'd owned it. The hay had been cut and stacked. We walked as far as a little slough, where frogs jumped in the grass and the water came through our shoes. I tried to put my arms around both those girls, but they pushed me away.

"We came to an agreement. I could see one of them each week, alternating weeks. I couldn't tell them apart anyway, but I liked them as a pair and said what was on my mind. No, they said; alternating weeks or nothing. So we shook hands on it. I planned to work my charm on them one at a time. Jealousy would take its toll, and eventually I would have my way with two. Or none; it could be double or nothing."

"So was it double, or was it nothing? Tempus fugits, Edward." *Tempus fugits* is what Karla's mom used to say while she was fixing a sandwich between the bra factory and the tavern.

Edward goes "Hmf" in his dry old voice. "What do you see out the window?"

Karla cranks her neck like a barn owl. "It's hot out there. Lawn's green in the middle because the sprinkler runs all the time, but it's dry and yellow around the edges. The sky is kind of yellowish blue, with a few puffy clouds that won't amount to anything. One back yard has sheets and pillowcases on the line. She's going to wish she'd used the dryer. Jack Keogh was out there but he's gone now. I guess somebody went and grabbed him."

"Look closer. Tell me one small thing."

"Hey, I know I'm stupid. Don't push me." Karla turns her whole body to see better. "OK, here's something. There's this ornamental crab tree by your window that isn't liking the heat. Every leaf has a curl around the edge. Well, all over the north side of the tree, each leaf has a baby spider on it, spinning off a line along the breeze. Kind of pretty, if you can stand to look at spiders."

"Parachuting. That's the white people's word for it."

"What would Indians call it? This Catches guy, what would he call it?"

"We— They— Tom Catches would see the thread, he would see the spider carried up, but he would never say it was only the wind that lifted. *Mitakuye Oyasin.*" Me Talk Oh Yeah Shin. All my relatives.

Voices in the corridor. Karla says, "'Thank you for telling me about the spiders, Miss Čapek.' 'You're welcome, Edward.' Now wind it up until I can get back to you. I'm going to have to put you on hold." She checks the grille of the heating unit for ashes. There are enough cigarette butts down there to start a prairie fire.

"I walked out there every Sunday. How's that for a windup?"

"Lame, but it'll have to do."

## Two

A NURSE MUST'VE BEEN IN THE ROOM, because Edward is not where Karla left him. He's in bed on sheets that were clean an hour ago, not sitting in the green chair, and she smells poop the minute she walks in. *The bedpan, Edward. If you can talk, you can ask for the bedpan.* She goes to fetch the basin and a towel, and wheels in the four-wheeled potty. Old Edward plays the dummy while she lifts him and sits him on it. Maybe she's a little rough, maybe she bounces him more than she needs to; it's a situation she's paid to deal with, but that doesn't mean she enjoys it. Edward's still off in his I'm-not-really-with-you space. Karla goes to throw his sheets in the shitbag and wash her hands, and on her way back with the cleans, she reminds herself how it's no good talking to residents. About the time you get yourself involved, they kick off on you. Back in Room Nineteen, she goes straight to the window and checks the crab tree. Late afternoon, so the building's now shading it. All the spiders are gone.

"To be the object of laughter is no joke," Edward says from his smelly seat.

"How'd you know it was me?"

"When you walk, you make things jingle."

Karla sighs. "I know all about being laughed at," she says. "Michael and me used to get it all the time, him being way tiny and me over six feet tall."

"Once I decided to make love to those twins," Edward says, "my baseball playing was jinxed. It wasn't that I played badly; I did the right things, but they would take a turn that made me look like a clown.

"It was one of those games where nothing happens until the fourth inning. We'd batted around, and it was my turn up. No outs, nobody on; all I wanted to do was get on base. The infielders were too far back, so I bunted one down the third base line. Well, both the catcher and the third baseman went for it and knocked heads; the third baseman collapsed on top of the ball, and the catcher was no use either. The shortstop rolled the third baseman over, and the pitcher grabbed the ball and fired a zinger to second base to head me off. Problem was, nobody was covering second; their second baseman was standing next to him, and I guess the center fielder was plucking his eyebrows. By the time the throw came in from the outfield, I'd scored. The scorekeeper marked it as an error by the pitcher, but it was the same as though I'd made a home run on a bunt. To make it worse, I tripped and fell crossing home plate. It looked as if the Keystone Cops were playing baseball.

"After we won that game, I went to watch some rodeo with my twins. The hometown boys didn't like it that an Indian had made them look like fools, and one of them beat me up; I think it was the shortstop. Are we having a smoke now?"

"This is going to get me canned." Karla takes out a Marlboro and lights it. "The bosses hire you to dust and fire you for sneezing." She takes the first puff; Edward gets the second. She snuffs the cigarette and slips the unused part back in the package. "Are you finished with your B.M. so I can put you back in your bed? Because at seven o'clock I go home and crack open a beer."

"With the girls it was the same," Edward says. "They laughed at me, even though I courted them in good faith.

"The first girl treated me with confidence and mockery. She'd pretend to let me hold her, then pull away. I'd get nothing from her but teasing for the rest of the day. The second twin's eyes were full of shyness and longing, but she felt shame because I wasn't fully white. At times she imitated her sister's cruelty; afterward, though, she would make some gesture that showed me a little bit of kindness."

"I'm not impressed with your twins thing," Karla tells him. "What if one of them had married you and then caught you in bed with the other one? Or was that a part of your plan all along?" She sniffs the air and wrinkles her nose. "How about now? Can I lift you off the pot and put you in bed? I want to go home."

His face takes on a sour-apple look. "To marry one would not have satisfied me. They weren't only identical; they were a single, hidden woman. Beneath the skin, their hearts were the same mystery. You may laugh, but to me it was serious.

"My job was not challenging. I worked on the roundhouse crew at Willow, greasing the locomotives and turning them around. It was grease and steel and steam and ashes, day in and day out. I dawdled through the weeks, and on weekends I cleaned up and rode the caboose to Turtle Lodge. But by the time baseball season was over, I saw that nothing would come of my desire. I fell into a decline.

"The corn ripened and the cottonwood leaves fell, but the winds of autumn did not lift my spirit. The first snow came and the sharp cold bit my flesh, but my blood was not stirred to meet the chill. I forgot to comb my hair; I developed a cough and was warned about carelessness on the job. Then, during the Christmas holidays, I cut my foot splitting wood. The axe turned and caught me between the second and third toes."

"Golly, look at the time," Karla says. She glances into the sink, to see if she remembered to clean it. "I'm listening," she tells him. "I just have to peek into the hall for a second. Then I'll wash your butt and tuck you in." She steps to the door and looks. All quiet out there.

"How can I talk with you jumping up and down?"

"I don't jump," Karla says. "So, you chopped your foot. Come to think of it, I've seen that scar. Hurry up, now."

"My two sons happened to be staying with me. They saw blood in the snow and followed my track inside, where I was adding wood to the fire as if nothing was wrong. They talked me into lying down, and the youngest boy held the wound closed while the oldest ran to get Tom Catches. I would've died, but my young son held my foot in his two small hands."

"You could've wrapped it in something." Karla is making his bed while he talks, flipping out and floating the clean sheets. They smell like air rising above the infield on a hot August day. Anyway they smell better than Edward.

"That's what Catches did. He sent my two boys to stay with my sister and got some people to help him carry me to his place. He had this shack on the edge of Willow, no bigger than this room, stuffed full of baseball equipment.

"First he washed the wound with Coca-Cola—"

"Coca-Cola!" Karla thinks, *Wait a minute.* "Phew, Edward, you stink."

"—then he bound it in a cast made of fabric and wet newspaper. He would have used cow manure for the cast, but I wouldn't let him. All this washing and bandaging was done out in the snow, so of course I was freezing. Finally he put me to bed on a panel door that had been cut down, so that my poor foot stuck out for him to bump whenever he went out to use the privy. It got so I clenched my teeth every time he stood up."

Karla finishes making the bed and looks around to see what else she should do. There are cobwebs up in the ceiling corners, but they're not hurting anybody. "Sounds like his bedside manner was about average," she says. "Okay, I'm going to move you now. Shall I put you back in bed, or do you prefer to sit in your chair?"

"He kept telling me my foot would fall off. One day he dropped a stick of firewood on it without making me squeal like a puppy; this was bad, he said. He straddled my leg so I couldn't see what he was doing and unwrapped and rewrapped my foot. That's when he started having me sing to it."

"Sing to your foot? Now I know you're lying." Karla slips one arm around Edward's back and the other arm under his knees; she lifts him up to the bed and sits him on a towel, and tips him back and cleans his old brown butt with a wet facecloth. His balls droop down and get in the way. Not much she can do about that. "What did you sing?"

"Cowboy music. Lawrence Welk songs. Polkas and waltzes. Catches said I should sing to my foot in Lakota, but I didn't know the language. I'd better make up something, was what he told me. My foot wanted its own special songs, not songs I'd heard on the radio."

"Do you remember any?" Edward looks guilty. Karla goes, "Yes you do, Edward! Come on, now, sing for me. If you don't sing, I won't give you any more cigarettes." She lifts him under the knees and slips the towel out from under him, and wads it with the shitty washcloth inside. She arranges him full length on the bed. "I'm waiting."

Edward clears his throat and sings. "'From my left leg they say you are going, I will miss your five toes and sweet smell—'" Karla starts snickering so hard she has to sit down. "You think it's funny," he says. "Wait until you're old and somebody bribes you with a cigarette and laughs at you."

"All right, Edward. By the way, there's a call button here for the next time you think you need the bedpan."

"Of course I had never sung a love song to the girl—"

Karla gets up to wash her hands at Edward's sink. She stops. "You mean those twins? We're back to that now, are we?"

"I made up lyrics for her—I wrote some down at different times—but I could never force myself to sing them. Where, with my foot, I could sing any foolishness you can imagine."

"Twins! Twins! You're talking as if they were one person."

"Catches kept after me: 'Sing! Your foot wants to divorce you!'"

"Look, Edward. You could not possibly have believed that singing would keep your foot from falling off. And, it was not one girl, it was twins."

"What about this Michael person?" Edward says. "Did you make up songs for him?"

It's Karla's turn to look guilty. "Michael was not a foot. And he didn't fall off. He transferred to a college up in Minnesota."

"Looking back," Edward says, "the songs I made up for my foot were better than the ones I made for the girl. At least I can remember them—"

"Old man, listen to me. A while ago it was twins, but now you keep saying 'girl', one each. What is the meaning of this change in number? By the way, my shift was up ten minutes ago."

"—silly as they were." His face has that suspicious look they get when the mind goes and they don't know where they are. "What twins? It was one girl and her ghost."

"You're changing the story, Edward."

"I don't know." Edward's voice is weakening. "When I first spoke to you, I thought I knew, but my life changed after that. Maybe it is I who am twins. Can you turn off the overhead light when you go? I can't see it, but it keeps me awake."

"Sure, no problem." Karla sighs. All her listening is for nothing, like her year at the U when the professors talked but all she heard was Michael, Michael. "Good night, Edward," she says. "See you in the morning."

# Three

ARE THEY GONE?

Edward knows this voice: Tom He Catches Them. "You can see for yourself," Edward says. "They're all down at the nurses' station, drinking coffee." Edward's not all that comfortable talking to Tom Catches because Tom's dead long since and buried up in South Dakota.

What about that giant housekeeping woman? Do you know if she'll be back?

"She's gone home for the night. What do you care? She can't see you."

I have a proposition for you. We need you to join our team.

"I can't play ball. I can't even stand up by myself."

Such things can be fixed. Don't you remember how I healed your foot?

"What I remember is your godawful cooking," Edward says. "You used salt instead of sugar and put gravel in the beans. I broke a tooth on one of your stupid jokes."

"I did it because you needed some cheering up." An old man peers into the room. He's dry and shrunken like Edward Stevens, but hale and lively on his feet. His steps when he enters are quick as a lizard's: he stops, looks around the room, then steps closer. He carries something in a paper grocery bag, which he sets on the bed. "You were taking your bad luck too seriously."

"I don't see how a broken tooth was supposed to cheer me up."

"Extreme measures," the spry old man says. "Radical thinking. Before you can change the world, you have to pull up your socks."

"Socks?" Edward blinks. "The day I first sat up—I felt better, even though my foot was falling off—you made biscuits with too much baking powder. Exploding biscuits. Once I'd tooted enough gas to fill a blimp, I took over the cooking."

"Pork and beans and potatoes. If you call that cooking." Uninvited, the old man sits on Edward's bed. Edward's feet are sticking up underneath the sheets, and Tom Catches slaps one of them and squeezes it. "How's the old hoof? Think you could run on it?"

Edward sucks in air between his teeth. "Ow! Ow! Ouch! There was nothing wrong with my foot a minute ago! Now it hurts like the devil!"

"If there's nothing wrong with your foot, get up. We need you at batting practice."

"What batting practice? Look into my eyes. Can I see to hit the ball?"

"You see me, don't you?"

Silence. "So what?" Edward says. "My seeing you proves nothing. You're dead. You can't possibly be here."

"It proves you can hit a few if you want to. When you're ready. Wouldn't you love to get out on the field again? Get some fresh air into those old lungs?" Catches stands and picks up the bag he brought. He does not open it.

"I can't move. I've got this cast on my foot," Edward says, and suddenly he does have a cast. There it is, sticking up underneath the sheet, big as a Black Diamond watermelon.

"Let's see this famous foot of yours," Tom Catches says, and whips the sheet aside. "Well, look at that filthy thing. It needs re-bandaging."

"Ow! Watch what you're doing!" Over Edward's resistance, Catches unwinds the cloth bandage that forms the cast. He uncovers ancient yellowed newspaper, which he uncrinkles. "Look at this! Hitler invades Poland. England and France declare war." He unwinds the bandage further, exposing Edward's foot. "That's a beautiful foot. All healed. It's as good as new."

"No, it isn't! It hurts! Wrap it up again!"

"This little piggy went to market, this little piggy stayed home—"

"Ow! Ow! Ow! Ow! Ow!"

"This little piggy ate roast beef, this little piggy had none—Almost out of piggies, Edward. Looks like you're down to your last piggy."

"Go away and leave me alone! I'll call Nurse Hazlett!" Edward reaches for the call button, but Catches grabs it first. "Give me that!"

"Here." Catches dangles the button from its cord. "Sit up and take it."

"I can't sit up."

Tom Catches shrugs. "As you wish," he says, and starts re-bandaging the foot. Instead of the cloth bandage, which has fallen to the floor, he uses fabric from the room: Edward's pillowcase, a towel, the extra sheet from the foot of the bed. He removes a baseball glove from the paper bag and studies the bandage, then sets the glove aside. He rises and gets Edward's bedpan and slides it inside the paper bag; he slides the pan with its paper bag over the bandage and fastens it with a flourish. He sets Edward's foot back on the bed, with the bedpan sticking up like a giant shoe. "There you go. All better."

"It's terrible. It hurts!" Rather than looking at his foot with the bedpan, Edward stares at the glove. "What's that?"

"What does it look like? It's your fielder's glove. Sit up, now. I've brought people to see you."

"What people? The only person in Turtle Lodge who remembers me is my son. He never comes."

"Here they are, now. Sit up. Try and be polite."

Nine men of different ages crowd into the room; they wear baseball gloves and uniforms that say Willow Warriors. All but one of them are Indians of various blood quanta, from full-blooded and dark-skinned to pale. One by one, they remove their caps and introduce themselves.

"Leonard Chambers. Second Base. Auto accident."

"James Buffalo. First Base. Measles and pneumonia."

"Billy Doolin. Shortstop. Jap bullet at Guadalcanal." Billy Doolin is all Irish and red-headed.

"Aristo Johnson. Catcher. Cirrhosis and pancreatitis."

"John Buffalo. Right Field. Esophageal cancer."

"Erwin Stone Soldier. Left Field. Auto accident."

"LeMoine Yellow Thunder. Third Base. Cirrhosis and Parkinson's."

"Darald Shield. Pitcher. Heart failure due to age."

"Samuel Wallace. Relief pitcher. Mortar round. Korea."

"Thank you, gentlemen." Tom Catches turns to Edward. "We need a center fielder. Sam Wallace can play center, but he's slow. And what would happen if one of them hurt his foot? We'd have to forfeit the game."

"These jokers can't play ball," Edward Stevens points out. "They're as dead as you."

"Maybe they are. What makes you so special?"

"I didn't say I was special. It's just that I'm not dead yet."

"So you tell me. If you're not dead, sit up."

"I can't."

"Here's two more to see you."

The baseball players shift to form a passage, and two identical women enter the room. Not young but not above middle age, they wear long old-fashioned dresses made of flour-sack material, and heavy brogans rather than women's shoes. They approach the bed and offer their hands to Edward. "Dorothea," one of them says. "Dolores," says the other. "Lupus, 1955 and 1959."

Edward glares at them. "Forget it. I'm too old."

"We should have married you," Dorothea says. "Our lives were miserable. I married a man who needed a slave to help him cook his homemade whiskey."

"I bore a child out of wedlock," Dolores says. "There was nobody to help me raise him. I was on my own."

"We're sorry we teased you, Edward," Dorothea says. "The men we knew were of no account. They're gone. It will be different now."

"We want to watch you play again," Dolores says. "You were like a little squirrel out there, all quick and bouncy."

"I don't bounce any more," Edward says. "Get away from me. You don't smell good."

The two women step back humbly, their heads bowed. A new person enters the room, rubbing her eyes: Karla Čapek. "Where am I?" she says.

Edward Stevens sits up in alarm. He looks at Catches. "Not her," he says. "Leave her out of this."

Karla approaches the bed. "Edward, is that you? You're sitting up by yourself, Edward. That's just wonderful!" She glances at the baseball glove lying on the bed.

"Don't touch that," Edward says to her. "Go back to your dream."

"I was at a baseball game—"

"That's it. You were at a game. Go back there."

"—Only you were pitching, not playing center field, and you had this monster bandage on your foot."

Edward sits up and swings around so that his feet dangle from the side of the bed. One of his feet is enormous. He picks up the glove and tucks it under his right arm. "Get out!" he says to Karla. "Go back to your own dream. You're not safe here."

"Careful, Edward," Karla says. "This is great that you're so active. Better let me help you." She moves forward to steady him.

"No! Get back," he says, and waves her hand aside. "Don't touch me! I can stand by myself." He slides off the bed and stands, a bit crookedly because his foot is still trapped inside the bedpan. He slips his left hand into the glove and slaps the pocket with his fist. He gives Catches a nod, and six of the baseball players lift him onto their shoulders, three on each side.

"All right," Catches says. "Get in time, now. On the count of three." He lifts his hand like a band conductor and starts to sing: *Take. Me out to. The ball. Game. . . .*

The other men join in: *Take me out with the crowd. . . .* The six bear Edward from the room, bedpan first, in a sort of slow-march: step, pause, pause, step. The remaining three players follow with their caps in their hands, and the twins in their flour-sack dresses go last. Karla is left standing, confused.

"Where are you taking Edward?"

"Edward has joined the team," Tom Catches says. "We need him at center field."

"Edward is ninety-seven years old. He can't play baseball."

"Too late. He's out there practicing, shagging grounders."

Karla yawns. "Center field," she says. "How funny. That's where they used to send me, back when I was a skinny kid and could run like a rabbit." She looks around; Tom Catches has gone. The room is empty. "Well, I'm no rabbit," she says to herself. "Can't run fast now." She turns to follow the others but can't find the door.

IT'S TWO IN THE MORNING. All the bars have closed. Light slanting down the hallway from the nurses' station makes everything look drunk. A twist, a push—*door, don't squea*l—and here's Karla back in Room Nineteen. "Edvaaard," she goes in her best Count Dracula voice. "Edvaaard, it's me-eee, your double header, your twi-night dopple banger. I've cahmmm to keeess you. . . ." She crashes into the green armchair, and since she now knows where it is, she sits. Air wheezes out of the vinyl. The room is as dark as the inside of a cow.

"It's me, Karla. Sorry to wake you, but it's been such a night! I have to tell somebody." A pissy glow seeps under Edward's door, and the fun starts to whistle out of Karla. "Sorry," she says again, and scratches her bruised shins. "Well, crap. Here it comes: mood swing.

"Sorry sorry sorry. I get gosh-darned tired of being sorry. Sorry for what's not my fault— My dad ran off before I can remember, and my mom had to work two jobs. Her night job was tending bar, and I used to think if she didn't have a daughter who ate too much and grew out of clothes faster than she could sew them, she wouldn't've come home drunk every single night. I was always apologizing to Michael, too. Remember, I told you about Michael? Well, screw Michael and screw the rest of you! Not you, Edward. Sorry sorry sorry.

"Edward? I wanted to ask you. Do you think the whole world is lonely? I mean, those little spiders floating away, each in its own direction. You here in Room Nineteen. Me on my porch swing with my twelve-pack, wishing for—well, somebody. Michael, or— Somebody—

"Growing up, I never knew what it was to not be lonely. See, girls never liked me, Edward. Too big, too rough, whatever. I played with boys. We played war—they wanted me to be a nurse, but I wouldn't—war, and cowboys and Indians—I liked anything where I could run, you couldn't keep me off the ball field, I wasn't afraid of grounders and could hit as good as any of 'em. I loved baseball just like you, Edward. Loved the patience of it, the running— I could throw hard, even if I was a girl. You said you played center field. That was my position.

"But those boys broke my heart, Edward. See, I thought they were my friends, but as we got older, they started—teasing me—wanting me to be dirty, you know, and I had to let them do it. I was twelve or thirteen, skinny as a rail, didn't have my period yet, I got that really late, but I was as tall as my mom almost. I didn't know anything or feel anything, except dirty. Like a used Kleenex. I guess I thought I had to do it, though to be honest I did have a choice. I could've told on them, but then who would I have had? Nobody. I wasn't a boy, so I couldn't be on the team, and I was too big and strong and tall to be like other girls. Like if a tree grew in an alfalfa field. Well, of course they'd never let it grow. It'd get cut down.

"Then came high school; overnight, I got all big and heavy and bobbley, and—kind of funny looking— And the boys didn't even want me for *that* any more." It seems to Karla that Edward ought to say something. But there's only silence.

"Somehow I ended up on the girls' basketball team. We played a funny kind of basketball called 'six-on-six' that they don't play now. We went to a tournament at Kearney, and this little guy who played trumpet in the pep band made love to me. He did it on a bet, I found out later, but he— Uh, he was like a butterfly, such a little moth of a man that he couldn't be anything but gentle. Physically. I fell in love with him, and he— Maybe he was lonely, too.

"That was Michael. I won an athletic scholarship, and we hung out together at the University. Then we broke up and I got expelled. I almost did die that time, Edward. Literally." Karla gets the urge and starts rummaging in her pocketbook for a cigarette. She expects to hear a lot of throat-clearing from Edward, but she's glad when he doesn't bum one. His old rotten tennis shoe of a heart's had plenty of nicotine for one day.

Karla strikes a match—staring into the flame—and goes, "I'll be feeling sorry for myself in a minute, and that's not what I came to tell you. I had this dream tonight where I was playing ball." She lights up and blows the match out just before it burns her fingers.

"After I got off work, I went to the store for my twelve-pack and a loaf of bread and some Polish sausages. Then I went home and left the bathroom door open and had myself a soak and a beer and read the newspaper. All this time I'm thinking about you and Michael and ghosts and stuff, and how apples don't taste red any more—If there was one thing Michael hated it was Polish sausages.

"After a while I'm sitting on the stoop of my apartment building, having another beer. Fireflies in the yard, and heat lightning, way off— I'm thinking how it'd be to just sit there with someone, you know, we could sit, and talk— I try not to think too much, Edward, because for me it's nothing but a bad habit, but tonight I couldn't help it, somehow. The wind must've gone down, I'm listening to the nighthawks buzz the roofs, and I guess I must've fallen asleep.

"That's when I had this dream, and you were in it.

"I was one girl batting against a whole team. It was a game like Workup, except I was stuck in the batter's box at home plate, and it was a real box with boards up to my waist. To get free, I was supposed to hit the ball. I didn't know how many strikes I'd get, or what would happen when I struck out, but something bad was going to happen if I didn't get a hit. Maybe they'd add more boards.

"The first team I had to bat against was that bunch of privileged turds who used to rape me. Yeah, rape; that's what it was. I can finally admit it. I was twelve years old, they were teenagers, and they should've been put in jail. But I was so ashamed! Edward, it was them that did what was bad, but it was me that felt ashamed. How do you account for that? Maybe it's just part of growing up female. Being ashamed.

"Anyway, I batted around and batted around. I kept hitting foul balls. Then their leader came out to pitch, and I could see that he had a special ball for me. This was the son of a man my mother worked for, the manager at the bra factory. He made a complicated, nasty windup with all kinds of gestures that don't belong in baseball. Finally he throws the pitch, and it's an easy one, right down the middle. I swing and smack it good. Blooie! It was a ball of shit, Edward. They tricked me. 'Strike one!' I was splashed all over.

"Next team I had to bat against was college people, coaches and professors. Some of them liked me, some of them didn't; each one had a different windup, a different way of throwing the ball. But I kept hitting fouls, keeping my turn at bat alive. Now comes Ruby Hoeft, my weightlifting coach. Instead of holding a baseball, she's got a giant pill. She winds up and throws it, but on the way to me it breaks up into tiny dots. They hit me all over like shotgun pellets, and every place one hits, a black hair grows. I never even get a chance to swing. The umpire calls, 'Strike two!'

"I never do get a look at that umpire, by the way. Sometimes I think it's a priest, sometimes it's my high-school guidance counselor. But I don't dare turn around to see, because the next pitcher might throw one past me.

"Next team I had to bat against were old guys in regular baseball uniforms. I never saw them before, but they acted like ballplayers. Then the pitcher comes out and it's you, Edward! I know you said you played center field, but here you were, pitching. You were old, just like you are now, except you could see; your old blind eyes were bright and could look right through me.

"You pitch me a blazing fastball. Strike one! (Somehow I get a new strike one.) The old guys laugh. You pitch again. This time it's a corkscrew curve that goes in a spiral. Strike two!

"Time is running out on me, Edward, but somehow I know I'm going to smack it. I'm ready; here's the windup. You kick your left foot in the air, wearing a boot that looks like a bedpan—" Karla crouches in the dark and cocks an imaginary bat. "—Here's the pitch. It's a changeup, floating toward me like the Goodyear Blimp. Thank you, Edward!" Karla mimes a powerful stroke. "She swings! She connects! KA-BLOOIE! That ball is GONE!" Karla drops the invisible bat and starts toward first with her chest held high.

Clangalang! She collides with the floor lamp, trips, and crashes.

This time it's not only a couple of bruised shins. She's cock-a-heap in the corner. Edward's chair lies across her legs, and she can feel the lamp pole under her. The metal shade's still ringing, off in the room somewhere, and she's afraid to move for fear of broken glass. She puts a careful hand on the floor and pushes herself part way up, and twists around in the dark and tries to set the chair on its feet, though it's hard to get a feel for which way the floor is slanted. "That's when I woke up," she says. "Well, Edward, that was the dream I had. What do you think?"

Silence. It's as if he isn't there.

"Anyway, there I was, back sitting on the stoop. I stood up to go and get myself another beer, and I noticed I could hear women hollering, must be six, seven, eight blocks away. It was the women's softball league out at East City Park. I could see the glow of the ballpark lights above the houses."

The room's still dark as seventy-nine black cats. Karla feels dizzy; to stand erect, she braces herself against the heating unit. "I wanted to go so badly, Edward, but I was afraid. Afraid I'd be too fat; afraid I'd be laughed at. Maybe even afraid they'd know I had been raped. But, by golly, I went. I had such a time! Such a time— It was the last game of the season, so we all went downtown to the bar. Met new friends, Jan, and Martha, and— Can't remember all their names— They want me to sign up, hippopotamus that I am. Can you believe it? I'm going to try out next summer! Maybe I can be a pinch hitter. I bet I can still swat one—"

There's a click over by the door and, SHAZAM! All the dazzle in the universe pours into Karla's eyes. She can feel her forebrain shrivel like a salted slug. "Shit, that is intense," she says, though foul language is not tolerated at the Sailors of Galilee. It's Hazlett on night duty, the last person Karla wants to see. Hazlett stands there frowning with her hand still on the light toggle.

"Miss Čapek! What are you doing here?"

"Nothing." Karla squints from under her paw. "I came to see Edward."

"Mr. Stevens? But he's not here."

"Hunh?"

Karla peers through the glare at the empty bone-white bed. The pillow is fluffed, the sheet's folded back, and the blanket is as flat as an ironing board. There's no dent, not a smudge, not a shadow. And Edward's chart is missing. The next thing she knows, Hazlett is holding her and shaking her, even though Karla's a foot taller and a ton heavier. There's a loud howling noise in her ears. It would seem she is screaming.

"MISS ČAPEK! CALM! The RESIDENTS, Miss Čapek!"

Sure enough, once Karla stops for breath, she hears them up and down the hall. Like it's dawn and they're starting with their morning noises. "AHHH!" She gulps air like a netted catfish. "Edward! He— He—"

"It's all right, Karla. Edward's gone. He's not here." As if that wasn't the whole trouble. "We sent him to the ER at eight forty-five this evening. The hospital sent him back to us, and we, uh— We've moved him into Room Twenty until we can reach his contacts." Room Twenty is where they store meat and dairy products. There's an extra space the size of a gurney.

Now Hazlett is holding Karla around the waist, waltzing her backwards toward the green-plastic-covered chair. Karla balks; something about that chair feels creepy. She doesn't want to sit. "But—" It still hasn't gotten through to her. "I was talking to him."

Hazlett quits nudging Karla toward the chair. She steps back and gives her a sideways look. "I hardly think so, Miss Čapek."

"He could talk as good as anybody," Karla tells her. "He only talked to certain people, is all."

"Right." Hazlett balances what's left of the floor lamp on its base. She looks down at the broken cone of glass. "I'm sure the two of you had a lot in common."

"We discussed baseball. Edward Stevens used to be a famous baseball player. Then we talked about love and ghosts, how a longing can steal the heart out of you till apples aren't apples and grass isn't green any more, and you can cut half your foot off and not see blood in the snow—"

When Karla looks up again, the Hazlett woman is gone. It's so quiet that the air is buzzing. Karla's sitting in the green chair, not standing, and she wonders if she passed out or fell asleep. She wonders if she's having a dream inside a dream.

Karla heaves herself out of the chair and goes to look down at Edward's pillow. There's not a trace. "Edward," she says, "I brought you something. After the game tonight, when they were getting into their cars and the lights went off and the field was dark and quiet, I walked out onto the diamond, just to see what it felt like. I remembered you and tried to think what would remind you of baseball. I thought of the umpire sweeping dirt off home plate—if I'm too fat to play ball, I could still be a darn good umpire, because I know everything there is about sweeping—and I took some dust from the infield and folded it in a Kleenex, and here it is." She takes out the tissue and unfolds it. Nothing there but a gritty pinch on soft paper. She hates to drop dirt on the clean pillowcase, so she holds it off to one side. Then it occurs to her: suppose Hazlett didn't just leave? What if she ran to call the dispatcher?

"Got to go, Edward," Karla says. "Who knows, maybe we'll see each other in the Hall of Fame." She spreads out the Kleenex and sprinkles dust on her palm, then rubs it into her hands like a batter stepping into the box. She takes a couple of practice swings. She goes into her stance.

Strike One. *I spit on your Strike One.*

Strike Two! *I patoo on your Strike Two.*

Next pitch, KA-RACK! She's a fly ball hit hard; she's over the fence and climbing. Then the wind gets under her and she's a spider, a speck of dust. She's free, floating steady like a satellite, shining down on the earth's green diamonds through August air.

# Gerard

KARLA ČAPEK WAS STANDING AT THE EDGE of Baxter's Pond, fishing for the stunted bluegills that crowded the water. Most weren't big enough to take the hook in their mouths. If she could catch five or six of the biggest ones, she'd have enough for a meal, though it might mean throwing back a couple dozen. It wasn't real fishing, just something to do.

The shadow of a man passed over the water, and she saw that it was the Indian who cleaned the floor at the bank. He was up on the abandoned trestle, walking carefully over toward her side. She acknowledged him with a nod, then tilted her hat to shade her eyes from the afternoon sun. Pretty soon he came up behind her.

"Catching any?"

"Only these stinkin' bluegills," she said. "Big Sid is down there somewhere, but I'm not after him." Karla weighed in at two-forty and was strong enough to knock the average man flat, so she feared no one. This man was big, but his voice was gentle. Soft Indian voice. Though when some of them spoke Lakota to one another, they sounded harsh.

"You'd need a bigger hook," he said. "Stronger leader, too."

"I don't care for catfish. Especially this time of year, they taste muddy."

"The ones out of the river are all right, if you catch them near the mouth of a creek."

"I thought Indians didn't eat fish."

"That was back in the old days," he said, "before we were corrupted."

Horse Looking was his name. Gerard Horse Looking. Since she'd passed through menopause, names came to her slowly.

"Catch me a few of them little bluegills," he said. "You're going to have plenty."

"All right," she said. "Do you have a way to carry them?"

"I'll figure out something."

Karla fished for another half hour without turning to look at him. Only an itching at the back of her neck told her he was there. He was said to have killed a young woman, his own sister, years before. No, others argued, the town cop had done it. That was long before she had moved to Turtle Lodge. She caught twenty little bluegills and threw back eighteen.

"Want me to take a turn?" he asked. "You been standing there a long time."

"I don't mind," she said. "Watch the poison ivy."

He came up close behind her and took the rod from her hand. Slow and gentle. She noticed that the fingers of his right hand had been broken, so that the fingertips pointed off toward Jones's. "I got 'em caught in the action of an M-60," he said. "There wasn't even any war on at that time."

"The worms are in that can by your feet," she said. "I'll stand over here."

Karla was big. Gerard Horse Looking was enormous. It was funny to watch him handle the tiny fish, so careful when he took the hook from their mouths. He tossed them far out into the pond, hoping they wouldn't come back to bite the same hook again. "My brother was in a car wreck, over in Europe," she said. "I only found out yesterday. He's a musician. Now he's out of work until his shoulder gets better."

"I'm sorry," Gerard Horse Looking said. "I bet he was driving a Fiat."

"Nope. Volkswagen. He could have been killed." It had been Karla and her mother and her brother; she had never known her dad, anyway not that she could remember. "My mother has passed. Are any of your folks living?"

"Maybe my mom is," he said. "She's a witch. She might live forever."

"Nobody lives forever. Not even Big Sid."

HOURS LATER, KARLA TURNED OVER in bed and found this gigantic Indian sleeping next to her. His skin was brown and warm. It had been so long since she'd had a sex partner, she considered it a miracle. She had melted onto him, then felt him melting into her; she hadn't come, but it had been wonderful all the same. Now, though, there was the problem of what to do with him.

She decided she would get up and cook him some fish.

She rose without waking him—no small feat, considering the poundage the mattress had to release—went into the bathroom, and then to the kitchen. She found cornmeal and salt and pepper and a little bacon grease. She'd already scaled and gutted the bluegills, out by the pond where the turtles would eat the leavings, and now she breaded them in a paper bag and put cooking oil in a skillet, along with the fragrant drippings. Before starting the fish, she made a pan of raw-fried potatoes and laid them out on a paper towel. She replenished the oil and laid in the bluegills and opened another beer. It was maybe her third. Whenever she cooked supper, she always liked to have a sip of beer to help her along. The fish were sizzling nicely when she felt that same tingle at the back of her neck.

"Hi," she said. "Welcome. Do you want a beer?"

"I don't drink beer," he said. "Thanks anyway."

"You sure?"

"I'm sure."

She wanted him to put his arms around her, but he did not do so. "I'm making us supper," she said. "You'll have supper with me, won't you?"

"I'd be glad to," he said. "Where's the bathroom? I need to wash up."

"You just passed it," she said. "It's right behind you."

The little fish were crispy on both sides when he returned. Karla nuked the potatoes twenty seconds' worth so they'd be nice and hot, and served them up along with the bluegills, two plates on the dinette table, no tablecloth, paper towels for napkins. She opened herself another beer. "What can I get you to drink?"

"Seven-Up or water," he said. "I don't need anything. Maybe coffee later."

She did not find it strange that they ate in silence. The little bluegills tasted good, as if they'd been living in clean fresh water, not the stale pond. Maybe it wasn't so stale; a trickle of creek flowed into and out of it. There was pond scum on the surface, but it didn't cover the whole pond, just the end away from the trestle. There hadn't been a train in years; the rails were somewhere in Argentina.

"Tell me about your brother," he said. "What kind of musician was he?"

"Let me get myself another beer."

Her brother was a classical musician, a violinist, a real artist, not one of the stars like Perlman but just as good. He played with passion and finesse, a kind of intensity that some listeners found unsettling. After he relocated to France, he swore he would never return to the United States. Any nation that could elect Ronald Reagan as its president could never be his home. He'd had four or five nervous breakdowns, and those were only the ones she knew about. His accident might not have been an accident. He had always felt he was not respected, and his rage vibrated along the strings of his violin.

"I never really knew him as an adult," she said. "They took him away from us when I was twelve. Later on, I thought I hated him. It felt like only one of us could have a life. He moved away to Paris, and I got stuck in Turtle Lodge, Nebraska. He kept writing to me for twenty years. I don't know how he found my address."

"Younger or older?"

"Younger. I was the one who protected him. I beat the crap out of any number of boys. Some girls, too. They called him a sissy."

"Was he?"

"I don't know," she said. "He never married. There's that."

"*Winkte*. That's what we call it. It's no big deal. That's how it used to be, anyhow. The old people say."

"I love you," she said. "Every day of my life has been the same until today."

"Think you could quit drinking?"

That stung. She felt the hair on her forearms rise. "Why would I do that? Fuck off." He started to laugh. "No, I mean it," she said. "I want you to go home now."

"All right," he said. When he stood, the floor boards creaked. "Thanks for supper. Let me cook for you sometime."

"That'll be the day."

The night air that pushed the door open was chilly. "I'll be around if you need me," he said. "For anything," he added. "I mean it."

"That'll be the day," she said again. The room felt hollow when he had gone.

KARLA WORKED THE CASH REGISTER at the dollar store. She knew everybody and nobody. She wished them all a good day and they thanked her. That was about the sum of their conversation.

Gerard came through pushing a cart of cleaning supplies. "Hey," he said.

"You," she said. "I don't know you."

"Want to go fishing on a real lake? I can get us a boat."

"Why would I do that?"

"Perch," he said. "Crappies the size of a dinner plate. Bass, maybe. Northern pike? You never know."

"Men and their promises," she said. "My mother warned me."

"We'll go Sunday."

"I have to work on Sunday." She rang up the supplies and charged them to the bank's credit card. He turned to go. "Tuesday," she said. "Tuesday is my day off."

On Tuesday they faced a sad comedy of automobiles. His was a van left over from the hippie era, with peace symbols painted on the rusted doors. Hers was a land yacht that she'd bought for 200 dollars, running on seven of its eight cylinders and lacking a muffler. It was a tossup as to which vehicle would make a 50-mile round trip over sandhill trails without leaving them on foot in somebody's cow pasture.

"We'll take mine," she said at last, wary of the horizontal space in the back of the van. "It's got a bumper hitch. It'll pull a little boat trailer all right."

"Fine," Gerard said. "Let me do something about that exhaust pipe, though. I don't want us to end up gassed to death."

He found a used muffler in the junk pile in back of the Co-Op station, but he needed help to get it attached; a man at the station put her car up on the hoist and welded it in place. He didn't say anything about money. Gerard had a sort of advocate in Turtle Lodge, a businessman named Rudy

McDonough, who let them borrow his twelve-foot boat and trailer, and they were all set except that the rigmarole had cost them the morning. The afternoon would be hotter, but it might be cool on the lake. Karla packed baloney sandwiches and iced a twelve-pack in the cooler, and they were off, with the windows down to let out some of the heat. There was no question of the air conditioner working. She had to admit that it was nicer to drive without the constant grumble coming from underneath.

"Dinosaur farts," Gerard said. "They make gasoline from dinosaurs."

Karla knew better, but she did not correct him, it being pointless to argue with anyone who happened to carry the Y chromosome.

Summer is not the prettiest time in the sandhills—spring is prettier—but the grass-covered pastureland was pleasant to drive through. They passed hay meadows with nodding cattails and red-winged blackbirds, climbed the sandy cuts through the high places, skirted blowouts and startled deer. "Thanks for inviting me," Karla said. "I should get out of town more often. I get claustrophobia and don't even notice I can't breathe."

"It's different up on the Rez," Gerard said. "I don't know why, but it just feels different somehow. You got relatives bearing down on you, but the town itself isn't such a *thing*."

"White people have been living in towns for a million years. We like to settle down together in one place and make each other miserable."

Hackberry Lake reflected a sky the color of an infant's irises. Some infants. The breeze was light, just enough to pick up a little coolness from the water. Karla backed the boat trailer down near the shoreline without too much difficulty, and they detached the aluminum boat and slid it backward onto the mud, and loaded the oars and anchor and the cooler and fishing gear. Rudy had lent them his pet outboard motor, a certifiable antique from God knows when, a dull-green putt-putt thing that advertised itself to put out three horsepower. Neither of them expected it to run, but it did, and soon they were off across the lake no faster than a goose could paddle, followed by an oily cloud of blue exhaust.

The fishing wasn't any good but the day was perfect. Karla spotted a yellow-headed blackbird on a muskrat house, a bird the book said was common in the area but one she'd never added to her list. A bittern called from across the water, a deep "Gump! Gump! Gump! Gump!" as if some giant were bouncing a ten-foot Superball. The deer flies were not too pesky, and the waves slapped against the boat with sleepy little taps. Karla's head was nodding when she felt the boat lurch and looked up to see Gerard standing in the bow, preparing to cast a bass lure. Up until this time they'd been fishing with bobbers, which she much preferred. "Watch out," she said. "You're going to tip us."

"Nah," Gerard said. "I've been doing this all my life."

If he hadn't, he'd at least done it more than once. He balanced as he cast; his feet moved with the boat's motion but his body stayed erect. She let him get his line out and click the reel to begin to bring it in, and then she gripped the gunwale and gave the boat a rock. He overcompensated and they rocked the other way, and Gerard hit the water with a splash appropriate to his size. Karla grinned in anticipation, but he did not reappear when she thought he would. She watched the cloudy water for a full minute. Little bubbles came up but Gerard did not, and she threw aside her hat and fishing pole and plunged into the water, holding her breath with her arms outstretched, feeling this way and that. Her fingers found hair—Gerard had plenty of it—and she wound and twisted it and yanked him toward the surface. Once her eyes cleared the water, she grabbed the rowboat's stern and used the leverage to drag him. He emerged shaking his head and spitting water, but instead of registering panic, his face was full of laughter. "Ha, ha!" he said. "I swim like a duck. I was messing with you."

"You big turd. How did you stay under? Were you holding onto the weeds?"

"I had hold of the anchor rope." He rose to the surface and floated on his back, his legs spread comfortably. "Oh ho! You should've seen the look on your face. You were worried about me."

"I was worried about hauling your waterlogged corpse to town."

"No, you were all concerned. You didn't want to see me drown."

"I'll see you drown yet," she said, and gave him a hard but measured punch in the nuts. She almost succeeded, too. By the time she got him back in the boat, he'd swallowed so much water that he caught a pneumonia that it took three weeks to get rid of.

IT REQUIRED SOME TIME FOR THE TOWN to get used to seeing them together. Two people whom everyone thought of as being settled in their ways, who had mostly managed to live without causing gossip, held hands when they walked like a couple of teenagers. To add, they were of different races; this was a thing not unheard of in Turtle Lodge, but it was unusual for such couples to walk together in public. Karla didn't mind the talk, what there was of it, because she'd always felt like a stranger in the community and thought she was past caring what anybody said. Still, the looks they sometimes got unsettled her nerves.

"Get used to it," Gerard said. "People are idiots."

"The other day, somebody smiled at us. That was fun."

"Did you know them?"

"I don't think so."

"Bet they're not from here."

So it went. Nothing special happened to them for a while. Karla started helping Gerard with his cleaning duties, which were not severe but which tired him nonetheless. Then one morning she spat out her coffee.

Karla's mother had made European-style coffee, blacker than black. Karla liked it that way and depended on her single cup to get her going in the morning. So when she spat out her coffee, that was an event. The next morning was the same, and her eggs didn't taste good either. She began to think she might have caught the flu, but she didn't get over it. Gerard told her she ought to see a doctor, but the thought of being probed and questioned repelled her. Still, she missed her morning coffee so much that she decided it might be worth a try.

The doctor was a woman five feet tall who looked as if she were eighteen. She examined Karla all over, not just her throat and lungs, and asked about her symptoms. Karla thought of lifting her and holding her upside down, just to see if her voice would deepen, but she remained passive and did as she was told, breathing in, breathing out, coughing, letting herself be poked and squeezed. "Have your breasts been aching lately, by any chance?" the doctor asked.

"What? Heavens, no. Why should they? Do I have breast cancer?"

"No, no. In fact, I don't find anything wrong with you. But I'm going to give you a blood test, and if you don't mind, make a urine sample in this cup for me."

*For you? Do you drink urine?*

Karla peed in the cup as requested, then waited in the lobby twenty minutes, which turned into forty. Luckily it was a Tuesday, so she wasn't late for work. When the doctor called her back in the room, she was smiling. "Congratulations," she said. "You're pregnant."

"No I'm not," Karla said. "I'm past that. Closed up shop. The lights are on, but nobody's home."

"You mean you're not having sex?"

"I mean I'm as close to fifty as forty. I haven't had my period in about three years."

"Well," the doctor said, "sometimes Mother Nature finds a way."

"Mother Nature can kiss my great big butt," Karla said. "All I wanted was to enjoy my morning coffee and not to feel so dragged out all the time. Now this? What am I supposed to do?"

"Your stomach will settle down after the first three months. Anyway, that's what usually happens."

"How would you know? You've never had a baby."

"Actually I have three little ones at home. The oldest is in fifth grade." The eighteen-year-old physician and mother-of-three grinned. "I'm older than I look. I was almost thirty by the time I finished med school."

"I feel older than I look," Karla said, "and when I haven't had my coffee, I look like shit."

That night Karla and Gerard lay facing one another. The ceiling light was on, and she fingered the scars on his chest, the sun-dance scars that ran like little ladders up both sides and the long vertical scar where his sternum had been split and his chest pulled open like a sliding door. "Don't cry," she said to him. "It's not the end of the world. I'll get an abortion."

"Is that what you want, Chiefy?" He had taken to calling her Chief White Thundercloud, for some reason.

"I don't know what I want, Gerry. I need time to think."

"Well, if you want my vote, I'd say keep it. People poorer and dumber than us have babies all the time."

"Honey, be honest. We can't afford to feed a cat. And besides, we're too old."

"We're not old, we're experienced."

"And where has our experience gotten us? To this town at the end of the road, where I can't even get a real job?" Karla sniffled. "And where will we live? In this apartment? In that trailer of yours?" Her apartment was in a creaking stucco building that had once been the Bachelor Officer's Quarters of a forgotten World War Two air base. It was cold, drafty, dark and dismal, and small.

"I'll get a bigger trailer. Or build a lean-to. You work days, I work nights. We'll take turns. It's going to be great."

"I can see myself at her graduation," Karla said. "I'll be the oldest and fattest parent in the gym. And look at you. You'll be in a wheelchair."

"*Her* graduation?"

"Hell, yes, *her*," Karla said. "If it turns out to be a boy, I'll drown myself." She touched the left-side ladder of little scars. "Does it hurt you when they do that?"

"It hurts if you think about it. I try not to think about it."

"Why do it, then?"

"It gives me an event to focus on, one year to the next. It helps me stay sober."

BERT, THE HIGH SCHOOL'S CUSTODIAN, was found in the furnace room in a pool of urine, where he'd evidently been lying for two days. He'd had a stroke and did not form sentences again, though he continued to live on in the nursing home, waving an arm and mumbling indecipherable questions. The school needed a new custodian; Rudy McDonough spoke to a man who served on the school board and got Karla the job. Christmas vacation came and went, and her no-decision about her pregnancy became a decision. When the word got out, or when her state became obvious, the board felt betrayed by Rudy, but the high school was cleaner than it had been in two decades and she kept the job and persevered. Meanwhile Gerard got a second nighttime cleaning job, this one at an auto dealership, and they were able to make a down payment on a single-wide and park it next to Gerard's dilapidated trailer, which they converted to a sort of annex for the mice. Winter turned into spring, and it snowed some days and didn't snow others, and the snowdrops and then the crocuses came up in the lawns, followed by grass and dandelions. Karla made it almost to the end of the term, until she dropped her broom one afternoon and said, "Oh, shit," and a pimply kid with a learner's permit drove her to the hospital. There they gave her some nice drugs and put her in a room, and she began the worst experience of her life.

Karla had lifted weights in college, but she'd never strained at anything so hard as she strained to deliver that baby. After the first day and a half, thirty-six hours in labor, she became so savage that the nurses wouldn't go near her. One of them suggested shooting her with a tranquilizer dart, but they didn't know what dose would be appropriate. Then the agony ended, the baby squirted out of her like a watermelon seed and landed at the foot of the bed, and Karla passed out and slept for three days. When they brought her the little peanut-brown baby with European-coffee-colored eyes, Karla looked at her and said, "Her name is Onyx."

"Is that a Lakota word? Ah Nix?" the nurse asked. "How do you want it spelled?"

The baby yawned and made a toothless little smile. "You spell it J. O. Y," Karla said. "Her name is Joy."

So they lived, this big-hearted couple in their house that was much too small, keeping the lights and heat on and plugging away at jobs that were pretty stupid but more useful than, say, a driving instructor's. Ten years slipped by the way they do, and little Joy went from diapers to gauzy pastel dresses to cowgirl outfits and glasses. In spite of her outsized parents she was a normal kid, not too skinny and not too fat, not too tiny and not too tall, bright but not eccentric about it, musical but not a prodigy. Of course she was brown in a community where blonde was the default, but she was well liked and successful and brought home good report cards. She even helped her dad on nights when he was too tired and Karla had to wash clothes or study algebra.

So they lived, until one day her dad went ice fishing.

Gerard fished in all seasons and all weathers, but at no time did he take it as seriously as in December and January when the ice froze hard and transparent and he could get out onto the lakes without a boat. They ate more fish than beef in the winter months, perch mostly but the occasional northern pike, sometimes bullheads which were firm-fleshed and free of worms in winter, though they were difficult to skin. On this particular day, Gerard was out for perch at a time of year when most fishermen went after northern pike; consequently he had the ice to himself, on a shallow lake dotted with muskrat houses known as Government Lake. He had his tip-ups and the five-foot iron spud he used to make holes in the ice, and he had his pole and minnow bucket and tackle box and a thermos of Karla's powerful coffee, all this gear piled on a child's Flexible Flyer sled with a box attached, pulled with a rope. He wore mittens and overshoes, unbuckled, and a pair of bib overalls over his pants and sweater and underneath his parka. He was a heavy man heavily loaded, and the ice creaked underfoot.

Gerard pounded a dozen holes in the ice and set out tip-ups, and he rigged and baited his favorite spinning rod and sat down on the sled to drink coffee and wait. Pretty soon one little flag went up and then another, and he was taking perch off the lines, rebaiting the hooks with minnows and tossing the fish onto the ice, where they flipped themselves like little pancakes and gasped and died. He got hot and removed his parka and looked around at the pretty scene—it was a sunny day on the lake, and brown cattails nodded near the shore; the bare bent shabby willows along the shoreline were picturesque in their dark crookedness. The hills beyond the lake rose softly, the dead grasses russet and purple and tan. The snow had melted, what there was of it—it had been a dry winter—and the ice of the lake had a pleasant blue-black tint independent of the blue sky overhead.

There was a certain roughness to the surface, and the chunks of ice he chopped had fallen into splinters and scattered, so he knew that the ice would be going out in a few days, all the more reason to catch fish while he could. The result was that he stayed out longer than he should have; he put his parka back on because he'd gotten chilled. Finally he pulled his lines and rolled them up and piled his gear on the sled, except for the ice spud which he used as a heavy cane. There was one last perch to pick up, one that he'd tossed a little farther than the others. It had landed where some rushes came up through the ice, a few feet away from a muskrat house, and as he reached to get it, the fish gave a wiggle and disappeared through an opening alongside one of the reeds.

"Oh, my." Gerard felt a chill that was unrelated to the fresh breeze that had sprung up. The evening sun still shone but he had a cold sense of dread as he eyed the distance to his vehicle, an old Ford pickup parked along the verge. He thought, *Thank God I didn't drive it out onto the ice.*

He began walking gingerly toward the truck, picking his way, staying away from the reeds and watching the ice. It crumbled underfoot when he kicked it; in places little pools of water had accumulated. He felt ahead of himself with the spud and towed the sled and slid his feet along as if they were on skis. He was passing another rat house when the spud went through the ice and he felt himself descending. *Well, this is how I die,* he thought, and then the ice water hit his skin and suddenly he did not want to die, not that way, not drowning in lake water the color of weak iced tea. Then his feet hit bottom and he found himself standing in water just above his navel. Cold as oncoming death but not dead yet.

Gerard thought of the half-grown badger he'd once kept, notable for its stink and for its ability to claw its way out of almost anything. He thought of Joy's bright eyes and impish grin when she brought home a prize for being the best speller, and he decided he would get himself out of there. First he tried grabbing the ice and pulling himself out, but the ice crumbled under his grasp. He tried smashing his way using the ice spud as a hammer, but by the time he'd gone ten feet he knew he'd wear himself out long before he reached the truck. He glanced around and saw the muskrat house rising above the ice, and made his way in that direction, smashing and pushing and breaking through, anything to get himself out of the water. He reached the little dome of sticks and reeds and pulled himself up onto it, and started taking off his clothes.

The boots went first; they were full of water and weighed him down. His shoes and socks came off, then the parka, which was soaked through halfway up and worthless. He kept the wool sweater on but took off his sodden overalls and jeans, removing the billfold and holding it between his teeth. Then, standing in his underwear, he lifted the sweater up around his neck and took off the flannel shirt that was underneath. Without his shirt to protect his neck, the sweater itched like blazes, but he knew it was better than cotton to warm him in the cooling twilight.

The cold hadn't made him stupid yet—that would come soon enough—and Gerard looked around for options. There was no one on the lake to help him if he yelled, no one to hold the other end of a rope. But, speaking of rope, he still held the rope that tied him to the sled, which floated behind him in the slush and broken ice. He pulled it up onto the rat house and looked at it.

He emptied the minnow bucket and threw it aside. He twisted the cap off the Thermos and drank the last cup of coffee, and threw that in the water as well. The box on the sled was easily detached, and it could go, along with his tackle box and fishing tackle and favorite spinning rod. He had no need of the heavy spud unless it was to smash his way through ice, which he hoped not to have to do. He laid it carefully on the rat house in case he had to come back for it.

Gerard slid the sled out onto the unbroken ice on the other side of the rat house. He eased his weight onto it, feeling the rotten ice settle and creak, and clawed himself along using his fingernails. By scrabbling and scratching, sometimes pushing with his toes, he made good progress until the sled broke through and he got a whole-body immersion in ice water. "Look at me, I'm a polar bear," he shouted, standing up in the wind. This time the water only came to his knees; the ice here was weak and crystallized, and he stomped on through, bruising and cutting his feet but getting himself closer to the truck. Finally there was no more ice, and he ran ashore, splashing and laughing because he'd been smart or lucky enough to leave the keys in the ignition.

When his wet rump hit the ice-cold seat he got a jolt, but the engine started without any fuss and he turned the knob and put the heater on full. He backed around and drove, with his bare feet bleeding on the bare pedals, and the engine gradually warmed until he felt the first tickle of heat from the blower. Then his teeth chattered and he started to shudder so violently that he was hardly able to hold the steering wheel. A powerful urge to sleep came over him and he shook his head to clear his vision. The truck swerved and jounced on the two-track sandhill trail, and the jostling helped him keep his eyes open.

Half an hour later, Karla looked out the window of their single-wide to see her barefoot husband, wearing only boxer shorts and a sweater, come lurching up the driveway like a zombie. He was fishless and tackle-less and pole-less, and she knew right away what had happened and ran to the door to haul him inside. "Get in here! Look at you," she fussed. "In bed with you immediately! No coffee until you warm up. Move! Move!" He stumbled ahead of her as she hustled him along; she threw the bedclothes aside and tumbled him in and climbed in after him, kicking off her shoes and pulling the covers up around them.

"I'm hot," he said. "I'm too hot. Take those covers off."

"You're not hot," she said. "You're a fudgesicle. Now shut up and go to sleep, or else I'll smack you."

She held him in an iron grip until he quit shivering. She got up and piled more quilts on the bed and went to reassure her daughter, who remained in front of the TV and had failed to fully grasp what was happening. "Your father fell through the ice," Karla said. "He's cold. He needs to rest and warm up."

"Why not put him under the hot shower?" the girl asked.

"You're supposed to let them warm up slowly," Karla said. "If you try to do it fast, they can have a heart attack."

"If you think he's going to have a heart attack, you should call the ambulance."

"Sweetheart, there's no way we can pay for an ambulance."

Karla made the girl supper, mac-and-cheese from the box and French onion soup from the can, and fried herself a couple of eggs and went in the bedroom to see about Gerard. He opened his eyes when she sat down on the bed. "Hello, Chiefy. What time is it?"

"It's a little after eight p.m. How do you feel?"

"I'm fine except that I can't feel my feet. I guess I'd better get up and go clean the bank."

"You're not cleaning any bank," she said. "You're staying where you are until I tell you. What would you like to eat? There's soup. There's mac-and-cheese. I could make you coffee and warm you up a slice of pie."

"I should've died today, Chiefy. I would've died, too, but I was afraid you wouldn't find me. It would've been dark out there. You wouldn't have known what lake I was on. It's a big country."

"I would've hired an airplane and spotted your truck from the air. I wouldn't have let the coyotes eat you."

"Hunh. An airplane. I didn't think of that." He sighed and closed his eyes. "My feet are numb," he said. "Take a look at them, will you?"

Karla flipped back the covers and exposed his feet. The tops of them looked like they always did, discolored in purplish patches, scaly and dirty-looking, though he mostly kept them clean; he was particular about showering every day. The soles were dead-white and full of cuts and bruises. "Christ, Gerry! What have you done to yourself? Your feet are in tatters."

"I don't know. The ice was sharp, I guess. You know how it gets when it's breaking up. Crystals like four-inch glass needles."

"We'll get some clean socks on you. And pants. You're going to the hospital."

His old beater of a truck was blocking the driveway. She moved it and started her car and left it to warm up, and went back inside and recruited Joy to assist her. Together they helped Gerard to sit up. When his feet touched the floor, it turned out they weren't numb after all. "Ouch!" he said. "How'd I ever make it in here?"

"You were staggering," Karla said. "I almost thought you were drunk."

"Haven't had a drink in sixteen years."

"So you keep reminding me."

They got him out to the car, one on each side, and put him in the front seat and buckled him in. "Do you want me to come with you?" Joy asked. Karla looked at the child, young and worried, too grown up for her age.

"No," she said. "You take your homework and get yourself over to the McDonoughs'. I'll call if there are any developments. They'll bring a wheelchair for him. No more heavy lifting."

Joy leaned in through the open car window to kiss her father. "Come home soon, Daddy. I don't want you to be in the hospital."

"I don't like hospitals," Gerard said.

From a previous job at the nursing home, Karla knew a few things about people dying. When the old people died, sometimes their feet went first. That happened a lot with diabetics, and Gerard was borderline. She kept her thoughts to herself as she crossed the town; if Gerard had any thoughts, he was keeping them in as well. "Well, here we are," she said as she pulled up onto the apron. "This is going to cost us money. I hope the fishing was worth it."

"I hate hospitals," he said. "I should've died on the lake."

"You weren't on the lake, hon," she said. "You were in it."

He was stripped and given a gown and taken to a private room, where, with the ridiculous gown on his front and his fat bare legs, he brought to her mind a ham covered with a paper napkin. The nurse on duty looked at Gerard's feet, said "Ugh," and cleaned them with alcohol and painted them with iodine. Together they arranged him on the bed—Karla had to help her lift him—and the nurse led Karla from the room. "We're going to put a heart monitor on him," she said. "It sounds like he's in atrial fibrillation. The top part of his heart's not working."

"I know what a-fib is," Karla said. "You can zap him out of it, right?"

"Only if the doctor orders it," the nurse said. "I'm going to call her now but I already know what she'll say. Keep watch on him overnight and we'll see how he's doing in the morning." She gave Karla a hard look and added, "You'd better go home and get some sleep. His heart's going to be all right. It's those feet I'm worried about. We'd better watch his blood sugar, too. Are there any antibiotics he's allergic to?"

"I don't know," Karla said. "He's only been sick once since I've known him."

"I'll ask him," the nurse said. "You can say good night to him now. Come in first thing in the morning. We'll need you to sign some papers."

Gerard was asleep, but he opened his eyes when she approached. "I feel funny," he said. "My feet are cold."

"I'll ask them to warm a blanket for you," she said. "I'm going now. I'll see you in the morning. Stay with us, OK?"

"You can leave," he said. "I'm not going anywhere."

"I love you, Gerry."

"I love you, too, Chiefy. Kiss our girl, our little *choonkshee*."

"She's fine. She's at Rudy and Ellen's, doing her homework."

TO SAY THAT KARLA WAS DEVASTATED when Gerard died is like saying that the French were disappointed when Hitler's troops marched into Paris. It happened like this. After the doctor came in the next morning—it was the same toy doctor who had diagnosed her pregnant, grown thinner and prematurely gray—and after Karla signed half a dozen forms, they applied paddles to Gerard's chest and back and hit him with 400 volts. His heart stopped cold and restarted in a normal rhythm, but within a few minutes he had slipped back into atrial fib. They tried three times, but the same thing happened. "We'll quit for now," the doctor said. "I'll give him more metoprolol and we'll try again later. I can see that he's had thoracic surgery. Has he had heart issues in the past?"

"I assume so," Karla said. "He never complains about his health. Last night he said he felt funny. That's the only time I can think of."

"The nurse gave him insulin last night. His blood sugar was off the charts. That happens sometimes when a person is under stress."

"He was up to his neck in frozen slush. I guess that counts as being under stress."

Gerard's heart never returned to its normal rhythm. Karla picked up Joy after school and took her to the McDonoughs' (Rudy and Ellen doted on her as if she were their grandchild) and went back to the hospital to keep watch. The squiggle on his monitor became more regular, but the rate stayed above 100 beats per second. Around seven that evening, after the meds had been distributed, three nurses came into the room. "We have to get him up," the lead nurse explained. "If a big guy like him stays immobile, bad things happen."

"I know all about that," Karla said. "Let me help you."

"Not allowed because of the insurance. Are you ready, Mr. Horse Looking?"

Gerard looked grim. "Give me a minute with my wife. Karla, have you got a pen?" One of the nurses handed her a pen and turned over a piece of paper on a clipboard. "Write these numbers down," Gerard said, and gave her three phone numbers, two of them with the South Dakota area code. "One of them is my auntie," he said. "One is a guy I sun dance with. The local number is my AA sponsor. If I happen to miss a meeting, he'll want to know where I am."

"Honey," Karla said. "They're only going to get you up and help you walk a few steps."

"Last night my feet were freezing," he said. "Today the ice moved up around my chest. Now it's at my neck. Don't forget that we have a daughter. Whatever happens, she'll always be my daughter, too."

The three nurses unhooked the monitor—its frantic beeping echoed down the hallway—and swung Gerard's feet around and sat him up on the edge of the bed. One of them got under his left arm, one got under his right, and the third helped to lift him from the front. He stood with an effort and turned to face Karla, and gave her one last look that said everything: *For God's sake get me out of here, what the fuck are they doing to me?* Then his eyes focused on something beyond the door and corridor, and his face turned deadly white, then black. Then he looked at nothing.

When Karla saw him buckle and go down, a fist of ice closed around her own heart and she lost consciousness. The trio of nurses looked at the two of them on the floor. One nurse nudged Karla's calf with the toe of her running shoe. "Great," she said. "Now we've got two to deal with. Doreen, get the crash cart and call code. I'll start CPR."

"What about her?"

"Slide her out of the way. She's among the living."

KARLA FORGOT SHE HAD A DAUGHTER. She would show up for work half blitzed and make it through the day, so she could get hammered on beer again as soon as possible. Joy took care of her as well as a ten-year-old child could, but she got no help from her mother, who spent her evenings in an open-mouthed stupor in front of the TV. In her mind Karla was reliving long hours without her own mom, who had worked two jobs in the town of Crete, Nebraska, sewing brassieres in the daytime and tending bar at night. The issues had been different but the result was the same, a lonely kid growing up with half a parent. Joy couldn't keep it up; Child Protective Services stepped in, and the girl went to live with the McDonoughs. Karla looked around and saw that she was alone, and increased her nightly beer consumption by half. She lived on Oreos and potato chips, with the occasional Polish sausage for a little comfort.

She made it through the school year without getting fired. Summer came, along with baseball season, and she sometimes broke her routine and went out to watch the games, though she never once thought of inviting the girl. Of course the child was miserable and put on weight, and nobody in town knew what to do with them. Joy could be helped a little bit—the McDonoughs took her to Disneyland—but Gerard's dying had left such a crater in Karla's life that people stayed away as if they might fall into it, too.

Things went on like this for a while. One July night there was a knock on Karla's door. Two Native American men were out there, one tall and dark and thin and drunk as a weasel, one short and solid and sternly sober. Their van stood idling at the curb, a van much like the one Gerard had owned when she first went fishing with him. Karla went with them without asking questions, taking only her purse and a sweater and a six-pack. They left town and headed north into South Dakota.

They drove beneath the stars and past the wheatfields, on up into the prairie country, and crossed the Missouri River at Fort Pierre. They drove on into the darkness, and the little lights that marked the farmyards became scarce and disappeared. Finally they pulled into a town that looked abandoned except for a former gas station that boasted a tall red lit-up sign: "Casino." The two men stopped the van and got out, and Karla followed. In the yellow light that fell through the open door, she got her first good look at the men she'd traveled with. The shorter of the two had a hard, determined face and was dressed in conventional "American" style except for the thin gray braid hanging halfway down his back. The skinny one's look was startling. A bullet scar traveled vertically up the left side of his face, past where half his teeth had been and ending at a glass eye. He had scars across his forehead and part of an ear was missing, and there was a groove across one of his biceps— he wore a sleeveless shirt and beaded vest—that appeared to go all the way around, as if his arm had been amputated and sewn back on. Karla thought of Gerard's bent fingers and glanced at the man's hands. They were scarred and tattooed but the fingertips were straight. The man looked back at her as if he was just coming out of a trance.

They went inside and approached a thick-shouldered man of middle height and middle age, dressed in a Western suit and a spotless cream-colored Stetson and playing a slot machine. He heard them coming and swiveled around in his chair. He sighed and placed his hands on his knees and looked up at Karla. "Last year I lost thirty thousand dollars," he said.

"This woman is Miz Gerard Horse Looking," the solid traveler said. "She drinks too much. Louie, here, thought it might be good if she came to see you."

"Pleased to meet you," the man said. "My name is Oliver Broad Moccasin." He rubbed his round face with pudgy hands. "Your husband pledged to dance four years," he said. "This year would've been his fourth."

"My husband is dead."

"Right." The two of them looked at one another. "No male relatives, am I correct?"

"He has one daughter," Karla said. "And there's me."

"Well, you're here, anyway," the man said. "Thanks for coming. I guess it was voluntary."

"I was brought," Karla said. "Where are we, by the way?"

The man waved his hand. "You're in Indian country," he said. "How do you like it?"

"It sucks," Karla said.

"Smart girl."

They invited her to attend the sun dance. Not as a participant, since she'd had no preparation, but just to be there. Just to be present in honor of Gerard's pledge. All they'd ask her to do, they said, was take off her shoes and watch. She could support the dancers with her thoughts if she wished, but all that really mattered was for her to follow a couple of rules. They would dance without food or water for four days. During that time, if she wanted to eat or drink, she would have to step away from the circle.

"No alcohol," Oliver Broad Moccasin said. "No drugs of any kind. As a supporter you can have coffee. We can't."

"I don't care," Karla said. "Just don't bother me with a lot of bullshit. I don't believe in a Great Spirit or anything else."

"None of us will bother you," he said. "We do this for ourselves and our community." He shifted his gaze to the thin man. "Louie," he said, raising his voice and speaking deliberately. "Do you think you can be ready to dance by morning?"

The man with the gray braid took hold of Louie's arm. "I've got him," he said. "He'll be ready. Don't you worry about Louie."

KARLA WOKE BEFORE DAYLIGHT to the sound of a man singing, a strange, clear, floating song that started out high and ended up low, sung in a sweet male voice that contained wishfulness and sorrow. It reminded her of a thing she'd seen in movies, the muezzin's call to prayer. The intervals were strange and hard to follow, and there were not a lot of notes. She suffered from drinker's insomnia, so she wasn't surprised to find herself awake. She was surprised to find herself in a tipi. Some women around her were putting on skirts. Karla didn't own a skirt, but one of them gave her a wide fringed shawl to wrap around her hips. She went with the others out into the blueblack morning.

As the sun approached the horizon from below and a colorless glow changed to turquoise and then to pink, Karla saw that they were on a hill with prairie all around. A distant line of trees marked the course of a river. A circle of shade had been constructed of poles and brush, with a shaded arbor for the dancers on the western side; the east was open and marked with flags, and she was instructed never to cross there. There was a fire pit and sweat lodge to the west of the arbor, in a closed-off area where only certain people were supposed to go. She didn't give a damn about any of it. The only thing good about the first day of dancing was that it didn't go on continuously. The drummers and dancers took breaks, so there were intervals of quiet. Usually someone took over the microphone to complain about her life and ask for prayers. There was an announcer who kept things moving with a jokey patter, half in English and half in Lakota. If anyone stopped to talk to Karla, she ignored them and they moved on. There was a cook tent where meals were served, but food had to be kept away from the dance circle.

Karla moped and snoozed her way through the second morning of dancing. Out of boredom, she tried to figure out what was going on, but what it looked like was a lot of confusion surrounding a tree. A young cottonwood tree, maybe thirty feet tall, had been stuck in the ground in the middle of the circle, and some of the dancers were tied to it. It had been green and fresh the day before, but already some of its leaves were falling.

"That tree is dying," Karla said to the person next to her. "Why did they cut it and bring it here? Why not make a circle where there's a tree already growing? Some great big cottonwood, not this poor spindly thing?"

The blonde woman next to her, whose pale neck was getting sunburned, smiled and nodded. "Special tree," she said. "The tree is praying. For the people."

"Why can't a good big healthy tree pray just as well?"

"Is healthy tree," the woman said. "Healthy tree is best. You marry one of the dancers?"

"I don't understand why they had to kill a tree."

"I am married to psychoanalyst," the woman said. She leaned closer and smiled behind her hand. "Big mistake."

The round-faced older man, Oliver, whom everyone seemed to defer to, passed by within the circle. "Hey," Karla called out to him. "Can I go home now?"

Roused from his thoughts, he gave her an absent look. "Two more days." Then he continued on toward the westside arbor. Karla thought about hitchhiking to Nebraska, but the summertime traffic went mainly east and west, and nobody picked up hitchhikers on a reservation. It would probably be quicker just to sleep on the ground and wait.

By late afternoon, both Karla and the tree were losing moisture; the moisture she would have preferred was beer, but there wasn't any. Even in the camp at night, when the dancing was done, nobody broke out a case and said, "Come over." The dancers were thirsty, too, having to go without water during the daytime through the whole four days. The maimed man, the thin one from the van, looked painfully dry and sober. The male dancers danced bareheaded, naked to the waist. It was clear they were suffering under the hot sun, but they stayed true to their purpose. Most were sunburned, whites and Indians alike.

The third day, from what she could discern, would be extra busy. There would be a "sobriety round" and a "healing round." What she wanted to hear about was a "let's go home early" round, but no one spoke of it. Her new friend and neighbor, the psychoanalyst's wife, seemed eager for the day's events. Karla liked her for her hopeful spirit. The woman was from Germany, as was her sunburned husband. In fact, a third of the dancers were white, some from places like Finland and Estonia. Karla supposed there were trees in Finland that could be cut off from their roots and stuck in the ground and prayed at until their leaves fell off, but there must be something special about South Dakota trees (though they had brought her so far north that she might now be in North Dakota) that drew tree-dancing lunatics from Europe. Then she remembered that her lover and soul mate had been a sun dancer. She had tended the inflamed little scars he brought home from the dance.

Gerard Horse Looking had not been a fool, and if he prayed, it would not have been to a tree. He had survived a hard life without becoming a hard person; his anger at the world's injustices had been balanced by an inborn kindness, and he had not outlived wonder. From whom had he learned to be tender? Maybe from the aunt he often spoke of; certainly not from his mother. His mother was a bad woman, crazy, and his father a face in a photograph. Except that Gerard had long since lost the photograph. Karla had imagined him alone in the universe, but he'd had such friends as these. It seemed that everyone at the sun dance carried a remembrance of Gerard, even those from Finland. They had set up an empty chair for him, with a quilt draped across the back. There were other chairs like that.

Karla looked up at the tree again. It was tired, but it still held most of its leaves.

The dancers' chests were pierced and attached by thin ropes to the tree, about as high as a man standing on another man's shoulders could reach. As his turn came, each dancer ran backward, jerking the slender cottonwood as he struggled to break the skin. It was a modestly bloody business, more like a calf branding than like war or surgery. There was smoke in the air, from the fire beyond the sweat lodge and from sage the "smudgers" carried around in perforated coffee cans. Karla stood as the dancers passed by two and two, the one with the bloody chest being led by another. The drone of the singing and the rhythm of the drum entered her bloodstream, so that she found herself moving her feet a little, one-one, two-two, left, left, right, right. Still, none of it made sense to her, most particularly the death of the tree. Why not dance around a flagpole and leave the tree with its relatives, drinking up water from the ground (tree beer) and holding its leaves out to the air and sun? Surely it had been happy where it was, in spite of the nibbling caterpillars and noisy birds. Maybe it had liked eavesdropping on the birds. Why not? They led fascinating lives, full of gossip and adultery.

Karla began to fear that she might be losing her mind.

One-one, two-two. Left, left, right, right.

A big man danced past her, blowing an eagle-bone whistle. For one second, she thought it was Gerard. Blowing a whistle? What did praying have to do with blowing a whistle? Gerard had owned such a whistle; he'd kept it in a drawer alongside his moccasins.

One-one, two-two. Left, left, right, right.

Late the third day, sometime after the healing round, the magnitude of her loss came crashing in on her, and she began to quake and had to sit down. She would never be truly happy again. She would never again know a man's weight upon her. There were further losses ahead, which she would have no choice other than to accept. At last the tears started to flow, for herself, for her daughter, for the vultures distant in the sky, for the little ants under her feet, for all creatures who love this green and beautiful world and have to die.

When the fourth day of dancing was finished, they dug and lifted out the tree; they brought it down gently using ropes and poles so that it would not touch the ground. They carried it through the east gate, singing, and took it out a quarter of a mile to a pile of sticks, and laid it there to be used for any purpose: firewood, temporary fencing, a broken stick to prop the door of a shed. The bright cloth offerings that were tied to it were given away. She took a red strip home with her, to remember the day and her husband Gerard, who should have been there.

# Shame

KARLA ČAPEK AND GERARD HORSE LOOKING, two enormous people both of whom were tall and strong-muscled and fat as September bears, produced a woman-child who was tall and slim and as beautiful a female human as anyone would care to see. More than that, she was smart and worked like a demon, as if to erase her humble start in life. Her name was Joy. After her father died, she got help from Ellen McDonough, who raised her during the years when Karla was unable. But when Karla gave up beer and got her act together, the girl was loving and grateful as if toward a perfect mother. Except, by then, she had gone away to college.

Joy took the name McDonough because, she said, calling herself Horse Looking caused people to behave awkwardly. Americans reacted one way, Europeans another, but she wished to be neither pitied nor adored, especially for something that had no basis other than in people's preconceptions. Joy was no ordinary girl—she was too beautiful for that, with her height and dark eyes and her glowing exotic skin—but she wanted to be valued for her accomplishments, not because she was some kind of Pocahontas.

As for the name Čapek, she said, she herself could not pronounce it. The opening consonant does not occur in English. Nor, for that matter, does it occur in French.

However that was—yes, Karla was hurt by it, how could she not be—when Joy slash Pocahontas telephoned from Paris to invite her mother to come, Karla was thrilled.

She was retired by then, had a pretty good pension from pushing a broom over at the school for twenty years, so she felt all right about taking a vacation in November. "You're sure about this?" she asked her daughter. "I've never been out of the country. Everybody there's going to know right away I'm a moron."

"It's time you started liking yourself, ma," Joy said. "Whatever you are, you're no moron. Besides, you've got weightlifting cred. That's one reason I'm bringing you, to see the World Weightlifting Championships. Strong women from every country will be tuning up for the London Olympics."

"I haven't touched a bar of weights in fifty years."

"All the more reason you should come. You'll see how the world has changed. Female strength is in style."

*I've seen how it's changed in Turtle Lodge,* Karla thought. *Everything that was any good has gotten sadder, and the young people left.*

"Since you mention style, I don't have any clothes. All those French are so elegant."

"You'll be surprised. They wear jeans and sweatshirts and running shoes, same as in America."

"Just what is it exactly you do over there, anyway?" Karla could have bitten her tongue. She'd asked the same question before, and she knew the answer. And the tone.

"I'm a consultant. I help people decide how to invest their money."

"Sorry I asked, baby. When I get there, maybe you can show me." *When I get there.* The thought terrified her. How many hours on a plane, flying over the ocean? Karla was a good swimmer, but nowhere near as good as the sharks.

IT HAD BEEN A SLOG, but after decades, Karla had acquired some friends in Turtle Lodge. (She did not count fellow AA members, whom she met in the Methodist church's basement every two weeks. As a general rule, members did not socialize.) Her bestie was Penny Raskonen, whose husband Alfred had recently "passed away." Penny still lived on their acreage south of town, but she was thinking about moving in. Too lonely.

"I'm afraid of flying," Karla told her, as she turned back the edge of a quilt someone had donated. Penny volunteered at the Historical Society and also at the library; she was always suggesting that Karla volunteer too, but Karla always said no. "I'm afraid my huge butt will get stuck in one of those seats. Then the plane will go down in the ocean, and I won't get out."

Penny Raskonen, whose butt was a foot wide, said, "When was the last time one of those planes went down?"

"You're missing the point," Karla said. "What if?"

"What if you went to Paris and had the time of your life?"

"What if my daughter is ashamed of me? I'll be the biggest and fattest and worst dressed person in France."

"When my youngest got married for the second time, I made myself this coral-pink dress with tons of ruffles. It looked good in the pattern book, but on me it was too much. I looked like a peony. I thought, 'Well, so what? I'll just go and have fun.' And I did. Then Alfred took me home and I put on my overalls and fed the chickens."

"I don't have chickens."

"Well, get some," Penny said. "Maybe they have chickens in France."

"I don't think," Karla said, "that the kind of people my daughter knows keep chickens."

"Speaking of chickens," Penny said, "why don't you come out for supper? Chicken and vegetables from my garden. Sweet corn and peas. There might be baby carrots, too. I haven't pulled any to see if they're big enough to fool with."

"I would love to come," Karla said.

PENNY BEING PENNY, IT WASN'T SIMPLY CHICKEN; it was chicken with homemade noodles, sputtering in a pressure cooker to make a lovely sauce. Karla helped by cleaning the little carrots. "Just wash them good," Penny said. "If you try to peel 'em, there won't be anything left."

"My mother had a pressure cooker," Karla said. "She ruined everything that went into it."

"If I ruin the chicken, there's hamburger in the freezer."

"I wish I had a garden. I don't know why I don't. I've got plenty of time."

"It's a lot of work," Penny said. "I raise five times as much as I can use. Any time you feel the need to weed, come right on out. You don't have to ask."

The carrots went into a salad—fresh lettuce, fresh cut-up baby onions—and Penny served pickled beets canned the previous year. The chicken, of course, was delicious, with just the right amount of pepper, and the noodles were thicker than any you could buy at the store. Karla pushed her plate away and sighed. "My God, that was good," she said. "It was also about twenty thousand calories."

"Alfred used to like to eat," Penny said. "I miss cooking for him."

"Gerard used to cook for me," Karla said. "He was a better cook than I am."

"Irene McDonough went into the nursing home," Penny said. "The rest of the McDonoughs are gone. Except for John."

"What's he doing now?"

"He works for the Chevy dealer. He drives all over the country, picking up used cars."

"I hope he's staying sober. We don't see him at the AA meetings any more." In fact, Karla was John McDonough's sponsor. She wasn't supposed to talk about the meetings, but Penny knew everything anyway. She was better than the *Thunderhead*, the local newspaper.

"Those McDonoughs," Penny said. "John is more like Baldwin than he is like Rudy. All three of Baldwin's boys turned out bad. Freddy was the worst. Their daughter Judy, they say she was a wild one, too."

"I knew Judy in college. In a way, she's the reason I came out here."

"You knew Judy in college?"

"It's a long story."

After a pause, Penny said, "Do you want to watch TV? I don't know what's on, but we ought to find something. I've got fifteen hundred channels."

"No, but thanks so much. I'll go sit on my porch and fight the mosquitoes. I've got some thinking to do."

"That plane won't crash in the water," Penny said. "If it does, you'll be dead before you ever get a chance to swim."

Karla grinned. "Thanks for that reassuring thought," she said. "I can always count on you."

PENNY RASKONEN WAS A TALL, stoop-shouldered, loose-limbed woman as dry and skinny as a matchstick. Karla sometimes pictured the two of them together, herself charging forward in her daisy-trampling manner, Penny loping alongside, her garden shoes pendulum-steady in their long slow swinging strides. Neither of them had given in to the gray creeping into their hair; Karla dyed hers its natural chestnut color, while Penny chose a pink-blonde tint and kept her hair permed in ringlets. She usually wore a sort of fisherman's hat, a pale cloth thing with a short circular brim that she could roll up and stuff in her pocket. Penny sunburned like a fancy tomato and wore a shade hat while she was hoeing. Karla didn't do any hoeing, or anything else that would give her proper exercise. Sometimes she thought about walking, but she couldn't get motivated.

Besides, nobody walked in Turtle Lodge.

One morning when she was having these thoughts, she realized that, rather than the plain streets of her adopted town, the two of them in her imagination were walking among blocks of apartment buildings on the boulevards of a city, with the Eiffel Tower in the distance. Penny in Paris! The idea amused her so much that she picked up the phone.

"Hey, it's me. Penny, why don't you come with me? We'll give those French people something to talk about."

"Karla, is this you? Have you been drinking?"

"No, I haven't been drinking. Why would you think that?"

"Well, for one thing, it's seven o'clock in the morning."

"Oh. Sorry. I always get up early. It's because I used to warm the school up for the kids." No point in telling Penny how her climb from the bottom of the ocean had been slow, how she still suffered from the alcoholics' insomnia that sometimes woke her at four a.m. "Do you want me to call you back?"

"Just give me a minute to nuke a cup of coffee." There was a brief sound of a faucet running and a microwave door being slammed. Penny always drank instant coffee, the wretchedest in the world. "Okay, so you're not drinking. Now, where did you want me to go? Are we shopping the thrift store today?"

"Paris, Penny. I just thought of us in Paris. It would be such fun."

"I thought you were afraid of sharks. I thought you hated the whole idea."

"Oh, pooh. I have to go, if I want to see Joy. She lives there now."

"Not in Paris, does she? Isn't it some little town? Marny Copenhagen?"

"*Margny-lès-Compiègne*. But she takes the train into Paris almost every day. How are your squash plants? Did you get the beetles out of them?"

"I poisoned the dickens out of those beetles. Are you sure you haven't been drinking?"

"No, Penny, I haven't been drinking. Come and talk to me one of these days. I'll make you a decent cup of coffee." After Karla put the phone down, she thought, Why would I want Penny with me in Paris? So they'd have someone to stare at even more ridiculous than me? Laurel and Hardy, that's who they would look like. Penny striding along with this big balloon at her side.

*Fudge bucket*, Karla thought. *I have to quit thinking about it, or I'll never go.*

She had Googled it enough to know that the weightlifting competition would be at Paris Disneyland. Karla had never been to Disneyland in California, never mind in Paris. Joy had been to Disneyland in Anaheim, courtesy of the McDonoughs, but that had been during Karla's 24-hour drinking days; even if she could have traveled with them, she might not have been allowed inside the park. Thinking about her past made Karla feel depressed. She'd been thinking about it a lot lately. Maybe she needed a trip.

She dug out her suitcase and looked it over. It was a hard-shell Samsonite piece of junk left over from the 1960s. Maybe the thrift store would have one of those suitcases with the little wheels.

*That girl of mine has lost her wits*, she thought. *Poor people don't belong in Paris.*

If a journey of a thousand miles begins with a single step, Karla's single step was getting out that old suitcase. She began to make preparations. She forgot all about inviting Penny and thought only of herself. She would need clothes that didn't resemble a janitor's uniform, so she shopped the farm store's sale on summer shirts. Men's, of course; no woman in town wore anything like what she needed, and even most of the men wore shirts that were too small. She got lucky and picked up a down vest on sale that would be just right for a chilly November evening. Shoes, as always, were a problem. Karla's feet were too big for women's sizes, and men's shoes never fit at the heels. She finally chose men's running shoes that had a gaudy neon stripe, with a French name, made in China.

KARLA ASKED, "IS IT ALL RIGHT IF I BRING A FRIEND?" She was on the phone to her daughter. They talked every two weeks, sometimes more often if there was news.

"A friend? Are you dating, ma?"

"Oh, no no no. Penny Raskonen is just a buddy. We've been hanging out since her husband died."

"Raskonen? Do I know them? That name is not familiar."

"I don't think so. They had a ranch south of Willow. Before they sold the place, they hardly ever came to town."

She could feel her daughter sighing over the phone. "Sure, bring her if you want to, ma. I'm not paying for an extra ticket, though."

"Her sons formed a corporation and bought their ranch. I think she can get her own ticket."

Karla hadn't really thought about Penny making the trip until Penny showed her a new pink blouse. Lots of ruffles; Penny the peony. "What do you think?" Penny asked. "*Très chic*, no? I cut down that pink dress I made for my daughter's wedding. She says next time she's going with cerulean."

"*Très bien*," Karla said. "I can't wear pink. Makes me look like a parade float. Does this mean you're coming to Paris with me?"

"Of course I'm coming," Penny said. "Somebody has to rescue you from the sharks once that plane goes down."

"Darned if I hadn't forgotten," Karla said. "We have to get you booked. Did you buy an airline ticket already?"

"Heavens, no. I thought you were going to do all that."

"Well, I am," Karla said. "You know we have to plan ahead. A few things like passports and visas."

"Do we need photographs?"

"We do."

"I hate to have my picture taken. I look so old."

Karla had to exercise a few brain cells she hadn't used in a while, but she shepherded them both through the process. They sent their passport applications in on time, got the necessary vaccinations, purchased plane tickets, reserved a hotel room, got a travel book and a big plastic-coated map of Paris. Karla watched her friend brighten at the prospect of travel. Penny had been a bit of a sad sack since her husband died; now her posture was more erect, her step quicker. Her enthusiasm was contagious, and Karla began to think the trip might not be a disaster.

The weeks sped by. Cicadas buzzed, the summer baseball leagues ended, school started without Karla (a young Honduran couple were keeping the place clean now) and, the first frosty morning, Penny's squash and tomato plants keeled over and died. Thanks to Penny, Karla had a hundred green tomatoes under her bed, wrapped individually in newspaper. There were jars of plum jelly, too; the local wild plums made a tart jelly for which a taste had to be acquired. The bounty of the season included pork that Penny's sons had butchered. Karla had a freezer full of meat and bins full of vegetables, and a pyramid of winter squash piled up in her extra bedroom. It was an insane amount of food.

"Honey, just stop," Karla said when Penny brought over a pail full of Brussels sprouts. "How am I going to eat all this? I hardly even cook any more."

"Oh, you'll eat it," Penny said. "It goes away fast. How's the itinerary coming?" She stood on the concrete step, looking around at the dark interior. Karla was no great housekeeper, but neither was Penny.

"I've got the first weekend planned. Joy wants us to leave the rest of the trip open; she's got something up her sleeve. I think we're going to get a tour of Normandy. Come in; we'll look at the map." Karla held the door for her friend; Penny slipped past like a gust of October air. "Can you drink a sip of my coffee?"

"I'll take half a cup. Half coffee and half milk." She set the bucket of sprouts on the kitchen table. "My kids don't want me to go."

"Who asked them?"

"I didn't, and that's a problem," Penny said. "Mostly it's the boys. They think it's a waste of money."

"Well, whose money is it? Yours or theirs?"

"It's mine, but they think it'll be theirs someday."

"Horse puckey." Karla ran some water in the coffee steamer. "The way you eat vegetables, you'll live to be ninety-five. You're as full of vitamins as a drug store." She pushed a button, and the thing started to hiss. It was a high-tech gift from Joy. Karla didn't understand how it worked, but it made wonderful coffee. "Take that bucket of green things off the table and unfold the map. I want to show you where we're going."

Penny sat down, but she did not remove her fisherman's hat. Karla's hand galloped over the Sharpie-circled places on the map, but Penny only stared out the window, fingers drumming her thin lip.

"All right, now, let's hear it. What's the matter?"

"My boys don't want me to go," Penny repeated.

"Those 'boys' as you call them are fifty years old," Karla said. "They can let go of the apron strings for at least a couple of weeks."

"There's terrorists," Penny said. "They blew up a train. They come over from Africa and blow things up."

"Since when are you afraid of terrorists? You never mentioned it before."

"Arabs, too," Penny said. "Muslims. They all hate us over there."

"Nobody hates you," Karla said. "You're the least hate-able person on the planet."

"I don't mean me, particularly. They hate everybody. Everybody who looks European."

"You've been watching Fox News again. I told you, stick to CNN."

"Alfred always had it on Fox. It's the boys. They don't want me to go."

Karla supposed the problem was temporary and that Penny would soon get over it, but then one night she heard a knock at her door. She opened it to find two men standing there who could have been twins but weren't; one was taller, and his snap-button shirt fit tighter where his five-pound-bag-of-potatoes drooped over his jeans. *Here they are*, Karla thought. *At least they didn't come in overalls.*

She was going to say, "Come in," but they were already pushing past her. They looked around with suspicion at the kitchen-dining room area of the double-wide. "Sons of Penny Raskonen, I presume."

"What?"

"I think I said, 'Who are you and what do you want?'"

Up close and in the light, they didn't look big. Just sunburned. "I'm Al Raskonen, Junior," the taller one said. "This is my brother Bert." They didn't offer to shake hands. "You know what we want. Where's that map you've been showing our mother?"

"The map of Paris? What's that got to do with anything?"

"It's got her all hypnotized. She keeps talking about the Loover. Going to see the Loover." He walked over to the fridge and opened the top freezer. He took out one of the green packages and showed it to his brother. "That's my writing," he said. "That's our pork. I wrapped it myself."

"Your mom gave it to me," Karla said. "Put it back."

He opened the refrigerator door and looked inside. "I suppose them's our Brussels sprouts, too."

"If you don't get your face out of my refrigerator," Karla said, "I'm going to put those Brussels sprouts up your nose."

That got their attention. The elder brother replaced the pork package and closed the door. "Who's paying for those tickets? Everybody in town says you're on welfare."

"I am not now and have never been on welfare," Karla said. "My daughter is paying my expenses. Your mother bought her own airline ticket, and we will share the cost of hotel rooms."

"Your daughter is half Indian, am I right? Gets a check every month from the government?"

"My daughter is a financial adviser, and she makes more money than you two boneheads put together. Now tell me in plain English what you want, and then you can leave."

"You can't tell us to leave."

Karla picked the bigger one up by his shirt collar and slammed him down onto a chair. The dinette was made in the fifties, and the chair could stand it. "You listen to me," she said. "Mommy is speaking. Your mother is a grown woman. If she wants to befriend me, that is her decision. If she wants to go to France, this is a free country. Women have the vote. If you ever come poking around here, looking in my refrigerator, I will punch your teeth in. Am I able to make myself understood?" He moved to get up, and she slammed him down again. "Am I?"

He lowered his pale-blue eyes. "All right." She let him up. He picked up his Pioneer seed cap from where it had fallen on the table, and he and his brother slow-walked to the door. With his hand on the knob and the door unlatched, he turned to glare at her, flushing scarlet between his freckles. "Our mother going to France? She's never been out of the state, except the one time we took that bay colt with the turned-back hoof to Lawrence, Kansas, to that vet college they have down there." He seemed to lose his train of thought. White bubbles had formed at the corners of his sunburned mouth. "She's crazy," the second brother prompted.

"You're crazy," Al Raskonen, Junior, said. "We're going to have you committed."

"Argh!" Karla picked up a cutting board and made a feint in their direction, and the narrow-shouldered brothers crowded one another out the door. "Crazy, am I?" Karla growled, slamming the cutting board on the counter. "Tell you what, that felt good, sitting him down like that." She flexed her fat arm and felt her bicep. "Didn't know I still had it in me."

KARLA AND PENNY DEPLANED AT ORLY and followed the crowd to the customs shed, where their passports were examined and their bags were passed untouched; the customs inspectors were smoking and having a discussion in French. They left the serpentine queue behind and headed for the escalator, Karla leading the way and Penny following like a dinghy following a barge. The airport was large and confusing, but there were signs and arrows to direct them, and they found their way to the ground transportation exit, where they were to look for a shuttle to the *Gare du Nord*. From there, per Joy's instructions, they were to take the subway to a place—a *Place*, which meant a circle—near their hotel.

As they approached the crowd that had bunched up near the exit, a man in a military uniform, carrying a submachine gun, began shouting and gesturing for everyone to move back. They were herded away from the exit, all the way back to the farthest wall, and stood among the travelers milling about. Nobody seemed to know what was happening, or if they did, they didn't speak English. Karla heard sirens just like in the French movies—boo deep doo deep—and an armored van drove up, escorted by two black cars. Uniformed men got out, some carrying guns and two carrying a dog-sized casket on two poles. Somebody in the crowd near Karla spoke the word "bomb."

More confusion followed, more milling about, more waiting. After what seemed like an hour, the man with the submachine gun began announcing something and made the gesture of covering his ears. People in the crowd began putting their fingers in their ears; Karla and Penny looked at one another, eyes wide, and followed their example. There was a funny little pop like a bottle rocket exploding, and everyone relaxed.

"What happened?" Karla asked Penny. "Did you see anything?"

"I bet it's those terrorists," Penny said.

A man in the crowd who looked like a bearded professor turned toward them. "They blew up somebody's suitcase," he said. "Don't leave your luggage. Any abandoned package could be a bomb. They can't take chances."

The two men with the casket-on-poles trotted back to their van, followed by their escorts. The crowd was released; as they returned to the exit, the professor nudged Karla and pointed to a scattering of fabric surrounding the burned fragments of a carry-on bag. "Whoever left that had better not come back for it," he said. "They could get a bill for ten thousand Euros."

The bus ride across Paris was encumbered by heavy traffic, and the distance was greater than Karla had imagined. They passed block after block of buildings all the same height, about as tall as Kresge's department store in Lincoln. There seemed to be no through streets or fast lanes; the bus repeatedly stopped to wait for an intersection to clear. There were many motorcycles. "This is terrible," Karla said. "It must be the rush hour. What time is it, anyway?"

"It's ten in the morning," Penny said. "I think all this bustle is exciting."

"I just want to get some sleep," Karla said. "That flight over the ocean wore me out. White knuckles all the way."

The *Gare du Nord* was a bus and train terminal that was bigger than the Omaha airport. There were several levels, with stairs from one level to the next. Karla stopped at an information booth and asked for directions and a map of the Paris Metro, the subway system. The two girls behind the counter looked Chinese; in fact, half the people in the terminal were of one shade of brown or another. Some of the women wore headscarves. "I didn't think Paris would be so mixed," Penny muttered. "I thought all the French were white people."

"Be careful," Karla said. "Remember what my daughter looks like. You don't want to upset me."

"I really have to pee," Penny said.

They found a kiosk and got French money for the restroom. "I think it's one of these yellow things," Karla said. She fingered a coin about the size of a quarter.

"I'm afraid to go, with all these—you know who I mean."

"All these foreign foreigners? I'll be right here. If you happen see an explosive device, just yell."

Karla and Penny were on their own in Paris. Joy would meet them, she said, at their hotel after her work day was over. They would have plenty of time to figure out the subway system. She'd advised them to use the subway because the walking distances were greater than they appeared. To walk in Paris, you went from *Place* to *Place* and looked for your new street name high up on the corner of a building; the French had more heroes than streets, so that even a street that went straight onward might change names. Also, you could forget about North, South, East, and West, because the streets went every whichaway. Karla thought she had come prepared, having studied her laminated map night after night. What she wasn't prepared for was not being able to find the subway terminal inside the *Gare* (it was on another level) and getting hungry and out of sorts. "Gosh darn this place," she said finally. "We have to sit down and eat something before I lose my composure and punch somebody."

"Let's see if we can find a donut shop," Penny said. "I already don't like Paris."

They didn't find a donut shop in the *Gare*, but they were able to find croissants. "Imagine this has a hole in it," Karla said. "Think sprinkles. Dip it in your coffee."

"It's actually all right," Penny said. "I wonder how they get them so light and full of butter."

"Now you're talking."

Being seated enabled Karla to think more clearly. "Subways are underground," she said. "We need to go down down down. Abandon hope all ye who enter here."

"What's that?" Penny asked.

"It's nothing. I've been poisoned by literature." Karla unfolded the subway guide. "We have to take the purple line to here. Then we take the green to here, and the yellow line to here."

"I don't know what you're talking about."

"You go by colors," Karla said. "It'll be a piece of cake. Let's have one more croissant."


THEIR HOTEL DIDN'T LOOK LIKE ANYTHING from the street—just an entrance and a brick façade twelve feet wide—but on the inside it opened onto a quiet courtyard where chestnuts lay among fallen leaves. Their room was on the third floor, with a balcony that looked out over the courtyard. "Thank God it's decent," Karla said. "Time to take a nap." *And a crap*, she added mentally.

The beds were high and narrow, and the mattresses were hard. Karla parked her suitcase and sat on one of them. It held her weight nicely.

"I'm not sleepy," Penny said. "I'm going to explore."

"No, you're not," Karla said. "If I lose you, your sons will have me committed."

"I'll go down to the courtyard, then. I want some of those chestnuts."

The first thing Karla did was remove her shoes. After she'd been in the bathroom, she lay back on one of the beds and was out, no dreams, no nothing, until Penny woke her with the news that her daughter was downstairs. For the first time that day, Karla felt panic. "Oh, God," she said, putting a hand to her hair. "I slept like a rock. I must look like what the cat dragged in."

"You look fine," Penny said. "That polyester doesn't wrinkle."

"It's not the polyester I'm worried about."

Karla splashed a little water in her face and hurriedly raked the tangles out of her hair; she'd noticed it thinning on top lately, but who ever got to see the top of her head? She made sure everything was buttoned and hustled Penny ahead of her down the hall. When she got into the elevator, it creaked. They stepped out onto the courtyard and followed a stone path toward the front, Karla leading the way.

The lobby of the hotel was long and narrow, with the concierge's desk tucked in along one side. Daylight shone strongly from the entrance door at the far end; a tall girl stood silhouetted against the light, and although Karla hadn't run in years, she thudded forward dangerously, tears blurring her daughter's image. "Oh, honey, it's been so long, I'm so glad to see you!" But at the last second, rather than crushing the girl to her chest, she merely held her by the shoulders and looked her hungrily in the face. "Gosh, you're so pretty! How'd you get so pretty? Your dad and I were never much to look at."

Joy laughed and kissed her mother on both cheeks in the French manner. "Oh, mummy," she said. "Mummy, mummy, mummy." She took Karla's hands and stepped back to look her up and down. "Oh, mummy, we need to get you some clothes."

"Honey, you know I dress to cover my nakedness, and to keep the gnats from biting me where I can't swat 'em."

"Well, you can't go around looking like the cleaning lady. Who's this? Is she your friend?"

"She'd better be my friend. If she isn't, we're going to have a miserable two weeks."

"And stand up straight. You're starting to get that widow's hump."

"I am a widow," Karla said. "And it's a while since I've been humped, thanks so much for asking."

Karla introduced her friend to her daughter. "Honey, this is Penny

Raskonen. Penny, you remember my daughter Joy. She used to dash around like a crazy little squirrel, trying to keep her feckless mother from falling apart."

"Hi, Penny," Joy said. "I'm very pleased to meet you again." They shook hands awkwardly; Penny wasn't ready yet to be kissed on both cheeks.

"Karla's told me a lot about you," Penny said. "She says you're a—a consultant?"

"That's right. I get paid for telling people where to invest their money."

"Maybe you can help me some time," Penny said. "I've got a few investments."

The three women drew back from one another a little. Joy said, "I suppose you two are starving. What would you like to eat?"

"I don't know," Karla said. "Mine is not the body of a picky eater."

"I don't know either," Penny said. "Can you get good roast beef in France?"

"How about *Boeuf bourguignon*?" Joy suggested. "I know of a little place just down the street. We won't even have to take a cab."

They left the hotel and moved off past a boarded-up storefront. In the gray light of evening, the neighborhood looked down-at-heels; a homeless man sitting in a doorway rolled his eyes up at them as a dog might do. Farther along, an old woman pushed a shopping cart loaded with the city's scrapings. Joy strode on ahead of them, unconcerned. She wore high soft boots with a modest heel, the leather supple enough to suggest shapely feet underneath. Two teenage boys, both black, came strolling in the opposite direction. They looked Joy up and down with interest; Karla bristled, until she felt Penny's hand on her arm. "Okay, okay," she said. "I'm not going to clobber anybody. Besides, they might have knives."

"What?" Joy turned back to face her mother.

"It's all right," Penny said. "She didn't care for the way those boys were looking at you."

Joy laughed. "Men in France are all like that."

The café was brightly lit and busy. Once they were seated across from one another, Karla studied her daughter at leisure. Joy had allowed her black hair to grow long; her dark cheeks were dusted with rouge, her chest and shoulders were strong but feminine. She wore an army-green wool jacket with a black blouse underneath. A worked-silver necklace graced her throat. "You've put on a little weight, I believe," Karla said. "It looks good on you. You used to be so skinny."

"*Touché,*" Joy said. "Yes, mother, I've gained two kilograms. That sounds better than 'five pounds.' What about you?"

"Oh, I never weigh myself. Too depressing." Karla glanced at Joy's perfect manicure, the almond-shaped, polished nails, then at her own large hands, which she tried to hide by fumbling with the napkin. Her daughter's makeup looked a little crumbly, signaling the end of a hard day. "What did you do today? Where have you been? Tell us a little about yourself, honey. I've been so longing to see you."

"You tell me about your day first."

"Oh, it was nothing. Just a plane ride."

"They blew up a suitcase," Penny said. "At the airport. Some men with this box on poles that looked like a baby's coffin. They made us all get back and put our hands over our ears."

"What?" The girl's eyes went wide and dark.

"Oh, that's right," Karla said. "Somebody left a backpack unattended. It was a pretty big deal, sirens and everything. We had to stand for an hour while they did their thing. It was disappointing, really; just a little pop instead of an explosion. Stuff from the backpack was burned and scattered. It looked to me like it was mostly underwear."

"Were you scared?"

"No."

"The police were carrying machine guns," Penny said. "Back home they don't have machine guns. I don't know what they have, but they're not machine guns."

"It must've been airport security," Joy said. "The cops have been nervous lately."

"They didn't even look at our luggage," Karla said. "At customs, I mean. I could've been carrying an atom bomb."

"Don't say that word," Joy said, leaning forward and glancing around. "It's not a joke here."

"I think your boobs are bigger," Karla said. "That's where those two kilograms went."

Joy laughed. "You don't miss much, do you?"

"Honey, you've got such a glow on you. You're just—vivid." It was Karla's turn to lean forward and lower her voice. "You're not in love, are you?"

Joy blushed. "I don't know. Maybe."

"Do we get to meet him?"

"I don't know. Maybe."

Karla leaned back. "I was in love twice," she said. "Of course with your daddy, and I wouldn't trade those memories for a million bucks. And once with this guy I met in high school. That one didn't work out so well." She sighed. "I'm lucky I didn't get pregnant. He would've dropped me like a hot potato."

A moment passed. Joy turned to Karla's companion. "Tell me about yourself, Penny. Is it Rasmussen?"

"Raskonen," Penny said. "It's Finnish, except my husband said his family were from Norway." A youngish, shortish, dark-haired man brought them menus. He looked too old to be in college and too smart to be a waiter. Karla wondered how he kept his white shirt sparkling clean.

"I don't know," Penny continued. "We got married out of high school and bought a little gravelly place, poor farmland with a few cows and a lot of flat pasture. Then some fellow down in Valley, Nebraska, invented the center-pivot irrigation system, and suddenly we could grow corn on land that would hardly raise sandburs. My husband bought more pastureland and converted it to cornfields. I had my three kids and my garden and we were busy, busy, busy, and now here I am in Paris. It's the first time I've been out of Nebraska, except we went to Kansas once. One of our mares had a colt that had something wrong with its foot."

"Were you in love with your husband?" Joy asked. Karla winced. It wasn't a question you could just spring on somebody, back home in Turtle Lodge.

"I don't know," Penny said. "We didn't have time to think about love." She sighed. "We didn't think about a lot of things. I never imagined I would ride a subway."

"Did you have your own horse?"

"No," Penny said, "but I had my own tractor."

"Where are your children now?"

"The boys are farming the place. My daughter is a flibbertigibbet. She's in her forties and still looking for romance."

"Time goes fast," Joy said. "I'll be thirty before you know it."

"You'll be sixty before you know it," Karla said.

The man who brought the menus came to take their order. They were not ready. "What is 'yellow chicken'?" Karla asked.

"It's a standard French recipe," Joy said. "I think you'll like it."

"I'll have that, then," Karla said. "Penny, are you going to try *boeuf bourguignon*?"

"It's a type of stew," Joy said. "They slow-cook it. Everything is tender."

"All right," Penny said. "I guess I can always eat the beef."

"I'm just going to have French onion soup," Joy said.

"Do you have to tell him 'French onion soup' in French?"

"No French," the man in the white shirt said. "I live ten years in Toronto. Yellow chicken, *boeuf bourguignon*, French onion soup. What to drink, please?"

"Just water, I guess," Karla said.

"Have some Perrier," Joy said. "That's what I'm having. This meal is on me."

"Can I have wine?" Penny asked. "I always thought it would be nice to have wine with supper, but my husband didn't drink."

"Sure," Joy said. "Red or white? Sweet or dry? What kind do you like?"

"I don't know," Penny said. "I don't suppose they have blackberry."

"*Sauvignon blanc* for you," the man in the white shirt said. He winked at Penny. "If you don't like, I drink it myself."

"Did you see that?" Penny whispered after he had gone. "I've been winked at by a Frenchman."

"I think he's Algerian," Joy said, "But welcome to Paris."

"So what's the plan?" Karla wanted to know. "Will we be sightseeing tomorrow?"

"Tomorrow we shop," Joy said. "We need to get you properly dressed."

"Why? Don't I look all right?"

"Depends where you go," Joy said. "This isn't Dunlap County."

The man brought Penny's wine and the two Perriers in bottles. Karla poured half of hers into the glass and lifted it. "Cheers," she said, though she suddenly felt uncheerful.

"Cheers," Joy said. She lifted her glass as if accepting a challenge.

"Boy, this is good," Penny said. "I'm going to need another glass of this."

"OH, BOY," PENNY SAID. "I'm never going to drink another glass of that." Light from the courtyard was showing through the hotel's curtains.

"If you think you feel bad now," Karla said, "try waking up the morning after you've been drinking for thirty years." *Or forty*, she added mentally. *Fifty? When do I start counting?*

"Don't talk so loud," Penny said. "And please don't open those drapes."

"Sorry," Karla said, opening the curtains. "We have to get you up and moving."

Following dinner, they had gotten into a cab. "*Tour Eiffel*," Joy had told the driver, and Karla had thought that meant they were taking a tour. Which they sort of did. The taxi had taken them past the Notre Dame cathedral, lit beautifully at night, and past the *hotel de ville*, the city hall. They crossed the Seine on one of the city's famous bridges and approached the Eiffel Tower from the south. Karla had seen the postcards, she had seen the little replicas being sold by every street vendor in the city, but she still was not prepared for the size of the thing, for the grandeur of its lighted bulk against the sky. Penny, already tipsy, had kept saying "Oooh" and "Aaah" in high startled tones and wishing she had brought along her Brownie. Joy had stayed mostly silent. They stood in line, bought lift tickets, and went to the top. It was fully dark by then, and they saw Paris in all her jewelry laid out before them.

They had paused for treats in the restaurant at the *Tour Eiffel*, and that was where Penny had the glass that did her in. Joy and Karla drank coffee. They were focused on one another and on the variously-clothed crowd, and did not notice that their friend was beginning to tilt.

Later, as they waited for another taxi, Penny said, "Oooh, that tower made me dizzy," and turned around and puked into the gutter. Karla had to move quickly to catch her before she fell onto her poor old bony knees. Joy had said, "I see I'm going to have my hands full with you two."

Karla laughed. "Oh, she's not like this. I bet she's never drunk two whole glasses of wine in her life."

Joy smiled, rather bitterly as Karla thought. "Just so long as you don't start."

"I think I'm pretty safe. I don't feel that urge so much these days."

"Everywhere you go in France, they invite you to drink," Joy said.

"I'm aware of it, honey," Karla said. "I think I'm ready."

They'd arranged for Joy to pick them up at ten o'clock. But this time, instead of hailing a taxi, she herded them toward the nearest subway entrance. "The Metro is the best way to get around," she said. "The surface traffic's bad, so the subway's often faster than taking a cab."

"I see a lot of steps," Karla said. "I suppose there'll be just as many when we come back up."

"It's hard for women with baby strollers," Joy said. "In that respect it's not ideal."

They left behind the bright November air for a world where everything felt made; light and air came artificially, and the grinding and bumping of the trains could be felt through the floor. The people crowding the turnstiles were animated and unique, not antlike in any way, yet Karla had the feeling of movement in a swarm, as if her purpose had been channeled and sublimated. Somehow it made her feel the lost summers of her childhood, her wild lonesome rambles along the weedy banks of the Big Blue River, where paths made by children resembled tunnels but not tunnels that looked like this.

Joy showed them how to navigate the subway lines by color and destination, lessons they'd had to partly learn the day before. To this end she'd made them each a small portfolio, which she brought along in a shoulder bag. Each got a subway map and a map of the routes of the *RER*, the light rail system. There was also a surface street map and a plastic magnifier, a ball-point pen and a pad, and a strip of Metro tickets, along with a tourist guide to museums and monuments. "Gosh," Penny said to her. "You prepared all this for us? This must've taken hours."

"I know. It's crazy. I'm OCD," Joy said. "I can't help myself. It drives my mother nuts."

After a long walk underground, punctuated by several flights of concrete steps, they reached the platform. People of all types and ages waited for the cars, some accompanied and some alone, the young in noisy clusters, the old seated on the benches, holding their packages. Thumps and rumbles could be felt through every surface as other trains passed invisibly. After a short wait, a light appeared far down in the tunnel, and a string of half a dozen cars rolled rapidly up beside the platform and stopped with a clash and squeal. The doors slid open, a wave of people got off, and Karla and Penny and Joy pushed through them and boarded. An announcement was made in French and the doors slid closed. The train started with a jerk, and Karla lurched against the pole, supporting Penny as she did so.

The subway car hopped and shuddered; the concrete walls of the tunnel flashed past at a jolting pace. "The trick is," Joy shouted to be heard above the rush, "to not think of the streets above you. You go from one node to another. There's no linearity, no proportionate distancing. You forget about the grid."

"What?" said Penny.

"You pop up in one place, then drop down and pop up in another. It's sort of like whack-a-mole."

"Like what?"

"Or a prairie dog town," Karla added, seeing her friend's bemused expression.

"Alfred hated prairie dogs, even though we didn't have any," Penny said. "I think they poisoned them out back in the 1930s."

THEY "POPPED UP" IN A DISTRICT where clothing shops and jewelry stores occupied the ground floor of every building. People sipping and chatting at the sidewalk cafés glanced up at them without interest, as if a dark-skinned princess leading a hippo and a llama passed by them every day. Indeed, on this street, Joy's beauty did not stand out. Women who could have been fashion models hurried past, clutching purses that cost what Karla might have paid for a car.

Joy noticed Karla's discomfiture. "This is not our street," she said. "I sometimes come here to window-shop, but we'll go around the corner."

"They won't have anything for me," Karla said. "These French people are five sizes too small."

"We'll see," Joy said. She had the fast-paced walk of an urban businesswoman. Just a bit stiff in the sacro, maybe, when seen from behind. Not quite the willow waist that her mother remembered. Joy wore the clothing she'd worn the evening before, except that she had ditched the soft boots for running shoes. Karla surmised that her daughter had spent the night in Paris. She didn't look as if she'd ridden half the morning on the train.

*Around the corner* turned out to be a street of discount shops, where bargains could be had if one was careful to find the flaw and it was repairable.

"Are we going to look in any of these stores?" Karla asked, feeling the strain of keeping up.

"Just a little farther."

They arrived at a storefront bearing the words *Taille la Plus Elegánts* (*Ell lay phantz*, Karla mentally corrected). The air was tinged with the clean scent of fabric, and brightly lit aisles displayed colorful blouses; there were skirts in solid colors, belts and purses, leather jackets. Best of all, the sales personnel were women of substantial size. Joy, ten steps ahead of her, was getting into a shopping mode; her gait became less businesslike, more relaxed. She chose a blouse from a hanger and turned and posed with it. Of course it was much too big for her, but the colors were pretty, large flower shapes in blue and mauve on a field of white. "How do I look?"

"You look better than I ever could," Karla said. She turned to glance behind her. "Where's Penny?"

"I need to find a rest room," Penny said. She had fallen behind and was hurrying to catch up. She clutched her purse with both hands, rather like a squirrel eating a piece of lasagna.

Joy spoke to a salesgirl in French. "What do you suppose is the matter with her?" she asked, as the woman led Penny away. Then she laughed. "You don't suppose it's morning sickness?"

"It's morning-after sickness," Karla said. "I know it well."

Joy posed with another blouse. "Don't you think I'll look good when I'm older?"

"You'll never have to wear a tent, if that's what you mean," Karla said.

"Now, don't be touchy," Joy said. "We're supposed to be having fun." Just then, tiny notes of music came from her purse. "*Excusez moi.*" She removed her phone. "*Ça va?*" She turned her back so that Karla couldn't see her face. The man's voice on the other end was warm and pleasant, and Joy's responses carried an affectionate tone. They concluded their call in French, and Joy turned back toward her mother, blushing. "He's nice," she said. "I hope you're going to like him."

"What's his name?"

"*Benoit*," Joy said.

*Ben-wah. One of those French names. Why couldn't it be Paul, or George? Or Ringo.* "I'll look forward to meeting him," Karla said, and wished she were better at lying.

The saleswoman returned leading Penny, who still looked rabbity. She spoke to Joy in French, and Joy answered with something ending in *merci*. "She thinks Penny needs to eat," Joy translated. "We can come back afterwards."

"I'll go willingly," Karla said. "I could use a bite myself."

They found seating at one of the little sidewalk cafés and ordered Penny a croissant with a sampler of preserves. She declined coffee, as did Joy, but Karla had an espresso that was so good that she asked for another. For brunch she ordered a *croque monsieur*, a version of cheese on toast that turned out to be delicious. Joy sipped her Perrier and watched the older women eat. "Penny," she said, "are you feeling all right? Do we need to go back to the hotel?"

"I'm all right now," Penny said. "What are these preserves? Is this one huckleberry?"

"I think that is *Bar-le-Duc*," Joy said. "It's a currant mixture."

"Well, I have to admit these are good," Penny said. "I like to put up jelly myself. Mostly sand cherry when I can get some. They don't ripen every year. Alfred liked wild plum jelly, but I can't stand the stuff. Too much pucker for me."

"My mom, your grandmother, used to make plum jam," Karla said to Joy. "She used it to fill kolaches."

"I've wanted to talk to you about her," Joy said. "What can you tell me about my grandparents?"

"My mother was Czech," Karla said. "First generation born in the United States. Her parents were farmers in the Bohemian Alps northwest of Lincoln. About my father I remember nothing. There were no Čapeks around Crete, nobody who had the same last name as him. I'm guessing he must have been a soldier. He was tall and he played the dulcimer. That's 99 per cent of what I know."

"What about, you know, Gerard? My father's side."

"I can't help you much there, either. From what little Gerard told me, his mother was a terror; he said that people were afraid of her and that you never knew what she might do. His great-aunt raised him, and I'm ashamed to say I don't know her name. Gerard's mother called herself Rose Stevens, but everybody on the Rez called her Bad Pipe. I don't know anything about Gerard's father, except the name Horse Looking belongs to a famous family up there. They're descended from His Horse Stands Looking Brave, which doesn't translate."

"So I'm the daughter and the granddaughter of wild women." Joy smiled.

"Honey, I'm no wild woman," Karla said. "I've been scared of my shadow my whole life long. I try to put up a brave front, that's all."

"What about you, Penny?" Joy asked. "What was your family name?"

"Hartgrave," Penny said. "Everybody had English names until I married a Norwegian."

"No wild women in your family tree?"

"Not that I know of." Penny laughed. "Here I am in Paris, so maybe I'm the first."

JOY TALKED KARLA INTO ACCEPTING the gift of clothing. She got solid skirts and light-colored floral blouses that didn't make her look like something out of the Rose Bowl parade. Karla insisted on buying a gift in return, and Joy chose a delicate silver bracelet that was perfect on her dark wrist. "Do you ever wear gold?" Karla asked.

"Gold makes me look Middle Eastern," Joy said. "Around here you don't want that. Besides, it'd be misleading."

They made Penny do a little shopping, too. She got herself a pair of designer jeans and some running shoes similar to Joy's. Before going back to the hotel, they popped up near the *Arc de Triomphe*. The shape was familiar from photographs, but the scale of the thing was startling. It, too, was at the center of a *Place*, surrounded by a traffic circle with more lanes that Karla could count; several broad avenues poured into it and sucked the traffic out again. The effect was dizzying. "That's big," Karla said. "I've seen pictures, but I never thought it was so big."

"You can go up in it," Joy said, "but we would have to stand in line. Maybe the next time you're in Paris."

"What about the Louvre?" Karla asked. "Penny wants to see it."

Joy glanced at her watch. "The Louvre will be packed," she said. "It always is. You really need an entire day for that."

"Don't you worry about me," Penny said. "Whatever you two want is fine. I'm just here for the experience."

Karla studied her friend for a second. She said, "Penny, you look a little peaked. Maybe we should go back to the hotel and take a nap."

"Alfred used to take a nap after dinner," Penny said. "About twenty minutes was good enough for him."

"I don't know about you," Karla said, "but I'm going to need more than twenty minutes."

"You've both got jet lag," Joy said.

They found a concrete buttress to lean against—it protected some stairs leading to the underworld; a stream of humanity descended, four and five abreast—and Joy made them get out their subway maps and plan a route back to the hotel. Penny was confounded. "I still don't get it," she kept saying. "Which way is north? I can't figure out these lines."

"It's schematic," Joy said. "*Gare du Nord* is near the top, and the Seine is near the bottom. The stop for your hotel is to the right."

"I don't see any streets."

"When you're in the Metro you don't think about streets. You only have to remember which stop to get off at. I mean, remember where you get off. I just ended a sentence with two prepositions."

"My bad influence again," Karla said.

"What are you two talking about?"

"Nothing. Now get out your street map. Find your street and find the nearest Metro stop on the street map—it's marked with an M—and then find that stop on the subway map."

"What?"

"Here, I'll show you." Joy confiscated Penny's maps and studied them. "Shit. Now I can't find it." She bit the edge of her thumbnail.

"I think I know where it is," Karla offered.

"You keep your big hands off," Joy snapped. "I have to figure this out for myself." She studied the map a moment, then looked up. "I'm sorry, ma," she said. "Something you said a while ago struck me funny. You said you were scared of your shadow."

"I was. All the time. Small groups of men especially."

"Remember when you decked that Hudspeth boy with the mop?"

"I didn't like the way he was looking at you."

"He sat up and you pushed him down again. You shoved the mop in his face and said you would make him eat it."

"I suppose I did," Karla said. "If he was a Hudspeth, he had it coming."

"You didn't seem afraid of all those Hudspeths."

"I was petrified, sweetheart. I was sure I was going to lose my job. I would have, too, if your Aunt Ellen hadn't stepped in. She threatened to quit if the school board fired me."

"Well, see, I didn't know all that at the time. I just thought you were—" Joy blushed. "Kind of mean. You know what the kids used to call you? Mrs. Hulk."

"You were fourteen, honey," Karla said. "What did you know about any Hudspeths? You knew zip, because Ellen was there to protect you. If you'd grown up like I did, with nothing between you and the world, you'd've had to learn it all on your own."

"A girl has to learn anyway, ma," Joy said. "That's just how it is."

"I'm getting cold," Penny said. "I'll never figure out that map. Can you please take us back to our hotel?"

On the subway ride to the hotel, Joy changed roles from "cheerful and patient hostess" to "busy young woman with too many things to do." She took time at one of their transfer stops to explain the two large maps set into the wall, one map of the Metro system and the other of the *RER* commuter trains that carried workers to the suburbs out in *Île de France*. Penny still didn't get it—Karla began to wonder if she was color-blind—but Karla was mulling her own disappointments and didn't pay a lot of attention. She and Joy had little to say to one another.

Back at the hotel room, Joy opened her satchel purse and produced two weekend passes to Paris Disneyland. "These will get you in the gate, and you can ride all the rides," she said. "Mother, your weightlifting championships are in the hotel complex. Opening ceremonies are tomorrow. The championships go on all week; you can decide how much you want to attend. Tonight I'm going up to Compiègne to feed my cat. I have to be back at work on Monday, and I meet with an important client after lunch on Wednesday. I've taken the rest of the week off, and I'd like you to come to Normandy, to see a little bit of the country and meet some people who've come to be like a second family to me. You'll be on your own in Paris for a few days. Is there anything besides the competition that you'd like to see?"

"I'd like to find out where my brother Boris is buried and visit his gravesite," Karla said. "Other than that, maybe just a little sightseeing. The weightlifting doesn't interest me that much, if you want to know the truth, and I expect Penny will be bored to tears by it. Maybe we'll go on some of the roller coasters. I've never been on a roller coaster in my life."

"They've got roller coasters in America, ma," Joy said. "You don't come to Paris to ride the roller coasters."

"They don't have any in Dunlap County," Karla said. "How would I find the offices of the Grand Slovenian Orchestra of Paris?"

"The concierge can help you with that. My train leaves from the *Gare du Nord* in about an hour. I have to run."

"Better hurry, then. It's good to see you, sweetheart."

"Good to see you, too. Kiss kiss. Goodbye, Penny."

"Goodbye," Penny said. "Thanks for everything. I'll figure out that subway map. I just have to find which way is north."

After Joy had departed, Karla sat on the edge of the bed in a funk. "She's forgotten she ever needed me," she said. "She was twelve when her daddy died, and all I could do was watch TV and cry. I was no use to her or to anyone. Now she's a grown woman with a lover and a career. What can I do? I'm a stranger to her."

"You're lucky she's independent," Penny said. "My daughter keeps coming to me for money. I'd like to strangle her sometimes."

"You were a good mother when she needed you," Karla said.

"Not always. It's when she needed a kick in the pants, that's when I was not a good mother."

"Now I know why she's trying to spruce me up," Karla said. "I'm being dressed to meet the in-laws."

"I've met three sets of in-laws for my girl," Penny said. "The third time around, it's no big deal."

126

Karla sighed. "'Second family' my patootie. That girl's never had a family. Not since Gerard died." She reached down to unlace her shoes. "I wish I could drink."

KARLA HEARD RAIN IN THE COURTYARD during the night. She got up and closed the window and sat on the edge of the bed, not expecting to go back to sleep, but her roommate's gentle snores amused and relaxed her, and she was able to sleep for another hour. By the time the buzzer went off—she and Penny had set an alarm to make the most of their day at Disneyland—the rain had stopped, though a drip could still be heard falling on the chestnut leaves.

The nighttime temperature was pleasant, probably in the low 50s; they crossed the dark courtyard and stepped up to enter the breakfast room, where they turned in their chits and went through the short buffet line. Karla took eggs, bacon, and coffee, and Penny helped herself to croissants and preserves. There were a kind of pickled apricots on offer, and Karla spooned a few of them into a side dish. Once at table, she tried an apricot first. Spicy-sweet with a touch of heat, it stung her lips in a way that was too familiar. She quickly removed it from her mouth and laid it on her plate.

"What's the matter?" Penny asked.

"Brandy." Karla pushed the little side dish across to Penny. "They're lovely, but I can't have them. Help yourself."

Of the other guests at breakfast, one couple were French, one couple were American, and one were Japanese. Thought the room was small, each couple conversed only with themselves. The man in a white jacket who served the buffet was the concierge of the day before. When Karla asked him which Metro line to take to get to the *Gare de Lyon*, he smiled. "You don't take Metro. You walk. It is one kilometer approximate."

"That's five-eighths of a mile, am I right?"

"Yes. It is not far. If you walk fast, fifteen minute." He shrugged. "You walk to Metro stop, ten minute. Wait for train, five minute. Ride to next stop, five minute. Wait for train to *Gare de Lyon*, you arrive after thirty minute. To walk is better."

"It's dark outside. We might get lost."

"Can not get lost. Straight line almost. I show you."

The female half of the young Japanese couple looked up. "Paris Disneyland?" Karla nodded. "We are going too." She took out her cell phone and held it up. "GPS. No problem."

Penny finished the side dish of apricots and went back for more. "These apricot pickles are good," she said. "I want to learn how to make them."

"Better not," Karla said. "Before you know it, you'll be getting pickled on apricots."

"Why shouldn't I? Old Alfred won't be around to make a fuss."

"You should eat your croissant. You don't want to pickle on an empty stomach."

They saw the Japanese couple again on their way to the *Gare de Lyon*; the two youngsters scooted past them, walking rapidly under the streetlights. Karla and Penny picked up their pace in an effort to keep them in sight, and succeeded to the extent that they were led in the correct direction. The *Gare de Lyon* was brightly lit, not so vast as the *Gare du Nord*, and they found their way down to the third level (which was labeled "Level 2") and the ticketing kiosk for the *RER*. The Japanese were there waiting for the train, and this time they smiled in recognition. "Do you go to see weightlifting competition?" the young woman asked.

"That's right," Karla said. "How did you know?"

"You are big," the girl said, and laughed. "I am lifter, too. 48 kilogram." She flexed her arm and made her bicep appear. "You see? Very strong."

"Are you competing?"

"Oh, no." The girl laughed again. "I start late. Hobby only."

They followed the Japanese couple and bought tickets on Line A of the *Réseau Express Régional*. The platform was similar to a Metro platform, only roomier, and they entered from the left rather than from the right. A few people remained standing for the first stops, though there were plenty of seats. The train ran underground until it reached the outskirts, where it emerged from its tunnel and speeded up, click-clacking along under a cloud cover that was beginning to break. By the gray light of morning, Karla and Penny got their first look at a landscape that was not so closely ordered as that of Paris. Many buildings appeared to contain apartments; the windows were lit as the tenants dressed for work. These apartment buildings were of unornamented brick, plain by contrast with the city's charming façades. Though there were trees and open green spaces, on the whole the suburban countryside was unattractive.

"I wouldn't want to live in an apartment," Penny said. "No room to garden." They passed a wall covered in graffiti. "Why do they make it ugly like that?"

"It's kids," Karla said. "They're bored. They don't realize how bad it looks."

"I'm going to see the Loover on Monday," Penny said. "I promised myself."

Their train dove into a slot in the ground and soon reached the end of its run. Karla and Penny followed the Japanese couple up a long escalator and to the right, and the theme park lay before them, bathed in morning sunlight. They presented their passes and entered amid a swarm of workers wearing ID badges on lanyards.

After spending two days amid the disciplined architecture of Paris, Karla could recognize a botch when she saw one, and the hotel they approached was a botch, a gigantic broad-faced toad with five hats and five hundred eyes, up whose tongue and into whose maw the workers marched. They passed a landscaped Mickey-face made of flowers, which Penny would've stopped to admire if Karla hadn't jerked her onward, and went through a sort of tunnel and into the park proper, where the colors of the rainbow were visible everywhere, if a rainbow could be made of plastic. The Japanese couple had vanished, and Karla realized that the toad hotel was their destination and that the Japanese had turned off into it. She caught the sleeve of Penny's trench coat and slowed her down. "Hey," she said. "I think we went too far."

"No," Penny said. Her face beneath the fisherman's hat looked betrayed. "I want to go on in."

"Well," Karla said, "'On in' is where the rides are, but I came here for the weightlifting competition. I thought you were going to come with me."

"Well, I was," Penny said, "but it looks so interesting. Will your competition take all day? We can split up, you know. There's no reason for us to do everything together."

"It goes on all week," Karla said. "Though to tell the truth, I expect I'll get my fill of it fairly quickly. If you'll stick with me for a couple of hours, we'll come back out and look at some of the rides. There are thousands of people here already, and it isn't even nine o'clock. If we split up, I'm afraid we might lose track of one another."

"This is like the Nebraska State Fair, only bigger." Penny sniffed the air. "And, it doesn't smell like manure. When I went with Alfred, if we got separated I'd look for him at the sheep barn. I don't know why he liked the sheep barn. We never raised sheep. After the boys got older, we'd find them at the shooting gallery."

"I doubt if there's a shooting gallery. Would they shoot little Donald Ducks? One point each for Huey, Dewey, and Louie?"

They tacked across the current of employees, fell into an eddy, and washed up on the step leading to the hotel lobby. Karla towed Penny inside and up to the desk, where she asked the clerk, "Weightlifting competition?" and mimed lifting a bar of weights.

He looked her up and down. "Which weight class are you in? Plus 105 kilograms?"

"You speak English really well," Karla said. "One more crack like that, and I'll tell you what I think of you in terms this whole room will understand."

He shrugged and gestured toward a posterboard propped on an easel. "Hotel map is at the bottom," he said. "If you get confused, just stop somebody in a funny-looking uniform."

"Wow," Penny said as they walked away. "He talked just like an American."

Their competition wasn't hard to find on the map, but it was a long walk to get there. Karla knew they were close when she caught the scent of analgesic balm; a fourteen-year-old seated at a folding table glanced at their tickets and waved them through. The theater-like space seated maybe a thousand. Once inside, Karla and Penny scanned the front of the room, where a stage supported a reinforced pad lit brightly for the TV cameras. A giant monitor high above the stage showed a silver-haired man wearing a sash full of medals. As he addressed the audience in French, a large blue dolphin painted on the wall behind him stood on its tail and balanced a bar of weights on its flippers.

"Wow," Penny whispered. "So many foreigners." Karla bristled but let it go. *You and I are the foreigners.* She hoped they would see the Japanese couple, but the room was filled with strangers.

The silver-haired official bowed, the audience applauded, and Karla and Penny took advantage of the clatter to scoot to a pair of seats in the second-to-last row. As Karla measured to make sure that her bottom would fit, a short man in the final row frowned up at them; Karla turned her back on this angry musclebrow, sat down, and wriggled herself between the armrests. She inclined her head toward Penny. "This is so different from what I remember," she said. "The only time I was in a competition, we could've had it in a church basement. My own mother didn't even come to watch."

After the silver-haired speaker vanished from the monitor above the stage, a backstage camera prowled the warmup area, showing the audience a row of pads where the athletes and trainers were busying themselves. Next the camera feed cut to the front, where three referees and a jury of five judges were seated; the scorekeepers stood up from their table, where they controlled the clock and the numbers on the display board. The camera team cut again to the area behind the partition, to a table where clerks kept cards for the trainers to write or "declare" the weights their lifters would attempt. "This is all too much for me," Penny said. "Do you get any of it?"

"Only because I've done it," Karla said. "Once the competition starts, it's not so complicated. Those three people, one in the middle and two at the corners, are referees. There's a table of judges who can overrule the referees, and another table for the scorekeepers. Everything else happens backstage."

The first round of competition was for men under 56 kilograms. The lifters had been seeded into groups A, B, and C; the first lifter in Group C was a dark-haired little man named Ruslan Makarov from Uzbekistan. His first declared weight was 115 kilograms. "That's eleven kilos more than I ever snatched," Karla whispered to Penny. "And look at him! He's practically a midget."

"I think he's a cutie pie," Penny whispered back. "Kind of hairy, but maybe all that fur is good. I bet those nights get cold in Uzbekistan."

Ruslan Makarov marched to the bar, bent down, spread his hands just so, looked up and into the distance above the audience, and, whip! Up went the bar as he squatted down and stood up straight again. He held the bar steady until the buzzer sounded, then let it fall in the correct controlled manner. There were lights on a scoreboard to replace the referees' cards; all showed white, signaling a perfect lift. Makarov nodded in acknowledgement, backed away, and turned and left the stage.

"He made that look easy," Karla said. "Great technique."

"I'd like to find out more about his technique."

"Penny! Girl, have you been hitting the *sauvignon blanc* again?"

The next man up was Yang Chin-yi, a citizen of Taiwan. He also declared 115 kilograms. He marched to the bar in the same straightforward manner, bent and spread his hands, adjusted his grip, and looked up. He took a breath and began his lift, but something happened and he released the bar and stood up, bowed, and backed away. "His balance wasn't right," Karla said. "He'll come back out and try again. He has two minutes to get ready."

"If Alfred had to try again, it took him more than two minutes," Penny said. "More like two weeks."

"Penny Raskonen! Are you OK?"

"It's those body suits they're wearing," Penny said. "Tight tight tight."

It was true that both Makarov and Yang were trim and good-looking. Karla, as a former contestant, felt her friend's unseemly regard. "They can't help what they have to wear," she said. "Their clothing contributes to their weight, so it has to be thin. They can't weigh in naked."

"Who'd mind?" Penny said. "I wouldn't."

The man behind Karla leaned forward. "You two should quit yapping," he said. "You're not the only ones here who speak English." His accent sounded Australian or South African. Karla would have turned to confront him, but she was wedged between the armrests; before she could think of a reply, Yang Chin-yi came out to attempt his second lift. This time he raised the bar overhead in a single sweep. There was a pattering of applause.

The next lifter to declare 115 kilos was Om Yun-chol of the People's Republic of Korea. He marched in like a stone-faced soldier, quickly positioned his hands on the bar, performed his lift with precision, and bowed and left the stage. "He's no fun," Penny whispered. "Like sleeping with a robot." The fourth lifter at 115 kilos was Cuban. He strutted to the bar and glanced from left to right like a rock star. "Now, there's a pretty little Communist," Penny said. "If I thought they were all built like that, I'd move to Cuba."

There was a rustle and a clearing of the throat. "I've heard enough of this," the man behind them said. "I did not fly all the way from Johannesburg to be forced to listen to your schoolgirl babble."

This time Karla turned around to face him. The man behind her was buzz-cut blond, with thick lips, pale blue eyes, and bulges above his eyebrows. His head was as round as a melon; he had the look of a rugby player who'd been squeezed down vertically. "No one's forcing you to listen," she said. "I bet we flew farther than you, and we were almost blown up at the airport."

"I regret the 'almost,'" he said.

A security guard who'd been standing at the back of the room moved toward them, holding a miniature walkie-talkie. The guard leaned above the South African from behind. "Surely there is not a problem here, no?" he said.

"No problem," Karla said. "This guy's too short, that's all. He's acting pissy because he can't see over me."

"These women are disrespectful," the blond man said. "I've asked them, but they won't be quiet."

"Ah," said the guard. He raised smooth eyebrows. "Perhaps the ladies will address one another more calmly. Eh?"

"Perhaps," Karla said.

"I'd move," said Mister Johannesburg, flexing his forehead, "but there are no more empty seats."

ACCORDING TO THE PROGRAM SCHEDULE, the second set of lifters would be Group C of the women's 48-kilogram division. Barring a miracle, these Group C women would win no medals, but they would strain to perform the same lifts as would those in Group A.

"Which ones are Americans?" Penny wanted to know.

Karla ran her finger down the list of names. "None of them," she said. "Except this one, Lely Burgos from Puerto Rico."

While the officials took a moment to stretch, the big screen showed scenes from the warmup area; Karla glimpsed young women going through their routines. Some lifted bars with no weights at all, doing reps to rehearse their technique; others already had the discs loaded and were taking single lifts close to competition level. Most coaches and trainers were male, and as they massaged the lifters' joints and muscles, these men passed their hands quite freely over their female trainees. "Look at that trainer," Karla said. "If he squeezed my leg like that, I'd smack him."

Penny said, "If a man squeezed my leg like that, I'd grab him and kiss him."

"Not this again," said the man behind them.

Karla swiveled in the cramped seat as best she could. "Mister, why don't you take a walk? Do something with yourself. These young women are here to be judged; we're not. You are out of line."

"I will call security. We will see who is out of line." The more the man spoke, the more Karla noticed a second accent flavoring his South African English.

Karla unwedged herself from between the armrests and stood. The South African rose as well and turned to summon the guard. He was a foot shorter than Karla, with muscles that stood out like potatoes on his stubby arms. A scar on his buzz-cut head showed that he'd been hit with something. Maybe a wall had fallen on him.

The security guard approached. "I am at your service," he said.

"This gentleman keeps harassing us," Karla said. "My friend and I are trying to enjoy the show."

The guard turned to the short South African. "And you?"

"These two old hens make filthy observations," he said. "They're obsessed with sex."

The guard's perfect eyebrows glided up and down. "Ah," he said. He glanced at Karla and Penny with the hint of a smile. "Americans in Paris, no? What can one do?"

"They could move," the man said. "This one—" he gestured to Karla— "blocks my view."

"You could try standing up," Karla said. He glared at her. "Oops. Sorry," she said. "You're already standing." Karla turned her back on the complainer and the guard. "I'm not moving. That musclebound runt can go and play with himself." She gathered the tails of her plastic raincoat and sat. The two men behind her did not speak again.

The first young woman to come out and lift wore a black sari-like garment that covered her arms to the wrists and her body all the way to the ankles, and a pale glimmering headscarf that concealed her hair and wrapped like a bandage under her chin. Penny's breath hissed. "There's one," she whispered.

"One what?"

"Terrorist."

Karla glanced to see if her friend was joking. She wasn't. "No, really," she said. "Look at her, Penny. What a sweet face." She checked the program. "She's from Pakistan. That's what they all wear in Pakistan."

The Pakistani girl's trainer declared 37 kilos, a weight that seemed ridiculous to Karla. Before lifting, she tucked her sleeves up to expose her elbows as the contest rules required. She bent, spread her hands on the bar, and lifted, but as she did so, one of her sleeves came down and obscured her elbow. Three red lights appeared on the referees' panel. "Two minutes to try again," Karla said. "She doesn't even lift her own weight. She has no chance."

"Why is she here if she has no chance? She's making me nervous."

"Maybe her country's just started a training program. Or maybe she's here to make a statement."

"What kind of statement?"

"A statement for women."

The Pakistani girl came out again, and this time her sleeves stayed up and her lift was successful. She got a scattering of applause, mostly for her courage. Karla clapped as well.

The next person to lift, a Brit, declared 57 kilos, and the weights went up from there. Because each lifter worked at the limit of her strength, injury was possible. One thing that Ruby Hoeft had taught, Karla now remembered, was how to exit a failed lift without losing control of the bar.

Ruby Hoeft. Karla's hand went up to touch her upper lip and explore her chin. For years after college, she'd had nightmares about Ruby Hoeft. The woman followed her across continents, offering pills of various shapes and colors and sizes.

KARLA WATCHED THE WOMEN'S COMPETITION with more interest than she'd watched the men's, but for Penny it was the opposite; a couple of times Karla caught her friend nodding. Lely Burgos, the Puerto Rican, was the best lifter in Group C, with a snatch of 70 kilograms and a clean-and-jerk of 92. Next highest was a girl from El Salvador, who put up numbers of 65 and 80. By the time each competitor in Group C had completed her lifts—three snatch attempts and three clean-and-jerks—Penny was asleep. Group B of the women's 48-kilogram class would not begin lifting until noon; Karla woke Penny and said, "From here on out, it's more of the same. Let's grab some lunch."

"All right," Penny said. "I need to find a rest room."

Others were taking advantage of the intermission, so that Karla and Penny were delayed in leaving the row. Coming slowly up the center aisle and holding back traffic behind her, a short white-haired woman as broad as she was tall beetled forward using a pair of aluminum canes. Something about her figure made Karla uneasy, and this uneasiness changed to alarm when the woman called out to her. "Miss Čapek! Wait, please. I'd like to talk to you."

"The name is Horse Looking," Karla said. "But how do you know me?"

The robust old woman came slowly up to her, breathing heavily. "Ruby Hoeft," she said. "I was your weight coach at the University of Nebraska. Surely you remember." She detached her right forearm from its cane and held out her hand.

"Coach Hoeft?" Karla touched the proffered hand and quickly released it. "What are you doing here?"

"Working, actually," the woman said. "I might ask the same of you. Hello, Miss—?"

"This is Penny Raskonen," Karla said. "A friend of mine. I'm in France at my daughter's invitation. She's too busy to see me today. She thought I might like to see the weightlifting."

Ruby Hoeft shook hands with Penny and retrieved the cane from her other hand. She resumed her four-legged stance and said, "I've had both hips replaced. I won't be needing these crutches forever. Let's move. We're drawing a crowd."

They moved on up the aisle and through the entrance, to join the line in the hallway outside the women's rest room. "How did you happen to recognize me?" Karla said.

"I noticed you when you stood up to talk to the guard. Not many women are as tall as you. What was that about, by the way?"

"Some guy from South Africa was harassing us," Karla said. "He was mad because I sat in front of him. There's something fishy about him. I think he's a cop or a detective."

Ruby Hoeft glanced back over her shoulder. "What makes you think he might be a policeman?"

"Thirty years of driving-under-the-influence. Also, my husband was large and Native American. He couldn't drive in Omaha without getting pulled over. We didn't even try to drive in Lincoln." Some women came out of the rest room, and the line moved up. "You said you were working," Karla said. "Do you still teach at the University?"

"Oh, no. I left Lincoln at the same time you did. There was some scandal about pharmaceuticals. They said I was prescribing drugs without a license." They moved up again. "I'm a consultant now," Ruby Hoeft said. "I work with the Ukrainian weightlifters."

"Are you still coaching, then?"

"Not exactly. As I said, I'm a consultant." She crutched herself closer to Karla and lowered her voice. "About that South African. He's a cop, you say? And you think he could be here professionally?"

"I don't know," Karla said. "It's just—he has a kind of bully attitude. Like he's used to people stepping aside for him."

"South Africa is not represented here," Ruby Hoeft said softly. "Not a single competitor. I don't think they even support a program."

The line moved forward. Ruby Hoeft said, "Are you going to be here all week?"

"No," Karla said. "In fact, I think we're just about finished. Penny wants to see Disneyland."

"That's too bad," Ruby Hoeft said. "There's somebody I'd like you to meet. Her name is Olha Korobka. She's twenty-six years old and weighs 332 pounds."

Karla rubbed her chin, a feature Joy had not inherited. "That could've been me, I suppose," she said. "In a different time." Karla grasped Penny by the elbow and pushed past the remaining women into the rest room.

"Our methods were primitive," Ruby Hoeft called out after her. "Things have changed. The rules have changed."

"Olha Korobka has my sympathies," Karla said. "Goodbye."

"WHO WAS THAT WHITE-HAIRED WOMAN on crutches?" Penny was eating a chili dog. They were having lunch in the hotel's dining room, where expensive food was served to Americans' tastes.

"She was the weight coach at NU," Karla said. "She had us all taking drugs. She's going to get that Olha Korobka disqualified."

"You were trying hard to be nice, but I could tell you didn't like her."

"That's an understatement. For years, I dreamed of killing her," Karla said. "Literally. I thought of different ways to do it." She looked at the chicken-fried steak on her plate and put down her fork. "Let's change the subject: roller coasters. After what Joy said to me, I plan to ride every roller coaster in the park."

"What did she say to you? You look ready to bite an alligator."

"She said that nobody come to Paris to ride the roller coasters."

"Maybe she just doesn't like roller coasters," Penny said. "You know what, this chili dog isn't very good."

Karla sighed. "It's got nothing to do with roller coasters," she said. "I'll let you in on a secret about me. Inside this sweet and loving exterior, there's a Texas chainsaw killer waiting to break out."

"I never saw that movie," Penny said. "Is there a roller coaster in it?"

"No roller coasters," Karla said. "We'll watch it when we get home. It's probably on one of your 1500 channels."

Their first ride together was a gentle boat tour past stiffly moving childlike mannequins dressed to represent a hundred national stereotypes. Children's voices sang "It's a small small world" over and over, until Karla wanted to take a chainsaw to the figurines. "If I had to listen to that song all day, I would cut my wrists," Karla said. "I wonder how the employees stand it."

"Look at those darling costumes," Penny said. "I wish they would stop the boat so I could check the seams. Do you sew?"

"I do not," Karla said. "My mother worked in a factory where they sewed brassieres. Eight hours a day, five days a week. She made my dresses all the way through high school. I swore I'd never touch a sewing machine." She smiled crookedly. "Though I do own a thimble."

At last they emerged from the small-world torture chamber. Karla took a breath of the crisp November air and blew it out again, and shook her head to clear the voices out of it. "Never again in this lifetime," she said.

"Funny how the two of us can have different impressions," Penny said. "I loved those cute costumes. I'd like to go on that ride one more time."

"You'll be going by yourself. What's next? Space Mountain?"

"Let's save that one. What about Temple of Peril? That sounds like what the Lutherans think of the Catholics."

"Or what Catholics think about everybody else. Let's go."

Karla and Penny rode "Indiana Jones and the Temple of Peril." Then they rode Dumbo the Flying Elephant to cool off a bit before tackling "Big Thunder Mountain." After that, they sat in a spinning teacup with a steering wheel in the middle. Karla spun them until they were dizzy. "What next?" she said. "We could ride the kiddie cars, except I can't fit into one."

"I can do one more coaster, if it's not too scary."

"Are you a Rock 'N' Roller?"

"I used to like looking at Elvis, but I don't listen to rock and roll."

"Elvis is fine," Karla said. "I don't think they've got a ride for Mozart."

The "Rock 'N' Roller Coaster" turned out to be too much. The jolts, the acceleration, the crashing and noise and lights all contributed to a feeling of whiplash, so that when they staggered back into the sunlight, they both felt nauseous. "These rides are not for old ladies," Penny said. "I'd better sit down." They found a bench—stationary, though it didn't seem so—and watched the crowd for a while. "They ought to warn us older people," Penny said.

"I've heard of people getting concussions on these things," Karla said. "Me, I've got a big hard head and very little brain. I don't think I need to worry about a concussion."

"There was a sign that said not to ride if you were pregnant." The riders getting off were about one-third their age. "I'm done roller coasting," Penny said. "I'm going to ride that Small World thing again. I want to see those adorable costumes."

"I'd need a lobotomy for that one," Karla said. "I said I was going to ride them all. Space Mountain is next."

They arranged a meeting place near the Small World ride, and the two of them headed off to stand in different lines. Penny looked outlandish but resolute in her trench coat and fisherman's hat. Karla hoped she looked resolute, too; the Rock 'N' Roller had daunted her a bit. But when she recalled Joy's snark about Paris and roller coasters, she flexed her shoulders and stiffened her spine.

As she joined the serpentine line to get in, Karla felt someone behind her. She turned to see if Penny had changed her mind, but it was the tough from the weightlifting competition. He attempted a smile. "Hello," he said.

"You've been following me."

"I have certain skills," he said. "I was with you on the Small World ride. You never noticed."

"You're not originally from South Africa," she said. "You have an accent. German?"

"That's all right for Johannesburg," he said. "I blend in."

"Do you want something from me? You have 'cop' written all over you."

"What is your connection to Dr. Hoeft?"

"I don't see why that's any of your business," Karla said.

The short man—little did not describe him—sighed. "While we are waiting in this line, with your permission, I will share part of my biography," he said. "You are free to disbelieve me, or to stop me at any time."

"Go on."

"My sister and I were born in the GDR; East Germany, as it was known in the West. Our parents were nobody special. We both became interested in weight training early and were singled out for attention. My own enthusiasm fell away; I had not the potential to become a champion. With my sister it was different. She was a fierce girl, not large but strong; she had an unusual power in her muscles. She trained like a demon.

"Before she reached puberty, my sister was sent to live in a special compound for elite athletes. Our family did not object to this, as it meant fewer persons living in a small apartment. We did not see her often, but when we did, we saw changes in her physique and her behavior. She became more manly; her shoulders broadened and her profile changed. Her breasts did not develop. She was still bright and attractive, but she became subject to fits of temper and wept easily."

"Let me guess," Karla said. "Ruby Hoeft was involved in this." The line moved up.

"Dr. Hoeft had come over from the United States," he said. "There were no weight training programs for females in the U. S. at that time. Hoeft portrayed herself as an academic who needed scope for her research, but in fact she was only interested in competition.

"As for myself, I joined a youth organization similar to the Boy Scouts. Of course I was being groomed for the Stasi, the secret police." He looked down at his hands and spread his stubby fingers. "I was taught to inform on people. I was rewarded when I told them my father sold his petrol ration. That sort of thing."

"And did you continue to lift?"

"I took up the martial arts. I enjoyed my training. All of it." The line moved up; he sighed. "I learned interrogation techniques. Basic electronics. Psychology. I learned to encode messages. I practiced spycraft, to become invisible in a crowd. I learned to notice everything and to be suspicious. Like my sister, I grew apart from our family. No one would confide in me. At the age of eighteen, I was given my own apartment and went into police work full time."

He looked up and smiled. "Then, one day, Reunification happened. The Wall came down and I was unemployed. That is when I emigrated to South Africa."

"Just in time for the end of Apartheid."

"Yes; bad timing. But for a man like me, there is always employment. So that is who I am. A cop. Not a good cop. Not a cop who rescues puppies and gives out parking tickets."

"And your sister?"

"My sister is dead."

They had reached the head of the line. A little train of cars pulled up, and the people ahead of them boarded until every seat was filled. Karla and the cop were held back at the last moment, so that they would be first to board at the next opportunity. "I am sorry," Karla said. "What happened to your sister?"

"Officially, she suffered an aneurism. After Reunification, the GDR's Olympic weight program ceased to exist. My sister swallowed a handful of Dr. Hoeft's little tablets. They would have caused a catastrophic rise in her blood pressure." The man fell silent. Then he said, "By the end, she was the only family member who would speak to me."

"So you blame Ruby Hoeft?"

"That is my belief, yes, that Dr. Ruby Hoeft is responsible. If not for Dr. Hoeft and her misuse of medications, my beautiful strong sister would be alive today."

"Are you going to kill her?"

"No. I could manage that easily. What I want is that she should be exposed. Discredited. Made to feel shame."

Their conversation was interrupted by the arrival of a train of vacant cars. Since they were first in line, they boarded the very first row, at the front of the train. The attendant, a young South Asian woman whose long hair and dark eyes made Karla think of Joy, came by to make sure the bar was down and they were clamped in. "Are you confident to sit in front?" she asked Karla. "This ride bounces badly. I ask because of your age."

"My age is none of your concern. I won't bounce out, if that's what you mean."

The girl drew down the corners of her mouth and made a fine French shrug. "It will be as you wish," she said. "*Bon chance.*"

The little train climbed into darkness. Points of starlight appeared above and along the track, but they were faint and illuminated nothing. Karla felt gravity pulling at her arms as she gripped the crossbar; as the string of cars ground to the apex, a flicker of light came from behind and there was the roar of a rocket motor. The roar cut off and the flicker stopped, and she felt herself floating into space; then the cars headed down and the screaming began in earnest.

Being seated in the front, with no one ahead of her, she had no opportunity to brace herself when the cars changed direction. The "bounces" the girl had spoken of were jolts as the wheels crashed over joints in the track. Karla's loose flesh wubbled and bobbled until she felt her fat disconnecting from her skeleton, and the points of light came at her like bullets or supersonic bees. When they reached a secondary summit and the cars dropped down again, she cried out as she felt the weight of her thighs press upward against the bar. The train zigzagged among stars and planets, snapping her head from side to side; it zoomed up, compressing her spine, and topped out into zero gravity, and her stomach felt as if she'd swallowed the contents of a washing machine. She forgot the man sitting next to her; all she could think was, "When will it stop?" At last, they returned to the platform and rolled to a halt. "My God," she said, aghast. "That was horrible."

When the dark-haired attendant unlocked the bar, Karla was unable to stand by herself; the girl and the South African policeman had to help her. The man continued to hold her arm as they left the platform. "Please don't make me ride it again," she said. "I'll tell you everything I know."

"Not amusing. Do you go now to meet your companion?'

"The Small World ride. If I can get there."

He guided her to the bench outside the Small World ride; she wouldn't have found it by herself. "I suppose I'm indebted to you," she said. "Or not. Maybe. I don't know."

"Did Dr. Hoeft say something to you? Any information that might be useful?" Karla hesitated. "The enemy of my enemy is my friend," he said. "You know something. Tell me."

"Olha Korobka," Karla said. "You can't miss her. She weighs 332 pounds."

BY THE TIME SHE AND PENNY got back to their room, Karla had a headache that rivalled her worst migraine. She lay on the bed face down, fully clothed, running shoes and all. "Can you find me some Tylenol?"

"I think I've got some in my purse," Penny said. "If I don't, the concierge will have it." She brought two pills and a glass of water. Karla tried to raise her head. "Ooh, ouch," she said. "I think I'm going to need a straw."

"Lucky for you I've got grandkids," Penny said, rooting in her purse. "There's a straw from a juice box in here somewhere."

Karla managed to get the pills down without lifting herself from the pillow. "Thanks," she said. "I used to get a headache once in a while. This is the worst."

"Was it the roller coasters?"

"Yeah, the Space Mountain one. That girl tried to warn me, but I didn't listen."

Penny sat on her bed across from Karla and removed her shoes. "Do you think I ought to telephone your daughter?"

"Good Lord, no. I don't want to hear her say 'I told you so.' Besides, it's Saturday night. Her friend might be there."

"Didn't Joy go to Compiègne? I thought he lived in Paris."

"I don't know," Karla said. "I don't know anything. Don't talk to me."

The next morning her head felt like that blown-up backpack they'd seen at the airport; in addition, she'd developed nausea. Penny brought a hotel wastebasket to put beside the bed. "I'm going to get some breakfast," she said. "Then I'm going to call your daughter. Where's her phone number?"

"There's a little notebook," Karla said. "Get my purse. It's in there somewhere."

Not long after Penny returned from breakfast, bringing apple juice and a croissant—Karla sipped a little juice through a straw—there was a tap at the door and Penny let in an amiable-looking young man who introduced himself as Dr. Lazcaré. "Madame Čapek," he said to Karla, "I am told that you have developed a severe headache following a ride at Disney. If you'll permit me, I will examine you." This young doctor had a nicely-trimmed little beard and brown eyes with a hint of mischief in them.

"I'll permit you," Karla said. "Just don't ask me to hop on one foot."

Dr. Lazcaré carried a leather doctor's bag and wore, around one of his forearms, a large white cuff, which he removed and set on the bedside table. He was dressed as a graduate student might dress to go to church, in a nicely tailored button-down shirt and slacks. He listened to her heart and lungs with a stethoscope (from the back; she did not sit up or turn over) and took her pulse. "I must read the pressure in your arteries," he said, all business now. "May you expose your left arm, please." Karla gave him her left arm to do with as he wished, just so long as he didn't joggle her head. "Do you take a medication for your pressure?" he asked as he Velcroed the cuff.

"No, but I should," Karla said. "So my doctor tells me."

"You must always listen to your doctor." He squished the bulb, then let the air out slowly. "One hundred forty-five millimeters of mercury over one hundred. That is high, but this cuff may not be accurate. It is for an arm that is not so large in diameter."

"Do you think I'm having a stroke?"

"I do not think it, no. Your presentation would be different. Do you feel tingling or numbness in your extremities? Hands, feet? Toes, fingers?"

"I guess not, no."

"May I touch the back of your neck?"

"Careful, Doc," Penny said. "She's a mean one."

Karla felt cool fingers on the back of her neck, probing gently, pushing a little. Then a skyrocket exploded in her head. "Ow! Ouch," she said. "I think you found something."

"Here is what I would like," he said. "I've brought with me a cervical collar. It is of a general type and may not fit you perfectly, but I would like you to try it. Then, if you are able to sit up, I will drive you to a hospital so that your neck can be x-rayed. If the x-ray reveals a stress fracture, your neck must be immobilized. This will be inconvenient, but preferable to being *paralysée*. It will not be expensive," he added after a pause. "In France, most medical care is free."

"If it's free, why not take me in an ambulance?"

"It is Sunday morning," he said. "This is the only time Paris is a little quiet. The ambulance is noisy." He smiled; once again, there was that concealed twinkle. Of course he thinks I'm funny, Karla thought. It's not his neck.

When Karla sat up, her visual field constricted to a bright circle surrounded by a black whirling darkness. Sparks danced on the screen of her eyelids, reminding her of the tiny lights of the Space Mountain ride, and the pain in the back of her head made her want to vomit. She managed to hold herself still while the young doctor fastened the collar in place; her hands crushed the edge of the mattress and the heat of seven suns passed over her. When he'd finished and the agony abated a little, she said, "If it's a cervical collar, shouldn't it go around my cervix?" No response. "Phoo," she said. "That had to be at least a ten point five."

"Once you are prepared to stand, I will help you," the doctor said. "You will need to use the chamber, is it not so? Perhaps Miss Penny will assist."

"It is so," Karla said, "if by 'chamber' you mean the bathroom."

Because Karla had lain down fully clothed, her hair was full of tangles. In the bathroom, Penny offered to help, but when the brush pulled at one of the snarls, a bullet went down her spine. "No, no," she said when she caught her breath. "That doesn't work. Leave it."

Dr. Lazcaré's car was a battered green Renault shaped something like a mailbox; he and Penny loaded Karla, and he got her to a hospital without her head falling off. There they gave her an injection and laid her on her back and sent her head-first through a donut that made sloshing noises. There was no fracture but a compression of the discs; the upshot was that she left the hospital wearing a much stiffer brace, one that held her chin forward and erect and prevented her from turning her head. It came up as high as her ears at the back and down almost as far as her shoulder blades. When she was released, they charged her twenty-five euros. It was twelve o'clock by then, and the effects of the injection were wearing off, so they gave her extra-strength Tylenol. It was difficult to drink or swallow while wearing the brace.

The young Dr. Lazcaré drove them back to the hotel and walked Karla to the door of their room. He handed her a card. "My telephone," he said. "If you experience a sudden increase in pain, or tingling in your extremities, you must please call me quickly. Take Tylenol for the pain and ibuprofen for inflammation. I advise you to drink orange juice plentifully. Please do not become dehydrated." He glanced at Penny. "Tomorrow you will rest. You will not go to the Louvre."

"Fine with me," Karla said. "I don't like art much anyway."

"Ah, don't say so." He smiled. "Art, food, music, these are the soul of France."

"Don't forget *l'amour*," Penny said.

"Ah, yes. There is always *l'amour*."

"What a nice boy," Penny said when he had left. "Imagine him being a doctor already. Do you want me to help you lie down?"

"I'd rather sit up for now. I'm afraid I might jostle my neck."

THE NEXT DAY, PENNY WENT BY HERSELF to see the Louvre. Karla stayed in their room with the shades pulled shut and wondered if she'd see her friend again. Penny made it back in the evening, after a misadventure; she'd taken the correct train in the wrong direction, and had ridden it to the end and back again. "You could've got off at any stop," Karla pointed out, "and crossed over and come back the other way."

"Well, I did think of that, but I kind of enjoyed the ride. Seeing all those different colored people gave me chills at first, but after a while it was like Small Small World. Do you want to get something to eat?"

"I'm game," Karla said. "I think I can walk to that little place down the street."

The same white-shirted Algerian brought their menus. "Ooh, I like him," Penny whispered. "Do you think he would open a restaurant in Turtle Lodge?"

Karla laughed. "Couldn't do it," she said. "The French eat snails, and the only snails in Turtle Lodge are the ones out at Baxter's Pond. They're barely the size of a kidney bean. Why don't you try the yellow chicken? I'll get the *beef bourguignon*, and if you don't like yours, we can switch."

It was awkward for Karla to eat while wearing the brace. "Damn this thing," she said. "Pardon my French." Both of them laughed. "That doctor," she said. "Where did you get his phone number?"

"I didn't call him," Penny said. "He must be somebody Joy knows. What will you do tomorrow? Are you going to spend another day in bed?"

"I don't know. I hate to waste the time. Would you go to see the Louvre again?"

"It's closed on Tuesdays."

That night, with the lingering headache and the neck brace, Karla found it hard to go to sleep. She sent Penny to ask the concierge for extra pillows and made a mockup of her old recliner on the hotel bed, but she could not get comfortable. Penny's snoring didn't help, nor did the *beef bourguignon*, which sat heavy in her stomach. When she did doze off, she dreamed that Ruby Hoeft was forcing cheese-and-pimento sandwiches into her mouth. At one point she rose, went into the bathroom, and, tilting herself carefully over the fixture, threw up. After that she felt better and slept until morning.

For breakfast, Karla had a croissant with jam, while Penny ate three of them. The Japanese couple was there, and the young woman greeted Karla. "Big news," she said. "They spot check for drugs. One person on Ukraine is disqualified. Ukraine coach is angry, saying team will go home."

Karla wiped a bit of jam off her brace. "I'm sorry to hear it," she said. "I feel sorry for the girl who got caught. She's put her whole life into it."

The Japanese girl looked puzzled. "Ah. You heard. Korobka. European champion."

"Too bad for her," Karla said. "It's probably not even her fault."

"They have to punish," the Japanese girl said. "Otherwise all would cheat."

Back in their room, Karla eased onto the bed and leaned herself carefully against the mound of pillows. "I think I'd better lie here and try to digest," she said. "That injection they gave me two days ago stopped my guts from working."

"That cute young doctor said you should drink orange juice. I'll get you some. While I'm down there, I'll ask the concierge if the rest of the museums close on Tuesdays. I want to see some naked Rodins, but if we can't, we can't."

"Maybe later we could take a ride on one of those tour buses."

"Or a boat ride on the Seine," Penny said. "Maybe that little restaurant guy would go with us." Her eyes sparkled with mischief. "France is way more fun than I expected. How's your head?"

"Better, but would you please get me more Tylenol?"

The TV in the room played VCR tapes, and Penny brought back a promo tape showing what they might see from a tour bus. Watching it made Karla restless. "We are wasting the day," she said finally. "You had better go out on your own."

"I don't like that idea," Penny said. "There must be something we could do that wouldn't jostle you. What about that boat ride?"

"I could agree to it," Karla said, "so long as I don't have to listen to 'It's a Small Small World.'"

Penny went down to the concierge's desk again and came back with a brochure and information. "He says we can join one of the boat tours just a few blocks from here."

"A few blocks is as far as I can go," Karla said, "but let's do it. I'm getting cabin fever."

The concierge's notion of "a few blocks" turned out to be a mile and a half. Their walk took them to Île de la Cité, from whose quais they could choose among boats of different sizes; for smoothness, they chose the longest. The day had begun cool and cloudy, and during their walk it had started to rain, so they took seats on the crowded lower deck. The drops on the Plexiglas windows obscured the view, but the cool weather and low wet clouds accorded with Karla's mood. "They say Paris is beautiful in the rain," she said.

"I should have worn more than a trench coat," Penny said. "I left my poncho in my suitcase."

They slid beneath the Alexander Bridge with its gilded angel statues. The tour guide called attention to important buildings, but the pleasure of being on the water (real water, not some carnival sluice where the customers bobbed along like plastic duckies) brought back memories of Gerard. Karla pictured her husband fishing in the staid old Seine; the quiet lapping of waves evoked the mystery of the double motion of rivers, how each molecule made its journey to the sea, yet the river stayed. How the river's drops and the raindrops were indistinguishable. How the mist that cooled her head represented a copulation of waters.

Penny had brought along her little plastic camera and was trying to take flash pictures through the Plexiglas. "I hope these come out," she said. "I need them to show the ladies in my book club. Alice Mitchell had pictures of Yellowstone two weeks ago. A fox was carrying a sandwich."

"You should buy postcards," Karla suggested. "Your flashes are bothering people."

"It wouldn't be the same as what we're seeing," Penny said. "Anybody can buy a bunch of postcards."

Karla went back to listening to the waves. Her chin rested firmly against the neck brace; her eyelids closed, and she fell asleep sitting upright. The chatting of the people around her and the tour guide's accented lecture all blended with the river sounds to become music. She felt herself carried royally along, like Elizabeth Taylor floating on the Nile.

"Wake up! You're missing the Tuileries."

"Am I? What's a Tuilery, anyway?" Karla refused to be diverted from her reverie, and the fifteen-Euro boat ride continued to be the pleasure cruise of an empress. She emerged only when the boat returned to the quai and the people around her stood and began to shuffle.

Her friend was staring at her, concern written on her face. Karla smiled to reassure her. "Isn't the rain lovely? But it's going to be down our necks. Maybe we can find a taxi."

"I don't like taxis," Penny said. "The drivers cheat you."

"So when were you ever cheated by a taxi driver?"

"It happens in the movies all the time."

By the time they walked in the rain to the nearest Metro station, then rode the jolting train, then walked in the rain again to their hotel, Penny was shivering and Karla's headache had intensified. A rivulet had found its way down the inside of her neck brace, and she had to ask Penny to help her dry her hair.

"Your gray is showing," Penny said. "And it's freezing. I'm going to ask them to turn up the heat."

"Take a hot shower," Karla suggested. "Once you get warm, dry yourself off and crawl in bed."

"What will you do?"

"I think I'll put on my jammies and try to read some of these brochures."

Penny went to the window and looked out at the wet chestnut leaves. "Did you notice the people on the boat? They were different from the people on the subway."

"How's that?" Karla asked.

"All of them were white."

IT HAD BEEN A DAY THAT SEEMED like evening all day long. When the true evening came and they walked to the little restaurant up the street, Penny had a glass of wine to warm her up, then another, then one more. Karla eyed the empty glasses longingly. "You're turning into quite the lush, my dear," she said.

"The more glasses I drink, the better that Algerian guy looks."

"I'd like to have one with you, but I can't," Karla said. "Joy comes tomorrow. There's more to see in Paris, but we're going to be out in the country. She knows some people who have a farm. This fish is good, by the way." Karla had ordered the turbot, which turned out to be flat like a crappie but with both eyes on the same side of its head. "They could've left the head off," she said. "I wouldn't miss having that thing looking up at me."

Penny had ordered duck. "We tried to raise some ducks," she said. "They tended to get out of the pen, and the coyotes would get 'em."

"How is it?"

"Duck is duck," Penny said. "They can put a nice sauce on it, but it's still duck. Do you think I should have another glass of wine?"

"Whatever floats your boat. You know my situation."

"I guess I'll skip it," Penny said. "Did Gerard drink?"

"Gerard was a dry alcoholic," Karla said. "I don't know how he could manage to live with me, but he did."

"Alfred was against drinking," Penny said, "so I never did. He was good to me; at least, he wasn't mean. Our sex life was kind of like this duck. You know? It was fine for a while, but then you get tired of eating duck."

Karla grinned. "Try a bite of my turbot. It's delicious."

Back in their room, Penny scrolled through the channels until she found Al-Jazeera, the only news program in English. Karla was studying a map of the city—she had gotten the concierge to mark the location of the Grand Slovenian Orchestra of Paris in her guidebook, a few blocks from the *Gare du Nord*—when Penny cried out, "Look at this! It's that woman with the canes." Karla looked up to see the apron of an airport, with a propeller-driven airliner parked at some distance from the jetway. A line of people carrying duffel bags was walking out to board, and the person at the rear of the line was Ruby Hoeft.

"Holy moly," Karla said. "It's my weight coach. That must be the Ukrainian team."

"That Oriental girl was talking about it at breakfast. Did they do something wrong?"

"One of the women got caught taking steroids," Karla said. "It's what that coach is known for."

"How did you find out about it, anyway?"

"I don't know," Karla said. "I must've seen something on the TV." She pretended to go back to her map, but it was some time before she could concentrate. She felt sorry for them all, for Ruby Hoeft and Olha Korobka, until she remembered the Johannesburg cop's dead sister.

"Philosophical question for you," she said, lowering her book of maps. "Do you think a person can do evil without knowing it? Can they believe they're doing the right thing even though everything they do is harmful?"

"I don't know," Penny said. "According to the Lutherans, we're none of us any good, so I guess that's possible. If we don't act according to our consciences, we risk serving Satan."

"But what if our consciences get turned upside down? What if Hitler thought he was doing God's work by cooking six million Jews in a gas chamber?"

"You don't believe in God," Penny said, "so why ask me?"

"Because you don't know either," Karla said. "We are partners in dumbness."

"Speak for yourself," Penny said. "When it comes to God, we are roommates, not partners. And," she added, "neither of us is dumb."

"This is why I like looking at maps," Karla said. "No ideas."

THE ORCHESTRA'S HEADQUARTERS WAS A WHOLE lot farther from the *Gare du Nord* than "a few blocks" would have been in Turtle Lodge. Karla and Penny stood in the rain, holding their roller suitcases by the handles and studying the contents of a shop window featuring rubber penises. "I like the green one," Penny said. "The pink ones are all too big. And what are those straps and buckles for?"

"That's in case you want to have sex with a woman and pretend she's a man."

"Poop," said Penny. "I had to do enough pretending with poor old Alfred."

The offices of the Grand Slovenian Orchestra of Paris—*Le Orchestre Slovene Grande de Paris*—were next door to the sex shop, in a stone building that had been built in the time of Mozart and neglected ever since. Karla pushed open the door a few inches and peeked inside. No one was evident, but the office was unlocked. The desks and furniture were Army green, left over from two world wars.

As she and Penny looked around the dimly lit room, dripping rainwater on the floor, a person emerged from a side door to confront them. This femalesque human stood over six feet tall and wore a red, floor-length satin cocktail dress; her breasts stood high and prominent and her platinum-blonde hair was fluffed, but her jaw was blunt and blue like Richard Nixon's. "If it pleases you, may I assist?" she said in the voice of a reedy bagpipe.

"I'm looking for information about a man who was once in your orchestra," Karla said. "He was a violinist named Boris Čapek, or possibly Kupesich."

The transvestite's eyes grew wide. "And you?"

"I'm his sister," Karla said. "Was his sister. When he was living."

"If it pleases you, I would see proof," the trans person said. "A man such as Boris, who is known to many, could have many sisters."

"I have copies of both our birth certificates. You will see that the information matches." Karla rooted in her purse for a zipper notebook that contained her passport, some American money, and the papers in question. The certificates were nearly identical, white letters in typescript on a charcoal background, registered in Saline County, Nebraska and embossed with an official seal; both Karla and Boris had been born in hospital, with a physician attending. The person in satin put on reading glasses and compared the certificates. "Certain of our members arrived prior to the collapse of the Soviet Union," she said. "They carry documents that look as *authentique* as these. Forged, to be sure." She handed them back. "Why did you not come forward earlier? Your brother has been dead for almost eleven years."

Because I was drunk, Karla thought. Because I'd lost my husband. Because I had no money to buy a plane ticket. "I had health problems," she said aloud.

"Mental and physical. I came to see if you can tell me where he is buried."

"Is it your wish to claim his property? He left some things for you."

"What things? Nobody told me he had anything of value."

"Hm." The woman-person looked Karla up and down; she took a ring of keys from a drawer behind the counter and said, "Wait here." She disappeared down a hallway and was gone for several minutes. There was a bustle and a metallic door-slamming of what sounded like gym lockers. When she returned, she carried two objects wrapped in black cloth, one substantial and violin-shaped, one long and thin. "These were your brother's," she said. "They belong to you."

"Really?" Karla accepted the violin and carefully unwound the fabric. The instrument that it revealed was a poor old shabby thing; the lacquer had all worn off beneath the strings, and the heads of the pegs were chipped. It felt light in her hands as the husk of a cicada. She smiled. "It's not a Stradivarius, is it?"

"It is not a Stradivarius," the person in satin said. "It was created in the workshop of Honoré Derazay in the year 1846. It is, *bien sur*, a Stradivari copy."

"I don't know—"

A drop of rainwater fell on the violin from Karla's sleeve, and the person in satin snatched the instrument and brushed away the drop. Karla looked up and was about to say something when a thin old man burst into the room, panting. He was a spry fellow with spidery hands, a large round head, and a thick shock of cotton-white hair. He drew himself up to his full height of five feet four and looked Karla angrily in the eye. "I will pay you six thousand Euros for that violin."

There were more footsteps in the hall. A much younger man, red-haired and dotted with acne, ran in gasping. "Seven thousand," he said. "I will pay seven thousand Euros." The two of them glared at one another like fighting cocks.

"Seven thousand five hundred," said the first man. "That's it. I will pay you in cash this afternoon."

Karla felt Penny tugging her sleeve. She followed her to a place near the door and bent to hear her friend whisper. "Ask for more money."

"How much more?"

"Double it."

Karla straightened and turned to face the two musicians. She cleared her throat to give herself some time and stop her voice from shaking. "Fifteen," she said. "Thousand," she added. "American dollars. I don't want Euros."

The two of them looked at one another. Suddenly the older man dropped to his knees. "Please," he said. "Please. I am only a poor musician. Please, I deserve this violin. I have waited a lifetime. Oh, please, please, sell it to me." Tears ran down his cheeks.

Not to be outdone, the redhead sank to his knees, too. "Sell it to me, not him," he begged. "He is old and will die soon. Besides, he plays horribly. I will play it beautifully for many years. Sell it to me."

Karla opened her mouth, but Penny grabbed her sleeve and wagged a finger. "I don't care," Karla said finally. "I'll sell it to both of you and you can take turns. But I want fifteen thousand."

The two men, one young and one old, went off in the direction of the hallway and put their heads together. When they finished whispering, they came and faced Karla shoulder to shoulder. "We will pay you fourteen thousand," the red-haired one said. "Euros, not dollars. That is all we can do."

Karla felt a little tingle at the back of her neck. "Show me the money," she said, "and it's yours."

The two men looked at one another and approached the person in satin. The red-haired one took the violin tenderly in his hands, while the older man touched the worn lacquer with a spidery finger. "We can have the money for you in one hour," the red-haired one said. "Charlise will arrange a draft for us and we'll repay it later. Is it not so, Charlise?"

"I can do that," Charlise said. "It may take more than one hour. After all, this is France."

Karla, feeling somewhat stunned, was turning to go kill time for an hour, but Penny tugged her sleeve again. "What about the bow?" she whispered.

"Doesn't the bow go together with the violin?"

"I don't think so," Penny said. "I watched a special program about violin bows. The wood comes from Brazil."

Karla turned and squared her shoulders to confront the musicians. "The bow is separate," she announced. "Fourteen thousand Euros does not include the bow."

"Ah." There was a collective sigh. The older violinist shrugged his shoulders. "Of course. How much shall we pay? One hundred Euros?"

"I don't know," Karla said. "Let me see it."

The tall Charlise person unwrapped the violin bow, keeping it beyond the reach of drips from Karla's plastic raincoat. She held it vertically and they studied it together in the dim light. It was stamped with the word "Vuillaume" and a number in the low thousands. "It is as I thought," Charlise said. "You would be a fool to sell this bow for one hundred Euros."

"Who was Vuillaume?"

"He was a luthier, a maker of stringed instruments. He did not make bows. It would require an expert to say who made this bow. Its value might be only two thousand Euros, or it might be higher than the violin. Of course," she added, "we do not know what the price of this violin might be if it were to be sold at auction. You are too impatient, perhaps."

Karla swallowed hard. "You mean that I might have priced it too cheap?"

"We will not know the answer until one of these men dies and the violin is sold. Even then, different times will value old things differently." Charlise turned the bow in her hand and studied it carefully. "I myself will take a chance on this," she said. "I will pay you two thousand five hundred Euros for this bow."

"Sold," Karla said. "Hand over the cash and I will run like hell."

Charlise did not laugh. "It will not be necessary to run," she said. "This neighborhood is more secure than it appears. Do you now wish to know the location of your brother's burial?"

"Yes, please," Karla said. "Maybe we can visit him while you get the money."

"The cemetery at Montmartre is extensive," Charlise said. "You will not find his grave unless you purchase a map. It will be wiser if you first obtain lunch. Enjoy your meal, drink a glass of wine, and return here. We will have money for you and you can search for Boris at your leisure."

That afternoon, Karla and Penny walked the boulevards of the dead, past mausoleums roofed like miniature stone houses. The necropolis had its narrow winding streets, its neighborhoods, parks, and greenspaces. The light rain and accompanying mist made the place seem both vast and claustrophobic; low clouds hid the domes of the Sacre Coeur basilica. As Charlise had warned them, it proved difficult to find Boris's grave, but with the help of a groundskeeper they finally reached it. Karla placed the flowers she had brought, then stood a few minutes over the stone. She could not picture Boris as anything but the child in her photo album: skinny, uncertain, always angry. His adult life was a blank. Yet he had had success, been famous in his circle. His stone was nothing more than a slab with his name and dates. "Let's go," Karla said at last. "We can do laps inside the *Gare du Nord* until we dry out."

"I buried Alfred in the graveyard south of Willow, next to his folks," Penny said. "It sure is nothing like this place."

"I had my Gerard cremated," Karla said. "I borrowed a boat and sprinkled half of his ashes on Hackberry Lake. The rest are in an urn buried next to his sister, in the McDonough plot at Hanes. That's where his marker is." Karla turned for a look back as they were leaving. "My name is on it, too. All they have left to do is to carve the date."

"I could never do that," Penny said. "When our boys wanted to put my name on Alfred's tombstone, I told them, 'Not till I turn my heels up.' What will you do with the money you got for the violin?"

"I want to pay back Joy for the tickets and everything," Karla said. "The way she dresses, I'm afraid she's spending every dime she makes. She should be saving her money. Things can happen. You never know about the future."

"The girl is a financial advisor," Penny said. "Of course she's saving."

"I wouldn't bet on it," Karla said. "Haven't you noticed how mechanics always drive some old clunker with the fenders falling off? She's probably putting her money in the stock market, where it'll all fizzle out in a year or two. Then she'll move back to Turtle Lodge and I'll have to clean out a room in my trailer."

Penny laughed. "If she was in one of my soap operas, she'd be pregnant."

Karla had to smile. "No, she'll have two kids and a border collie. And a boyfriend who kicks holes in the sheet rock."

"Now you're talking about my daughter."

Dripping, they towed their bags to the Metro stop. The air underground felt warmer but no less humid; the people on the subway were dripping, too. They arrived at the *Gare du Nord*, rode the crowded escalator to street level, and joined the wet lineup at a coffee kiosk. The *Gare* was noisy; it had no green spaces, and no one was there to remember anyone else. It was a space dedicated to a speedier kind of passing-through.


AS AGREED, JOY FOUND THEM at the terminal following her meeting. She seemed pleased with herself and said that the meeting had gone well. "How was your adventure in Paris?" she asked the two of them. "As you see, in winter it rains here half the time. I hope that didn't put a damper, pun intended."

"I've been damper than this," Karla said. "My gosh, you look delicious."

Joy blushed and glanced down at her outfit. She wore a black skirt over a black leotard, with a black blouse and a rust-colored jacket; a silver chain set with uncut amber lay against her neck. The boots she had on were black, patent leather or plastic. "My clients are nearly all male," she said. "It doesn't hurt my business that I was not born ugly."

"Indeed you were not," Karla said. "You were a gorgeous little black-haired baby. After thirty-six hours in labor, I was never so glad to see anyone in my life."

Before Penny could open her mouth about the violin, Karla told how they had gone to find Boris's former orchestra and then the cemetery. She described the Sacre Coeur Basilica as if they had actually visited it, and exaggerated the difficulty of finding the grave. "He is resting in a beautiful spot," she said. "I'm sure he felt more at home in Paris than in Nebraska."

"You showed me Grandma Čapek's house in Crete," Joy said. "Giant weeds all around it and thorns crawling up the screens. Like Sleeping Beauty's castle."

"Her Handsome Prince never came," Karla said. "I feel rotten every time

I think of her, all alone in that wreck and drinking herself to death. After she died, the county took it. I couldn't pay the taxes."

They bought tickets and had them stamped at one of the yellow ticket thumpers. "I'm sure there's a point to these machines," Joy said, "but to me it's just a dumb thing you have to do." Destinations, times, and track numbers were displayed on an overhead screen, but Joy knew where to go. "I ride this thing two or three times a week," she said. "Sometimes more often if I have to meet somebody."

"Why don't you live in Paris, then?"

"Too expensive. I could never buy a house in Paris."

Once they'd boarded, Joy got out a laptop and started typing; Karla and Penny watched the landscape hurtle by. The fast train flew rapidly along on dedicated rails, slicing through a wet countryside that was mainly industrial, warehouses and rainy construction sites from which new apartments were rising. The architecture was uninspiring until they passed some half-timbered houses. They began to see orchards and gardens, livestock and farm machinery. "I like the look of this country," Penny said. "You could make a living here."

"I see little pastures with one cow in them," Karla said. "You don't get rich doing that."

Joy glanced up. "*Salers*," she said. "They make the best cheese."

Karla's experience of cheese was that it came from the government in five-pound blocks; there was also that orange powder in the mac-and-cheese boxes. Velveeta came in slices that you put in a kid's lunchbox. Cheese was the kind of thing you swallowed without thinking about it, like the cheap weenies wrapped in Wonder bread that had fed her growing up. Cheese was food. You ate it. Of course she knew of other kinds, cream cheese for desserts, blue cheese for your baked potato at a fancy restaurant, cottage cheese that was supposed to help you lose weight if you ate enough of it, Swiss cheese with the holes, et cetera, but she had never thought of cheese as a *thing*.

Now mushrooms, that was different. Karla's mother had taught her about mushrooms. Some of them you could eat, some you couldn't. There were even hallucinogenic mushrooms. There was no hallucinogenic cheese.

"Wake up. You're snoring again." That was Penny.

"Sorry," Karla said. "It's this neck brace. I get tired from holding my head up straight."

Joy looked up from her laptop. "Someday you're going to have to tell me how you got that," she said. "All I know is that you had a bad headache. That doctor I sent you told me nothing. He said it was a case of doctor-patient privilege."

"Someday I'll tell you. But remember, it's not nice to laugh at your mother."

The houses in Margny-les-Compiègne were narrow and tall, jammed together brick wall to brick wall like the downtown business buildings in Turtle Lodge. Joy's house on a street near the station had a walk-in basement, a ground floor with two rooms and a galley kitchen, a second floor with two bedrooms and a bath, and a third floor up under the roof. "You bought this?" Karla said when they arrived. She was looking up at the stairs leading to the bathroom. The ceilings were high and the stairs correspondingly steep.

"It's been a good investment," Joy said. "Though you can never tell about real estate. It needs some fixing up, as you can see." A gray tabby came to the top of the stairs and looked down at them with yellow eyes. "That's William of Ockham," Joy said. "I call him Ockie. If he rolls over in your lap and starts to purr, watch out for Ockie's razors." Joy ran lightly up the stairs and grabbed the cat; she cradled him in her arms and turned to grin at them, and Karla saw a black-haired child holding her Barbie. "It's safe to come up. Old Ockie won't bite you."

Karla collapsed the handle of her roller bag and began the steep ascent. "I see now why there are no fat people in France," she said. "You have to climb stairs or die."

Joy had made up the guest bedroom for Penny. She offered Karla a choice. "You can sleep on a foldout couch in my office," she said, "or I can take that one and you can have my upstairs bedroom."

"I'll take the foldout rather than the extra stairs," Karla said. "We'll be staying here one night only, is that correct?"

"That's right," Joy said. "Tomorrow I'll be driving you to Normandy. We'll be staying with some friends there who have a B&B. Maybe later we can drive on up to the coast."

"What about Ockie?"

"He doesn't mind," Joy said. "He has the run of the place when I'm gone. He's a mouser, my little Ockie. You won't see any mousy critters when he's around."

Penny's room had the accoutrements of a bedroom: frilly bed cover, arty objects on the dresser, pictures on the wall. Joy's office had none of these. Besides the couch, a desktop computer with a floor lamp, a swivel chair with a mesh back, and a television filled the space. "This is where you watch TV," Karla said. "I'll be intruding."

"It's no big deal, ma," Joy said. "Put down your stuff and hit the bathroom. You and Penny can have a snack while I shower off a little bit of this Chanel."

Once they'd parked their roller bags and descended, Joy seated Karla and Penny in a narrow room next to the kitchen while she got out crackers and a cheese slicer. "I have Gruyére and Salers, and some soft cheese that tastes like

Gouda," she said. "I'm out of cheddar. I can offer you sparkling water or cider; I don't keep wine or beer in the house."

"Sparkling water would be lovely," Karla said.

"I subscribe to the *Wall Street Journal*," Joy said. "Let me get it for you."

Karla and Penny read the day-old financial news while Joy went upstairs to shower. When she came down, she wore soft pajamas and was devoid of makeup. "There's the girl I remember," Karla said. "Gosh, you look so pretty."

Joy had twisted her black hair up in a bun to keep it out of the wet. "I feel like a different person in Compiègne," she said. "Paris tightens my back up. If I had to stay there twenty-four seven, I'd end up with piles." Penny burst out laughing. "No, I'm serious," Joy said with a smile. "In Paris, I'm swimming with the sharks. Here I can relax."

"Maybe you should find a different job," Karla said.

"No, I love my work," Joy said. "I just have to be on my toes every minute. Can you stand to eat omelets for dinner? That's about all I know how to cook."

"Why not let me make fried potatoes?" Penny said. "I miss being in the kitchen. Scrambled eggs and fried potatoes? How does that sound?"

"It sounds like heaven," Joy said. "I'll put my feet up in bunny slippers and read the paper. And thank you from my heart."

While Penny cooked, Karla pretended to look at day-old headlines, but in fact she was only interested in her daughter. Joy read the financial news with Ockie on her lap; girl and cat looked comfortable and content with one another. Outside, water trickled in the downspout. Joy had cracked all the windows open, and the room felt chilly and damp. Karla helped herself to the good French cheeses, and the aroma of frying onions drifted from the kitchen. Joy's head snapped erect with a jerk. "Oh!" she said. "I fell asleep."

"What do you normally do in the evening?" Karla asked. "Do you go out?"

"Not lately," Joy said. "I usually waste my brain in front of the TV. I tell myself that I'm learning French, but really it's just mind candy. Or mind tapioca pudding. Something to fill up time."

"Sounds like me when I was working," Karla said, "except I drank beer."

"You don't drink at all any more?"

"Your mom's an alcoholic, kiddo. I wouldn't dare."

"I worry about becoming an alcoholic," Joy said. "I know I've got the genetics for it. That's why there's no wine in the house. My French friends think I'm crazy."

"So who's this boyfriend you keep not mentioning? Does he drink?"

"He has it all under control," Joy said. "You'll meet him tomorrow." She dumped the gray cat off her lap and stood to see how Penny was doing. "Penny's amazing," she said when she returned. "She's cleaning up the dishes as she cooks. Maybe you could leave her here when you fly back to the States."

"It wouldn't work out with Ockie," Karla said. "She doesn't like indoor cats."

Karla and Joy set the table, using dishes from a hutch along the wall. "These are pretty plates," Karla said, turning one over to look at the back. "I bet you didn't get them from the hospital auxiliary."

"Within my means, I like to live well. It's what the French do," Joy said. "Someday I plan to cook like Martha Stewart. Right now, I don't have time for it. Also, in order to cook, you have to shop for food. There's a farmers' market half a kilometer from here, but I don't have time for that, either."

"I can teach you to fry fish and boil hot dogs," Karla said. "That's what my mother taught me."

Joy sliced a loaf of tough peasant bread and made toast to go with Penny's eggs and potatoes. It was a satisfying meal, rounded out by more cheese and some table grapes. Afterward, Joy brought out three different kinds of chocolate, and Penny and Karla sampled it with delight. "Life in France is good," Penny pronounced. "There's no chocolate anything like this in Turtle Lodge."

Joy suggested that they go to bed early, and Karla and Penny made no objection. Since Penny's bed was made up, she took the opportunity to shower while Joy and Karla converted the foldout couch in Joy's home office. "You really should sleep in my room," Joy said. "It's a queen-sized mattress up there. I'm afraid this little couch won't be comfortable for you. I'll get more pillows, if you think that'll help."

"I don't want to put you out," Karla said. "You need your rest if you're going to be driving us. Besides, one more flight of stairs might kill me."

The contour sheet didn't fit the foldout bed; Karla woke in the night to find both sheets bunched up around her neck brace. Somewhere in the house, Joy was talking on her cell phone. "We're all right," she was saying to her lover. "She's sober. So far, so good."

IN ADDITION TO THE NECK BRACE, the young doctor had prescribed prednisone, the steroid Hoeft gave Karla back in her lifting days. She swallowed the tiny pills with reluctance and monitored herself for side effects: irritability and sleeplessness, hunger, palpitations. As her daughter had said to someone during the night, so far, so good. They ate oatmeal with brown sugar and berries and packed up their roller bags; Joy carried a gym bag of her own, and they left the narrow house through a door at the rear of the basement. Joy's car was parked at the back, in a narrow parking space off a narrow alley. It was a stubby box on dinky little wheels that promised neither comfort nor safety. Joy opened the back and stowed their luggage behind the rear seat, and Karla observed with relief that the steering wheel was on the left. She hoped that the car's dinky wheels wouldn't joggle her neck.

The streets of Compiègne and the country roads beyond were laid out on the same scheme as the streets of Paris, that is, from one roundabout to the next. Joy drove them first to the Forest of Compiègne, where the Armistice of World War I had been signed. They got out in a drizzle and toured a museum displaying artifacts and photographs of the war; the peaceful order of the museum contrasted with the muddy misery shown in the photos. "One of my uncles fought in both world wars," Penny said. "He was Canadian. He built a bridge across one of these canals."

"People here feel grateful toward Americans," Joy said. "Canadians, too."

The second place Joy showed them was a real Prince Valiant castle from the Middle Ages. The plaque said it had been demolished by a jealous prince, then rebuilt on its original plan in the 1800s. It had turrets and parapets and crossbow ports, but what most impressed Karla was the architect's lodging alongside. The architect's house, but not the castle, had been hit by a German shell during one of the wars, and the blackened ruin had been left standing. There were pockmarks on the castle walls, too, but the walls were intact. Karla figured that if the Germans had wanted it gone, they'd have blown it up.

They had lunch at a workmen's tavern beside the Somme, where a set of locks lifted boats to be floated eastward toward the Canal du Nord. The gloomy tavern and the dampness of the place suited Karla's mood. "I love the smell of water," she said. "Not so much the clear flowing streams—they don't smell at all—but rivers and lakes where the water moves slowly. They smell of life. Like a newborn baby."

"Newborn babies have a smell?" Joy asked.

"Yes, they do," Karla said. "Isn't that right, Penny?"

"Let me think." Penny closed her eyes and inhaled through her nose. "They smell a little bit swampy and a little bit like bread. Baby calves have a smell like that, too. Except, you know. Humans don't smell like cows." She opened her eyes and smiled. "Please pass me another one of those rolls," she said. "I haven't had butter this good since I made it myself."

"That's something I want to try," Joy said. "I want to make butter."

Penny laughed. "First you have to feed your cow," she said. "Then you have to milk your cow. Then you have to crank the handle of the cream separator—"

"Okay, okay," Joy said with a smile. "I get it."

After they left the valley of the Somme, Joy drove them to a second museum, this one commemorating a battle from World War II. Outnumbered Polish troops held a hilltop for two days and two nights. They lost twenty per cent of their men but helped to prevent a successful Nazi retreat. Beneath the gray cloud ceiling, the valley below the ridge was a lively green, and the feeling was one of deep peace rather than hellish slaughter. Falling rain muted the steady sound of a distant tractor. "Don't show us any more museums," Karla said. "This whole French countryside is starting to look like one big cemetery."

"You don't want to drive to the coast and see Omaha Beach?"

"Not today," Karla said. "My headache's telling me I've had enough."

They left the scene of the Poles' heroics. Joy herded the boxy car along country lanes. She said, "A friend and I bicycle in this area. I kind of know where I am, but don't be worried if I stop to look at a map." Their route took them through villages of half-timbered houses; every valley had a cathedral with a spire that reached into the mist. It felt odd to pass through a centuries-old town and encounter a giant blue Ford tractor. "They've removed a lot of hedges to make the fields bigger," Joy said. "Farming is pretty lucrative here. I've advised some people who invest in farmland. They tend to do well."

They passed under the highway from Paris to Rouen and entered the town of Les Andelys. Here Joy became anxious, taking a couple of wrong turns before they left the town to follow a narrow road. They passed fields both fenced and unfenced until they came to a low stone wall among hedgerows. Joy turned the little car into a driveway, and two shaggy black-and-white dogs came bounding to meet them. Before a modern-looking farmhouse centered in a square of far older buildings, she parked her car next to a familiar green Renault. A tall robust woman halfway between Joy and Karla's age came out on the porch to greet them. "*Bonjour*, Fanny," Joy called out. "*C'est bon de vous voir.*" It's good to see you."

"*Bonjour*," the woman replied. After scolding the dogs in French—they ran up onto the porch and entered the house, pausing for a final woof—she descended the step, wiping her hands on the back of her pants. She and Joy embraced, kiss-kiss in the French manner; their embrace was a little awkward, as if they hadn't had much practice.

Karla got stiffly out of the car, scraping the top of her head, and went to meet this woman who might soon become her in-law. Not at all the elegant Frenchwoman of the perfume ads, Fanny was tanned and vigorous, with red cheeks, a freckled nose, and a fair amount of middle-aged broadening. Though she might possess a countrywoman's reserve, she had the look of a happy person, or at least of a contented one. Enough money and a life she liked. "*Bonjour*," Karla said, bowing her head as far as the neck brace would allow. "Karla Čapek. My husband was Gerard Horse Looking. I am pleased to meet you."

"*Bonjour*," the woman replied. She grasped Karla's hand and released it with a smile. "Welcome. How are you? I am Frances. You should say Fah-NEE."

"This is Penny Raskonen," Karla said, introducing her friend. "She's my companion on this trip."

"Pen-NEE. I am good to meet you."

"Same here," Penny said, shaking hands. "I see you have chickens."

"*Oui*," the woman said, looking around. "*Les poulets, les vaches, un cheval—*" She shrugged. A burro's "hee haw" came from somewhere. "*Une gran ménagerie.*"

A young man came out of the house followed by the dogs, who kept themselves between him and Fanny. Karla recognized the student doctor who'd come to her hotel. He approached Joy with a smile, and they touched noses before kissing. "You came safely," he said. "No problems, eh?"

"No problems," Joy said. "We stopped at the little museum at Mont Ormel. It's been raining all day."

Joy's lover turned his warm brown eyes to Karla. "*Bonjour* again," he said with a smile. "How are you feeling? Still some headache, maybe? No more roller coasters?"

"A roller coaster!" Joy said, laughing. "She didn't tell me."

"You! You played a joke on me," Karla said to him. "Yeah, *bonjour*, my head hurts. The cervical brace is helping, but I'll be happy to be rid of it. How much longer?"

"One week longer, I think," Joy's doctor-boy replied. "It irritates, is it not so?"

"It rubs me at the base of my neck," Karla said. "It's worse when it rains."

"Tch," the young doctor said. "We will look at it later. In the meantime, I am Benoit Lazcaré. You have met my mother."

"I am pleased to meet you a second time," Karla said. "I see that the two of you are tricky."

"Your daughter and I? Oh, yes, we are very clever," he said. "She is the more clever. She is very good at games."

"He thinks I'm smart because I beat him at dominoes," Joy said.

"She didn't learn that from me," Karla said.

They unloaded their bags from the cubical little car. Rather than carry them into the house, they crossed the driveway and a strip of grass, dodged the claws of an ancient apple tree, and entered a long two-story farm building that had been converted into rooms for paying guests. Joy led the way up a tall flight of stairs and showed Karla and Penny their quarters. The walls were newly sheetrocked—a whiff of latex paint remained in the air—and the rooms were spacious, with big windows that opened out onto the courtyard.

Karla lifted her roller bag and laid it halfway on the bed, and went into the bathroom to get tissue to wipe the mud off its wheels. The bedcover was a quilt, homemade and hand-stitched in the wedding-ring pattern, and she regretted not having put a towel down first. The dirt on the wheels was rust-colored and would have stained, but she got it all off without incident. "Nice place you've got here, Fah-NEE," she said to no one. "I hope I don't wreck it."

Joy stood in the doorway. "It's all right, ma," she said. "These people are just folks. They're planning to start a B&B here. They only bought the place a couple of years ago."

"Did you advise them?"

"Not in my official capacity," Joy said. "They're family, so I could tell them what I thought. Up to a point," she added.

Karla looked up, still holding the muddy tissue. "Am I family?"

"Of course you are. Why do you ask?"

"I don't know. I feel like you're evolving. If I'm a fish and you're a salamander, are we still family?"

"You sound like those people on the Rez," Joy said. "That old bucket-of-crabs thing."

"Listen, baby. I love you, and I'm all for you. It's just that I'm out of my depth. I'll try not to embarrass you, but I'm too big to make myself invisible. They'll see who I am."

"You'll be all right, ma," Joy said. "You have a good heart. That's what they care about."

"I'll trust you on that, honey," Karla said. "Provisionally. Go see if Penny wants to take a walk. I need to stretch out for an hour. Your car's a bit small for me."

After riding all day in the cramped vehicle, Karla was glad to relax on the queen-sized bed. She stripped to her underwear, then took those off, too, and put on her soft old pajama top; her need for sleep was powerful, and she saw no reason not to satisfy it. It was getting dark when she woke up flat on her back. The person rapping at the doorframe was Penny. "Hey," she said. "Are you awake?"

"Oh my gosh!" Karla said. "How late is it? I can't sit up. Help me."

"It's after five o'clock," Penny said. "I just thought—" She took hold of Karla's right wrist, supported her head, and tipped her upright. Penny's stringy old gardener's muscles were as strong as wire.

"Thanks," Karla said once she was vertical. "I needed to wake up. Did you have a look around their farm? What's it like?"

"Well," said Penny, "the soil is good, I think. It's a kind of clay loam that will hold a lot of moisture. It doesn't wash away. They grow several kinds of crops, but their main crop is sunflowers. They keep a small herd of half a dozen cows that they milk by hand. Some of the outbuildings are four hundred years old; stone walls, but they're wired for electricity. There's an apple orchard. Joy says the pigs get most of the apples. They don't press them any more."

"Press the apples?"

"It's a special kind. They make a drink called Calvados. Do you need help standing?"

"I'll be fine," Karla said. "Turn around so I don't flash you." She bestirred herself and pulled on warm tights, and unpacked the skirt and floral blouse Joy bought her the day they shopped the Gucci district. She thought of adding lipstick but decided she might as well skip it; she ran a washcloth over her face and brushed her hair. "I'm as ready as I'll ever be," she said. She lifted her broad fat shoulders and let them sag. "I'm not applying to be their housekeeper."

The same gentle rain was falling from the same heavy sky. Karla and Penny crossed the yard to the big house; the two dogs announced them and circled around behind to have a sniff. The people were all at the back of the house, in a farmhouse kitchen the size of Karla's living room. "*Bonjour*," they all said, raising their glasses—they were having wine—and came forward to either kiss-kiss or shake hands. Karla met Benoit's father and an aunt who lived with the family, and an ancient grandmother who didn't rise from her chair. There was a girl a few years younger than Benoit, just on the edge of becoming a teenager. And, of course, the dogs, Bernard and Benjamin, whose names were the only ones Karla could remember. She held up her hand, palm outward, when Fanny offered her a glass. "Please, no," Karla said. "Once I start, I can't stop. I'm one of those people."

After she thought she'd met everybody, a white-haired, blue-eyed geezer came into the room. He was tall and bony and as fair of skin as Penny, splashed with liver spots and freckles; his neck was leathery and his hands were callused, and he had the look of the farm about him. "*Bonjour, bonjour*," he said, coming up to Karla. "I see that you are embarrassed. Me, too. Ah, but you are welcome here. Most welcome." He turned to Penny. "And who is this lovely person?"

"I am Mrs. Penelope Raskonen," Penny said. "Who are you?"

"I am the spirit of the farm," the thin man said. "I come with the place. No one can get rid of me." His alert blue eyes turned to Karla, then to Penny with a smile. "These city people can't manage without me," he said. "They wouldn't know what to do."

Joy helped Karla to a seat at the table, where a plate with several kinds of cheese was being passed around. There were chewy slices of baguette to go with the cheese. "What is this?" Karla asked as she cut herself a slice. "I like the smell of it."

The woman Fanny smiled. "Is good," she said. "We make."

"You made this cheese?"

"No, no," Fanny said. "*Les vaches*. They make the milk. The *camion*, it takes."

"There's a co-operative," Joy explained. "The co-op makes the cheese. It's called *Salers*. It's made from the milk of a special kind of cow."

The couple's daughter, the youngest person at the table, spoke up. "Salers cows are red," she said. "You'll see them. We thought you'd be an Indian."

Karla laughed. "Not me," she said. "I'm nothing but a Bohunk girl from Crete."

"You are from the island?"

"No, no. From Crete. It's a small town in Nebraska. In America. They have a dog-food cannery."

Joy's doctor boyfriend looked up with a smile. "Does the cannery require a special kind of cow?"

"They require them to be dead."

Karla watched the wine animate the family; their warm conversation contrasted with the dreary sky outside. More and more, she was envious of Joy, that she had come to be welcomed by this confident and materially untroubled clan. At the same time, on a deeper level, she knew she should be happy for her daughter's good luck. Her feelings were complicated by her not being able to join in; they tossed her a remark in English from time to time, but it was only done from politeness. Also, her abstinence made her strange to them, so that each time the wine was passed and she refused, there was a moment of tension.

That evening at table, Karla and Penny were placed on either side of the blue-eyed geezer, who responded by flirting with each of them, though as the meal progressed he paid more attention to Penny. Karla was unsurprised to find herself left out; she thought, *They always go for the skinny chicks.* She focused on her food and on her daughter's new family. Benoit's father was a retired bank executive who'd had a mild heart attack and decided that enough money was enough. The pubescent girlchild was a brat, but of the refreshing kind, and Karla thought she'd come to enjoy her, given time. The live-in aunt was untalkative and resentful, and the grandmother took no part in the conversation. That left Fanny, to whom Karla felt drawn. "Fanny," Karla said. "Can I help you in the kitchen? Your dinner is so good, and you haven't had a chance to sit down and eat a single bite." Benoit translated.

Fanny flashed an embarrassed smile. "Ah, no no," she said. "I am better myself. Thank you, thank you." She continued to bustle back and forth; the steaming dishes accumulated, but Karla felt rebuffed.

The main course was lamb, an animal Karla associated with memories of dormitory food. This roast, however, was exquisitely prepared and dripping with flavorful juices. Karla took a second serving, not realizing that she was being reckless and that there were three more courses to come. At some point someone filled a glass with wine and placed it at her elbow, and at some point further along, she drank it.

Karla knew in a second that she'd made a mistake. She felt a lunge in every vein, like the tug of a northern pike taking the lure. *Oh, my God,* she thought, *I need to call Oliver.* Oliver Broad Moccasin was her AA sponsor, up in South Dakota.

No opportunity to call Oliver presented itself, and Karla felt the rush cool down and thought she would be all right if she got plenty of sugar. There were jellies and preserves on the table, and a basket of delicious fresh-baked bread, and if people noticed she was vacuuming up the sweets, no one said anything. The dinner progressed merrily until all were pleasantly stuffed, and Fanny proudly carried in a plate of flan.

The round of quivering custard topped with caramel gave off a luscious aroma of peaches and vanilla. They all handed in their plates—the dour aunt collected them—and received fresh forks and little dessert plates. The flan was cut in wedges, and each person held forth her plate to get a serving. Karla had gripped her fork and was about to dig in when a hush enveloped the table. The banker host, Fanny's husband and Benoit's father, was coming around with a bottle wrapped in colored wire. He dolloped clear liquid onto each person's plate of flan and used a Bic barbecue lighter to set fire to it. Each plate flared for a moment with a pale blue flame.

"*Voila! Mangez.*" That flan was the best dessert Karla had eaten in her life. High in proof, like strong vodka or ouzo, the liqueur tasted lightly of plums. The soft tissues of Karla's mouth absorbed the alcohol like a mother embracing a lost infant. Tears came to her eyes.

That first quarter of a mouthful worked on Karla's tongue like grease to a dry axle; suddenly she could say things. "My God, this flan is good," she said. "Fanny, you're the best cook ever. Here's to Fanny!" She raised her water glass. "And to Fanny's mom and to—" She'd forgotten the name of the aunt. "Here's to everybody." She took a sip of water. "Do you think I could have one more tiny little slice?" From the corner of her eye, she saw her daughter look up in alarm.

"Oh, please, just half of that," she said as her new friend Fanny began to cut her another wedge. The man, the husband, Banker What's-his-name, held up the bottle with a questioning look. "Do I want fire on it again? That would be so lovely." She handed over her dessert plate and watched it filled, then watched the delicious plum liquor splash. It was set down in front of her and the flame leaped up. "Oh, wow," she said, delighted. "This is like, I don't know, this is like eating the fucking Fourth of July. Oops! Dang. Pardon my French." Blushing, she aimed her hot face in the direction of her plate. The aromatic flan seemed to lift itself to her tongue. When she had finished, she put down her fork and used a spoon to dip the sauce.

Joy scooted back her chair. "Mom, we need to talk," she said.

"Talk?" Karla glanced toward her daughter's end of the table. "What do we need to talk about? We never talk."

"Oh, God," Joy said with a little shudder. "Here it comes. I was so afraid of this."

Karla put down her spoon with a clack. "All right," she said. "I'll shut up. Not another word out of me."

Conversation slowly resumed in French. Karla knew they were either discussing her outburst or talking trivia to avoid discussing it; she glared around the table from under her eyebrows, looking for allies. Fanny? Fanny was carrying dishware to the kitchen. The surly aunt? She saw no help there. The grandmother? It was hard to tell if the old lady even knew what was going on.

Banker-hubby-just-beginning-to-be-tubby seemed sympathetic but un-committed. The twelve-year-old-brat daughter had only eaten half her flan. Ben-wah and Joy were evidently on the verge of a fight, too intent on one another's faces to be interested in anyone else. That left Penny and the geezer, who at least spoke English.

"What do you do around here?" Karla asked him. "Are you some kind of a hired man or something?"

Her question seemed to amuse the blue-eyed fellow. "Ah, no," he said. "For that they would have to pay me. George over there is a skinflint." He meant the banker. Zhorzhe.

"But what do you do, exactly?"

"I supervise the cows. I drive the ducks to water. I do everything." He took a sip from his wine glass. "And nothing," he added, laughing. "I do whatever I want."

"He shoots grouse," Penny said. "He was just telling me."

"Ah, yes," the man said. "I must shoot those grouse. Otherwise they would become too numerous."

"And do you fish?" Karla had noticed a river flowing through the village, tributary to the Seine.

"*Mais, oui.*" The man seemed startled by her question; he regarded her seriously for a moment. "I often fish," he said. "I find it calming to the mind."

"Me, too," Karla said. "Calming." *As if I had a mind,* she added mentally. A champagne flute appeared at her elbow, and someone tapped a glass with a spoon. "What kind do you catch?" she asked, ignoring the flute.

"I fish for carp," he said with a twinkle. "I do not say I catch them. Zhorzhe is making a toast."

"Where I come from, carp is not a game fish," Karla said. "You can trap them in shallow water and toss them out with a pitchfork."

Someone tapped the glass again, more insistently; Fanny passed behind the diners, filling each flute with bubbly champagne. When everyone had a glassful, including the *grand-mére* and the twelve-year-old, Zhorzhe the banker stood carefully up and cleared his throat. *"Mes amis,"* he announced. "Friends and ladies from America. *S'il vous plaît*, I am to announce the *contracture* of my son, Benoit Lazcaré, and the American daughter, Joy McDonough, to be married. Hurrah for marriage! It is a pleasure everyone must endure."

"Hear, hear!" Penny and the geezer said. Everyone else said the French equivalent. Karla put down her empty champagne flute and wiped her lips. She said, "Nobody asked me."

"Ma," Joy said in a pleading tone. The rest of the table was silent.

"Well, they didn't," Karla said. "Pass that bottle over here. No, the other one. The one with the wire."

It was Joy and Benoit's turn to make a speech; they stood with their hands clasped and faced one another, and took turns saying something in French. *The usual bullshit*, Karla thought. She weighed the colorfully wrapped bottle in her hand and poured herself a flutefull. *Tsuika* was the name in Romanian; it had another name in Czech, which she'd forgotten. You steeped ripe fruit in grain alcohol, the higher the proof the better. Once it sat for a year, it was ready to be drunk. It would leave you with the hangover of a lifetime.

The young couple finished speaking and another toast was proposed. Karla downed one flute of the high-test, low-tech booze and poured herself another. The room had become quite warm; if she'd been at home, she would've stripped to her bra, but she understood that was not appropriate here. Besides, it would've disadvantaged Penny, who had no more tits than the wallpaper.

Penny and the geezer were discussing tomatoes; the twelve-year-old and the grandmother were sopping up the champagne. Everyone else chattered away in French. Karla polished off the bottle of bootleg Balkan lightning and looked around to see if there was any cheese she'd missed. She nibbled this and she nibbled that, nuts and olives and tiny pickled onions, and tried to think of a way back into the conversation. Meanwhile George and Fanny presented the couple with an elegant package the size of a deck of cards. Joy insisted that Benoit open it, which he did in the awkward manner of a male, damaging the silver ribbon and destroying the paper. The box contained a set of car keys, and the embarrassed couple oohed and aahed and protested, until Joy detached one of her earrings and threaded the key ring through the lobe of her ear. She posed and shook her head so the keys jingled, and everyone clapped their hands.

"Dang!" Karla said. "I have to go get my purse." She pushed back her chair and stood up, while the blue-eyed geezer steadied the table. "Be back in a minute." Her doggy friends, Bernard and Benjamin, followed her, wagging their tails, as she left the house and crossed over to the guest lodging. She ascended the hundred steps, pausing halfway up to breathe, and went to her room and secured the purse. Her room contained a dial telephone; she sat on the bed and stared at it for a moment, then got out her little address book. But when she dialed the South Dakota prefix, she was interrupted by a righteous female speaking French. The voice recited useless instructions, and the telephone honked in her ear.

"Well, what would Oliver say? He would tell me to stop. I can stop any time."

By the time she got back to the party, the mood had changed. Everyone was a little tipsy, and they were eating chocolate. Karla set her purse by her place at the table and stood holding the back of her chair. "I, too, brought a gift," she announced, "but I didn't have time to wrap it." She opened her purse and took out two envelopes, one with the fourteen thousand Euros for the violin, the other with the twenty-five hundred for the bow. The thinner of the two she put back. "Here," she said, passing the thick envelope to Benoit and Joy. "It's for you both. I wish you happiness."

The table chatter quieted a little. "Gosh, mother," Joy said, fingering the envelope. "Do you want me to open it here?"

"I don't care," Karla said. "Open, don't open. But first I need to sit down. Those steps made me dizzy." Her champagne flute had been replaced with a deep-bellied glass. The host reached across the table with a bottle that had an apple on the label and poured a little bronze liqueur. When he'd finished, Karla lifted the glass. The liquid inside swirled invitingly, and she remembered her first love, little Michael, when the world was new. "To love!" she cried. "To sex. To lots of babies." She tossed off the contents of the glass and nearly choked. "Whoo! That's powerful," she said. "What is it?"

"Calvados," Zhorzhe the banker said. "We grow the apples."

"Better pour me another." Karla caught Joy's disapproving eye. "All right, all right," she said. "I promise to sip it."

"I think I'd better look into this," Joy said. She opened the flap of the envelope, which was not sealed. "For God's sake, mother," she said. "Have you been to the casino?" She fingered the tops of the bills, not counting but estimating. "This is Euros, not dollars. You didn't bring it with you on the plane."

Karla lifted her fresh glass of Calvados, sniffing and tasting like an epicure. "You won't guess," she said, "so I'll tell you. I sold your uncle Boris's violin."

"Boris's violin? What violin?" Joy put the envelope on the table and sat back in her chair. "You need to tell me about this. And I hope you weren't drinking when you sold it."

"Of course I wasn't drinking. I haven't had a drink in years," Karla said. She looked at the empty glass in her hand and put it down carefully. "Penny and I went to the office of Boris's orchestra. I wanted to find out where they buried him, but it turned out they had kept his violin. It had been there collecting dust ever since he died."

"What kind of violin was it?"

"I don't know. It was old. It had some wear and tear on it."

Benoit, in a quiet voice, had been translating for those at the table who did not speak English. Now the twelve-year-old spoke up. "Was it a Stradivarius?"

Karla laughed. "Oh, no," she said. "I made sure of that. They said it was just an imitation Stradivarius."

"An imitation made by whom?" It was Zhorzhe the banker who asked. *Shit,* Karla thought. *He thinks he can question me. I'm not asking him for a goddam loan.*

"They made out a receipt," she said. "There's a copy of it in the envelope. The name is on there." She glanced around the silent table. "It was old," she said. "I've been to antique auctions. In America, those old fiddles are a dime a dozen."

Joy riffled through the contents of the envelope and pulled out a piece of paper. "Derazay," she said. "Eighteen eighty-six. Did you have it appraised?"

"Have it appraised? How would I do that?"

"You'd take it to a dealer of antique instruments. Did you look on the Web?"

"Listen, darling," Karla said. "I wasn't about to be lugging some old fiddle around Paris, looking for a dealer. I'd have probably sat on it."

Joy took out her ever-present phone and began tapping the screen. Benoit said something to her in French, but she brushed him aside. "You shut up," she said. "I'm going to look into this."

"One of them was an older gentleman," Karla said. "He literally got down on his knees and begged. The other one was a young guy about your age. With pimples." She took a sip from her glass, which had somehow filled itself. "The old guy was crying," she said. "He must have loved Boris a lot."

"If one of them was my age, he couldn't have known Boris," Joy said. "Here's a Derazay. It sold at auction for twenty-six thousand Euros."

"No shit," Karla said.

"No shit," Joy said. "Here's another one, a viola. Thirty-two five. Here's a violin in playable condition. 'Playable.' Whatever that means." She put down the phone. "They're asking thirty-eight thousand euros."

"I don't care," Karla said. "They were two of the nicest men you ever saw."

"God damn it," Joy said, "you should have asked me. Do you even know what I do all day? I manage money. Other people's money. I move around chunks of money that are a hundred times larger than this. People like George, here, ask for my opinion. Ask, hell! They pay me for it. They pay me!" She looked ready to cry.

"Well, I'm happy for you, getting to play with money," Karla said. "You didn't learn all that growing up with Gerard and me. We didn't even own a set of Monopoly."

"Not playing! Don't you understand? Money is a real thing. You do not play with it. Money is your life! You can't do a thing without money!"

"I can do something," Karla said. "I can go and look for a beer, that's what I can do. I'm tired of this apple booze that you sip, sip, sip. God damn it, I'm thirsty." She stood up, jostling the heavy table so that a champagne flute tipped over. "If I don't come back in a day or two, send a search party."

She turned and left the table and the house, and walked out into the rain. The two dogs, Bernard and Benjamin, followed her as far as the gate.

KARLA DIDN'T KNOW HOW FAR SHE'D WALKED. She'd come to an on-ramp of some kind and caught a ride, and had gotten out at an off-ramp several minutes later. She walked some more until she saw a tavern that overlooked a river. Men's voices came from inside.

*Home. Home. I knew it entering.* It was dirty and badly lighted, and smelled of fish. She was the only woman in the room except for two girls in mesh hose and thigh-high skirts who sat looking bored and resentful at the end of the bar. Karla went up to the bartender and asked for a depth charge. He didn't understand English, so she pointed to a couple of glasses—a beer mug and a shot glass—and set the shot glass inside the mug. Then she pointed to the bottle with an apple on its label and to the beer pull. A depth charge made with Calvados and French beer. Maybe she had invented something.

The bartender charged her ten euros and picked up the telephone.

Karla set herself up at one of the tables and laid a fifty-euro note in front of her. She planted her elbow on the table with her hand in the air, and cocked an eyebrow at the first man who came by. She glanced at the money and at the seat across from her. The man sat down, but he pushed the note toward her with a finger. Evidently he didn't have fifty euros. Karla retrieved the note and got out a ten-euro one, and the man put down ten euros and took up the position for an arm-wrestle. He was blond and stocky, with a mustache and an unshaven jaw, and wore canvas coveralls and rubber boots. She liked that he did not return her smile and was serious about winning her ten euros, so she let him push her arm back an inch or two before holding him there. Pretty soon his arm started to tremble; his face turned red and he twisted himself to put his shoulder in play. She decided that if he was going to cheat, then the hell with him, and without more ado she shoved his hand to the table, bumped it twice to show she was ready to do it again, and picked up his money. Then she drank off her depth charge at a draft, handed him the glass and his own ten euros, and pointed to the bartender.

Her next customer was small, dark, and intense. He cheated right away, so much that he practically stood up to get leverage. After she put him down and took his money, he refused to go get her another depth charge, so she made the third man bring her a drink before she would play. She caught the bartender's eye and held the shot glass and shook her head. Plain beer, that was best for a bender. Number Four was a redheaded boy, not yet out of his teens. She was getting a little foggy and sentimental, and she held his thin white hand in hers and blessed him with a thought before she crushed him. His arm collapsed so quickly that it felt like snapping dry spaghetti.

They were fishermen or bargemen, heavy-booted and wet-smelling, carrying odors of man-sweat and the river, and she loved them all. Still, she could see that they were not pleased that a massive American woman wearing a neck brace had stumbled in out of the rain to put them down. A little group gathered around her table, and the betting increased, so that she was taking in fifty or a hundred euros at every round. Finally they ran out of candidates and began to argue; she kept hearing the word *souris* or *la souris*. One who knew a little English looked at her. "Mouse," he said. "They are sending for The Mouse."

Two or three beers later, a man came in the door carrying a sleepy four-year-old girl and followed by his wife. The Mouse was five feet tall and four feet wide, but in spite of his bulk, he stepped lightly. He came up to Karla's table and studied the situation with a pair of kind brown eyes, all the while jogging the child. Karla planted her elbow and showed him her open hand.

The Mouse turned and handed the child to his scowling wife. He went over to the bar and ordered a shot of cognac, and brought the little glass and set it on the table across from Karla. He sat down carefully, as if he had sometime or another broken a chair, smiled at her, raised the glass in salute, and took the tiniest sip. "*Allons*," he said, and raised his hand into position. His forearm, tapered and shorter than hers, was thick as the leg of a snooker table. His fingers resembled thumbs except for the fifth finger, that had a tip that bent sideways at an angle.

Karla pushed her winnings to the center of the table. She took his gentle hand in both of hers, but instead of trying to twist it sidewise, she closed her eyes and drew it blindly to her lips. Then she broke down and began to bawl like a forsaken baby.

PENNY AND THE BLUE-EYED GEEZER arrived in a black Citroën driven by a duke. The duke turned out to be the geezer's nephew. The oddly-shaped car looked like it was designed to be driven underwater, but the ride was as smooth as cream. Or as Fanny's custard.

Karla cried all the way home, and she cried walking up to the door, but when she met Joy frowning down at her, her crying stopped. "Does that phone of yours make international calls?" she asked. "There's somebody I need to talk to."

"Anything you say, ma," Joy said. "If you'll tell me the number, I'll dial it for you."

Karla gave her a number with a South Dakota prefix. Joy dabbed at the instrument and handed it to Karla. "Don't hold it too close to your face," she said. "If you touch it, it might disconnect you."

After a few clicks and buzzes, the little plastic slab made the telephone-ringing noise. On the other end, someone answered. "Hello?"

"This is Karla Čapek. I married Gerard Horse Looking," Karla said. "I need to talk to Oliver Broad Moccasin. I'm calling from France."

"Who is this?" The woman's tone was suspicious. Oliver had his admirers.

"Tell him it's Karla. He'll know who I am. He's my AA sponsor."

"Oh. You're that Karla. Oliver is at the casino."

"Can you give me the number, please?" Karla gestured to anyone around her for a pen and paper. The duke, who had followed them inside, produced an engraved card and a silver ball-point from an inside pocket of his dinner jacket. The woman on the phone gave Karla a different number with the same prefix. "He may not come to the phone," she said. "They don't like to interrupt him when he's losing money."

Karla gave Joy the phone and the card with the number on the back; after thirty minutes without a drink in it, her hand was becoming uncontollable. Joy wiped the phone on her sleeve and punched the number in and gave it back.

"Hello?" A male voice this time.

"I'm trying to reach Oliver Broad Moccasin," Karla said. "It's an emergency."

"What is the nature of your emergency?" *Who the hell do you think you are?* Karla wanted to scream. *A dispatcher?*

"I have gotten myself damned drunk," Karla said. "He's my AA sponsor, and I need him to help me."

Evidently that was something the man could understand. The phone went dead for several seconds, but there were distant voices and bells, and soon the familiar soft voice came on the line. "Oliver Broad Moccasin speaking."

"Oh, Oliver!" Karla burst into sobs. "Oliver, Oliver, Oliver! Nobody loves me."

"This is Karla, isn't it," he said. "Karla, take a deep breath and think of the drum. One, one, two, two. BOOM boom BOOM boom. Breathe. I'll stay on the line. Talk when you feel ready."

Karla wiped her eyes and hiccupped a few times. "Okay," she said. "Oliver, I relapsed. It's bad."

"How many days?"

"Just tonight. I was drinking depth charges. I tried to outdrink the Navy."

"Where are you? What were you doing with the Navy?"

"There's no navy, Oliver. They're fishermen. I'm in France." Karla took in a shaky breath. "Oliver, I'm sick and the blue meanies are coming for me. I don't know what to do."

"Can you get to a hospital?"

"I don't know, Oliver. I don't think so. I don't even know if they have alcoholics in France."

"Well, listen," he said. "Let me think. Is there a river?"

"There's a river. Are you telling me to jump off a bridge?"

"No, no," he said. "Don't jump off anything. Maybe you should go fishing."

"Fishing? Why would I go fishing?"

"It's what I do." She could almost hear him shrug. "It sits you down. It gets you quiet so you can talk to the water."

"It's raining, Oliver."

"Wear a raincoat," he said. "The fish bite best when it's raining."

"You're crazy, Oliver," Karla said. "I never know when you're joking, but I love talking to you."

"Is your daughter with you? If she is, tell her hello. She was about the prettiest kid I ever saw."

"She's a beautiful young woman now. She's getting married, Oliver."

"Is that what set you off? Something's going on."

"I don't know. Send me good vibes. I want to come home."

After Oliver hung up, Karla explained to the gathered clan what she needed. "I'd like dry clothes and better rain gear, and a lawn chair and some fishing tackle and a flashlight," she said, "and a place on the riverbank to sit."

"Are you intending to go tonight?" Joy asked. "Is this a serious proposal?"

"Do you want to lock me in my room and listen to me scream?"

"No." Joy shuddered. "Only please stay out of the water."

George the banker was a fisherman, and close enough to Karla's size. He owned a hooded slicker and plastic overpants, and the lawn chair and the flashlight were quickly found. Karla chose a spinning rod and a treble hook. "Bait," she said. "If I'm going to wait all night for a fish, I need stinky bait."

They stood in perplexity for a moment. Then, "*Bon!*" Fanny said. "You will use *la pâte!*"

So it was. Karla, drunk and in the middle of the night, using *pâte de foie gras* for bait and the duke's engraved card for a license, went fishing in a tributary of the Seine. She sat all night without a nibble and let the river and the rain do the talking. By morning, the rain had let up, and the mouth-drying gut-twisting meanies had backed away.

THE PERSON WHO BROUGHT HER A COVERED PLATE was Penny's geezer. "Did you catch something?" he asked, standing on the bank and looking down at the river. "If you catch a flounder and let her go, you can make a wish."

"There are flounders in the river?"

"Not so far from the sea," the geezer admitted. "They need a little salt. Have you checked your bait?"

"I haven't," Karla said. "It's probably gone. Does your nephew own the river?"

The geezer laughed. "He owns the village but not the river," he said. "If you happen to catch a whale, he owns the blubber. It's a right that was granted by Charlemagne. Our family has lived in this neighborhood for a very long time."

The food beneath the cover was an omelet of mushrooms and spinach with a side dish of salted tomato slices. The aroma made Karla's mouth water, but her stomach was far from ready. "Did you bring any coffee? My brain needs a boost."

"Here is a Thermos bottle. I would offer you cognac, but—"

"Heavens, no!" Karla said. "Please, please, do not offer me cognac."

The geezer poured dark warm coffee, which she drank from the silver cup that capped the Thermos. "Oliver was right," she said after a time. "The river makes me calm."

"I like to watch the birds," the old man said. "In summer, as the sun comes up, they are comically busy."

"My favorites are the chickadees," Karla said. "They don't care if they're right side up or upside down. When my husband and I went to one of the sandhill lakes, we used to see yellow-headed blackbirds. You don't see those as much these days."

"Your husband was a Lakota Indian? I have read that the Lakotas don't eat fish."

Karla laughed. "That was before they were corrupted."

"You must smile more," the old man said. "Your smile looks very natural. You must have smiled frequently, sometime in your life."

"Where did you learn English?"

"In England, during the war. My brother the duke stayed and fought in the Resistance. He was tortured and killed by the Nazis. Nearly all of them were."

"My brother Boris was a brilliant musician. Nobody tortured him, but he died anyway."

The two of them shared the Thermos of coffee, taking turns with the silver cup. "I think I'm ready to go in," Karla said at last. "Except for being hung over, I don't feel too terrible. No snakes this time. I dread to see those snakes."

"You were once an alcoholic?"

"I am an alcoholic," Karla said. "Alcoholism is like diabetes. You don't get over it."

When she started to reel in her line, Karla felt something heavy and inert, as if the treble hook had snared a piece of trash. But when the thing surfaced, it turned out to be a fish, slick of skin like a catfish but long, almost like an eel. The old man helped her to pull it out onto the grass, where it lay looking up at them, alert but passive. "This is a burbot," he said. "We call it *la lotte de rivière*. They are rare. I have not seen one in decades."

"Do we keep it? Are they good to eat?"

"Very good," the man said. "But no, you may not keep her. She is only hooked through the lip. I am confident she will live." He dipped his hands in the water and unhooked the snaky creature, handling it with tenderness. "There you go, my dear," he said as it disappeared with a wriggle. He turned to Karla and smiled. "Did you remember to make a wish?"

"I would wish for my daughter to have a good life," Karla said, "but that fish was not a flounder."

"No matter," the geezer said. "You should wish it nonetheless."

TO STIFLE ANY YIPS AND HOWLS from the meanies, Karla accepted a sedative from Joy's young doctor. She spent the rest of that day in bed and slept through most of the night; she woke before dawn, to find Fanny already in the kitchen. Together they mixed a sweet dough and set it to rise, and Karla sat on the porch with the dogs to watch the chilly morning. After she'd drunk her second cup of coffee and nibbled a croissant, she went back in and began tearing the dough and rolling it between her palms, making doughballs the size of duck eggs. She asked for some jars of Fanny's preserves, and when her daughter Joy came in, she was flattening the doughballs and pressing an indentation into each of them with her thumb.

Joy slipped her brown arms around Karla and gave her a hug. "We showed them our asses, mama, didn't we?" she said.

"We showed them our panties," Karla agreed. "Maybe they'll adopt us anyway."

"I love the smell of bread dough rising," Joy said. "What are you making?"

"Fanny's helping me make kolaches," Karla said. "These are going to be good."

# Room Nineteen

THE FACELESS MAN WITH THE NET made of rainbow fire: that's who Karla Čapek is waiting for. There's not a damn thing interesting about it, only once in a while, when the medbot and the mopbot have an encounter. They regard one another as furniture, and each is baffled when the other moves. The door is automatic, too, and sometimes it gets into the act, opening and closing itself. Karla imagines one day there'll be a bedbot to change the sheets, and maybe a docbot to prescribe drugs and take her temperature. For now, though, real people do those things, and they are the only people Karla sees for days at a time. Once a week, her old friend Penny Raskonen comes to visit, but Penny would rather be working in her garden.

Karla has already fallen toward the net a couple of times, but some force pulls her aside. The net is made of lines of colored light, woven into a spiral in the shape of the whirlpool that forms when you pull the plug from an old-fashioned bathtub. Dots of light move rapidly along the lines, and the whole thing spins like an irresistible magnet. As for the faceless man, he is someone Karla imagines must carry the net.

She herself has become a giant slug, so heavy that they have to bring a crane to turn her over. The Weight Liftress is now a weight, a balloon of flesh that contains a scrap of life. And what does the life weigh? Nothing. It could float away at any time, and mostly she just wishes the hell it would. Just go ahead and float. If only they would leave the window open.

Though of course she is terrified of the man with the net.

When she thinks things couldn't get any worse, they bring a letter from her daughter. *I have lots of time to myself here*, the letter says. Joy is spending three years in a minimum-security prison, over in France. She is a financial advisor who started thinking of her clients' money as her own. Karla's grandkids, twelve and fourteen, are living with Joy's husband on a farm in Normandy, where they ride horses and feed apples to the pigs. Fanny, the French *grandmère*, sends notes on their birthdays.

*I have lots of time to myself here, and I wish I knew you better. I would like to ask you about my dad.* . . .

Gerard. Gerard whom Karla had loved more than herself. Gerard who broke her heart by dying and set her off on a binge that lasted half a year and caused her to lose custody of her girl.

*. . . who he was, and what he did before he met you.*

Now that is the million-dollar question. All she knows about Gerard is that he had a crazy mother. People up on the Rez used to say she was a witch.

EVERY SUNDAY, PENNY BRINGS KARLA a smuggled bottle of beer. (The Sailors of Galilee Christian Care Center is currently run by Sikhs, who don't approve of beer any more than the Mormons did, or the Nazarenes who built the nursing home in the first place. The Nazarenes had their reasons for a no-beer policy, as their forebears, at least the ones in Turtle Lodge, had all been drunks according to Penny. Penny has no information about the Sikhs.) The beer is usually warm by the time it gets to Karla. She sips it in pure delight, even though she has to drink through a straw while Penny holds the glass.

"So tell me about your garden," she says to Penny. "What's blooming, what's growing, what's dying? How are the weeds?"

"The pigweed is perfect," Penny says with a twinkle. "The whole thing'd grow up to pigweed if I'd let it. Then there's that prickly stuff we call honeysuckle, that the bees like so much. In the afternoon the bumblebees are so busy that I don't go out there. That's about the time I take my nap."

"Must smell sweet," Karla says. "I wish I could smell it with you."

"Tell you what, I'll bring you some of those weeds so you can sniff 'em."

"Nah," Karla says. "Just keep on bringing me beer."

There isn't much to talk about, just gossip about the local people. Some of them Karla remembers and some she doesn't. Karla and Penny never talk politics, since Penny is a Fox News person and Karla watches CNN. Penny was married to a Norwegian, and Karla married an American Indian. Their politics are as different as can be, to the point where, if they were male, they'd probably have to shoot one another.

"What do you hear from your daughter?" Karla asks. "Mine's in jail."

Penny laughs. "Oh, she's getting married again. He's ten years younger than she is, so maybe he can keep up with her. There won't be any bridesmaids this time. She wants a chartreuse wedding dress."

"Joy wants to know about her father," Karla says. "Trouble is, I know almost nothing about him. I never met Gerard's mother. He said they called her Bad Pipe in Lakota."

"Rose Stevens," Penny says. "She was a piece of work, all right. Did you know she was half-sister to George Smith? Edward Stevens was their father. George's mother was white but Rose's must have been pure Indian."

"I did not know that," Karla says. "So my Joy is related to the Smiths?"

"They do DNA testing now," Penny says. "You should tell her to look into it."

"You've been good to me," Karla says. "I hate to put you out, but I need you to do something. Can you write my Joy a letter? Tell her what you know about Gerard's side of the family."

"Aw, honey," Penny says. "You know I'm no good at writing. For one thing, I can't spell doodley."

"She doesn't care," Karla says. "She just wants the information."

"Somebody up on the Rez would know that better than me," Penny says.

"I can't get there from here," Karla says. "I don't think Indians write letters. Gerard never wrote a letter in his life. He wouldn't even sign a Christmas card."

"I don't think I own any writing paper."

"Please try," Karla says. "I'd appreciate it so much."


KARLA STILL HAS DRUNKARD'S INSOMNIA, and when she lies awake at night, she slips back and forward in time. Sometimes she even slips sideways into parallel universes. For instance, there are times when she remembers being married to her first love, Michael, even though the marriage never happened. They never had two blond children named Nadine and Zaphod. She doesn't know where that second name came from, but there it is.

There are times she remembers going to the Olympics in Paris, not as a spectator but as a lifter.

Mostly she remains stuck in the here-and-now, though there is nothing in the present to attract her. She can see out the window a little, when someone opens the curtain. The crab tree that used to shade the bricks is missing. If she can manage to shift her head sideways, she can just see the edge of Turtle Lodge Butte.

The medbot brings her medications, even though she can't reach out to take them. A nurse has to put them in her mouth and hold a glass of water. The mopbot cleans the floor, but a worker still has to sterilize the sink. The electric door doesn't open half the time, and God knows what they would do if there was a fire. The television works by voice command, so she can turn it on and off and change the channels. The one thing in the room that doesn't work is Karla. Her body is dead weight, a bag of Jell-o.

Karla doesn't remember what year it is, or exactly how old she is, but she remembers that Anderson Cooper is gay.

She knows she is always waiting, and that the things she is waiting for won't be pleasant. Sometimes it's to be turned over, sometimes it's for a bath, sometimes it's for the sheets to be changed, sometimes it's for a meal or the bedpan. The food is bland, and she gets no pleasure from peeing. The bath water is cold.

In one of her parallel universes, she's the captain of a fishing boat in the Gulf of Alaska. What a time she has there! There are storms, and breaching whales, and brawls with the fishermen. Snowcapped volcanoes jut from the water. Dark undercurrents of human nature are revealed; she solves mysteries and unravels ancient curses. Then she finds herself back in bed and falling asleep.

Waiting.

Sometimes the therapist comes in. "How are we doing today? Any luck with those toe exercises?"

*You've got to be kidding me.*

THE DOCTOR IS WEARING A MASK when she comes in, but Karla would know her anywhere. She has white hair, no tits, and is the height of a garden gnome. "How are you?" Karla asks before she can begin. "I haven't seen you in a while."

"I'm preparing to retire," the doctor says. "Thirty years is enough."

"Doc Cameron hasn't retired, and he must be ninety."

"Doc Cameron should have quit practicing twenty years ago."

The doctor is there to do the required six-weeks exam. She pops a thermometer in Karla's mouth and unfurls her stethoscope. "Cough," she says.

"I canck," Karla says. "I've gock a fermove'er in my mouf."

"Well, then, be quiet so I can listen to your heart." The doctor wrinkles her brow and concentrates. "Hm," she says. "Maybe I'd better put a monitor on you."

"I don't think so," Karla says after tucking the thermometer in her cheek. "What's the point? I've got a DNR on me."

"Do you want us to do nothing, then?"

"Maybe."

Despite Karla's wishes, half a dozen tabs are stuck to her skin and connected to half a dozen colored wires. They lead to a monitor whose screen she cannot see. Something's going on, she thinks. Maybe this is it. But the episode comes to nothing.

The Raskonen brothers built an ethanol plant where the roundhouse used to sit south of Willow. They recruited their workers locally, and, Willow being Willow, there arose a black market in straight grain alcohol. Karla got hold of a gallon in order to make plum brandy as gifts for her drinking friends; that is what she'd believed she intended. In truth, the demon had spoken to her, and she'd relapsed spectacularly. She woke up on the floor of her living room, unable to move, and that's where Penny had found her.

Now she lives on pointlessly, breathing sterile and regulated air, chewing and swallowing whatever is put into her mouth. The therapist comes in twice a week to move her limbs, but Karla shows no interest in moving them herself. Where she is touched, she feels the prick of pins and needles. The therapist says that this is a good sign, but Karla wants no signs of any kind. What she wants is to move out of Room Nineteen.

What she does not want is to go on like this forever.

"I want to go to the top of the butte," she says to no one in particular. To her surprise, a male face appears in her line of vision. It's the hippie kid from Willow who cleans the sink. He's cheerful-looking with clear young skin (darker than Karla's but not so dark as Joy's) and eyes that shine with warmth and interest in life. He smells of marijuana.

"Why the top of the butte?" he asks. "Do you want to do a vision quest?"

"It's just that I've never been up there," Karla replies. In her experience, young white males who talk about a vision quest are people to whom you don't loan money.

"There's a trail for mountain bikes," he says. "You carry your bike up there and ride back down."

"I'm a little beyond that," Karla says. "More power to anybody who can do it."

"The butte used to be full of rattlesnakes. That's what everybody says."

Karla assumes that will be the end of it, but one day the kid reappears. "My dad has a mechanical wheelbarrow," he says. "It's got a five-horse motor on it. He uses it for concrete work."

"What are you talking about?"

"Your vision quest," he says. "You asked to go up on the butte. Don't you remember?"

"I never said anything about a vision quest," Karla replies. "And I'm not going anywhere in a wheelbarrow."

"Well, you might as well try and have a vision," he says. "It's going to be a lot of trouble getting you up there."

"I was only talking to myself," Karla says. "I can't leave this bed. You know that."

"We can put you on a mattress," he says. "We'll rig a travois. That'll work better than a wheelbarrow."

"No, no, no," Karla says. "This is nuts. You don't know what you're saying."

"My dad's a buckskinner," the kid says. "You wouldn't believe what he can do. He does these incredible things all the time."

"What does your father have to do with it?"

"He owns a pack mule. It'll be a piece of cake."

"You're wacko," Karla says. "Forget I ever talked to you. Go away."

PHILIP AND KYLE SANDERS HAVE a five-room house in Willow, where they live along with Sylvia, Kyle's girlfriend. They subsist on frozen pizza and MDMA, a drug known as "molly" to its friends. Kyle's are the puppy-dog eyes that looked down with warmth and empathy at Karla; he cleans sinks at the nursing home in Turtle Lodge. Phil works construction alongside their father and attends buckskinners' rendezvoux on weekends. Phil can tan a deer hide, knap an axe-blade out of flint, and cook stew in a kettle over an open fire. Kyle can do none of these things, but he doesn't need to. When Armageddon comes, as everyone predicts, he will hang out with his brother until they are raptured. Phil will see to it that they're fed until Jesus takes over.

Sylvia used to waitress at the Willow Café until some joker poured ice water down her buttcrack. Right now she's between jobs and spends her days surfing the World Wide Web, looking for bargains in the retail drug trade. She takes her shipments via USPS and resells the contents at a profit, either to workers at the Raskonen Brothers' ethanol facility or to employees at one of the local feedlots. Sylvia, Philip, and Kyle are all three similarly shaped, with round heads and round shoulders, round moon faces, and no more waist than a toad. The boys are dark-haired, while Sylvia is a natural blonde; she dyes her hair periodically with Kool-Aid just to keep herself interesting. Once in a while, when she feels especially down in the dumps, she will cut herself with a razor blade someplace where it won't show; usually, though, she maintains a cheerful exterior with help from molly.

Philip is a veteran of the war in Afghanistan and has no bad habits, except that he sleeps with a knife in his hand and occasionally wakes them up with his screaming. For that reason, he has his own room and mattress, though Sylvia sometimes goes over to him out of kindness. The drug they take fills them all with brotherly love, and what's a little extra sex between friends? Living well is the best revenge, and these young people live well as life is measured in Willow. They're cold in winter and hot in summer, like most people in Dunlap County, and they carry their deficiencies with dignity.

"So why do you want to take an old lady to the top of the butte?" This is Sylvia.

"I want her to have a vision," Kyle says. "Everybody needs to have a vision, to take control of their life."

"Why not give her some peyote, if you want her to have a vision?"

"Have you tried to buy peyote lately? It costs forty dollars a button."

"Mushrooms, then. Black Elk ate a prairie chicken that ate mushrooms. That's how he got his vision."

"These Indians that go on a vision quest don't take mushrooms. They go up on a hilltop and wait, and pray and sing until the spirits come. Then they find their spirit animal."

"What if her spirit animal is a grubworm, or just another fat lady who can't move?"

"You're being negative. Didn't you ever want to do a favor for someone?"

"If I have the urge to do somebody a favor, I sit down until I get over it."

Their debate ends when Philip comes home. "Dad needs help pouring concrete this weekend. Is either of you available?"

"I don't think so," Kyle says. "I have to hang loose in case they need me at the Sailors of Galilee. I'm always on call, sort of."

"I'm expecting a package," Sylvia says. "I have to stay home until the mail comes." Concrete is usually poured first thing in the morning, when the air is cool. Because of her fair skin, Sylvia needs her beauty rest; she prefers to sleep until nine or ten.

"I'll get somebody from the ethanol plant," Philip says. "Those people are always looking for extra hours. What the Raskonens pay their mill hands is crap." He goes to his room to take off his work boots and load the bong.

After supper they discuss Kyle's plan, insofar as he has one. It goes like this: during the upcoming Dunlap County Alumni Weekend, when the residents of the Sailors of Galilee are brought out onto the lawn to view the parade, he and Sylvia will roll Karla out the back door and lift her into the bed of a pickup truck. The truck will be hitched to a trailer with Brownie the pack mule already loaded. They will drive Brownie and Karla out to Turtle Lodge Butte, where there is a four-wheeler-and-bike trail carved into the northeast slope, and unload Karla and the mule. There they will quickly fashion a travois (Kyle has never made one, but he's seen his father do it) from a couple of poles and the mattress from Kyle and Sylvia's bed. Kyle and the mule will drag Karla to the top of the butte, and Sylvia will follow with provisions. Philip will remain below with a twelve-pack and the truck. Kyle has formed this plan without consulting Philip, or Sylvia, or Brownie, or, for that matter, Karla.

"What do you think?" Kyle asks through the smoke.

"What does who think?" is one response. "About what?" is another. Kyle clarifies that he's talking about Karla.

"Who's Karla?"

Kyle patiently starts over, though it is tiresome talking to stoners. Once they have comprehended his plan, they begin to find fault with it.

"What if the mule won't go?"

"What if the trailer breaks down?

"What if they won't let us take this Karla person?"

"Everything will work out," Kyle insists. "The spirits will help us."

"What spirits? The spirits of dead Indians? Why should they help us?"

"Why would they not help us? We've never done anything to them."

"What if they think we're idiots?"

"That's no way to talk about your brother."

They spend the rest of the evening playing a game on Sylvia's laptop. Kyle has a computer more suitable for gaming, but it's down for repairs. Philip is the one trying to fix it.

FIRST THING THAT GOES WRONG IS, the mule won't load. Brownie does not like the beat-up horse trailer. Philip has put air in the tires, but the floorboards look iffy, even to a mule. Sylvia finds three sugar cubes in Kyle's backpack and gives Brownie one of them, with the promise of the other two once she steps inside the trailer. Problem solved! On to the next thing, which is to load Karla. For her part, Karla expects nothing and has not been looking forward to the parade. She would have been cleaning floors in the school when some of the alumni were teenagers, but what she remembers is their disrespect. The nurses' voices in the hallway carry an extra octave of false cheer, and the rattle of walkers and wheelchairs is continuous.

Outside, the day is a pretty one; sunshine streams in Karla's window, which faces twenty degrees to the north of east. This would be a good day to go fishing on a sandhill lake, herself and Gerard and little Joy in their twelve-foot boat. She wonders who now owns the boat; she knows that her possessions have been sold and her double-wide stands empty. Her retirement from the school goes into a fund administered by the bank, to which she might have access if she could write a check. A disbursement goes to the Sikhs who run the Sailors of Galilee, but there's a portion reserved for her personal expenses, like shampoo and nail polish. Penny Raskonen is the one who buys her toffee and paints her toenails; twenty dollars a month takes care of all of it.

Meanwhile the tipi poles Kyle plans to use for a travois, which have been lying on the ground for two or three winters, have come to be weak and brittle. Philip and Kyle choose two of the heaviest and lash them to the trailer along with the mattress. Brownie, already skeptical, is not going to like dragging these stiff and awkward poles up the side of the butte.

Karla hoped that Penny might come by—the time drags—but there's a lot going on, with the carnival and the parade, so it's no surprise that Penny has something better to do. Karla moves her head to the side a little so she can see the edge of the butte, and wishes someone would put her in her wheelchair. She can't do much, but she can hold herself erect if she is propped in a chair. It's been a week since anyone wheeled her outside. The only residents who receive less attention are the ones parked in Room Twenty, waiting for the undertaker while their corpses are cooling.

She seldom wishes to see her therapist—in fact, she's often rude to her—but at least if the girl would come by there'd be somebody to insult. The therapist's routine consists of moving Karla's limbs while Karla tries to resist. She always says, "Good! Good," even though, from Karla's point of view, nothing changes. True, her joints have stayed flexible and her muscles haven't tightened, but of what future use her floppy joints and mushy muscles might be is not evident to Karla.

Back in Willow, one more thing goes wrong. Kyle can't find the three hits of LSD he intended to take to the top of the butte. "I don't get it," he says. "It was here a minute ago."

"Don't look at me," Sylvia says. "I never take acid by myself. Besides, that last stuff you got is scary. I was, like, all turning into bubbles."

"I didn't take it," Philip says. "It's hard to drive while you're hallucinating."

"I thought we weren't bringing any drugs," Sylvia says. "You told us the Indians never took any."

"They stayed up there four days and four nights," Kyle says. "We have to get the fat lady back before supper. We don't have that kind of time."

"Were you planning to give her acid without telling her? That's a mean trick to play on somebody."

"Well, it's kind of moot at this point," Kyle says. "Those three cubes were all I had, and now they're gone. Do you think that mule is acting funny?"

"I wouldn't know," Sylvia says. "It's hard to tell with mules."

Somehow Karla is not surprised when the shaggy sink-sterilizing specialist shows up with his grape-Kool-Aid-haired girlfriend. "This is Sylvia," the hippie says. "We're here to take you to the top of the butte. You know. For a vision quest. We talked about it the other day."

"I never spoke to you about any vision quest," Karla says. "You must've been talking to someone else."

"But we've already made sandwiches," Kyle says, and the puppy-dog eyes show up.

"As far as I understand it," Karla says, "you do not take sandwiches on a vision quest. You need tobacco ties, and you need a pipe that has a history of some significance. And what would be your motive for seeking a vision?"

Tick tock, tick tock. Blink blink.

"Let's just call it a picnic," Kyle says. "You make everything sound too complicated."

"Oh, please, come with us," Sylvia says. "It's a beautiful day."

Karla looks at Sylvia, for the first time, really. She sees purple hair and a pale and bloated indoor face and reads, with the little wisdom she's acquired in seventy years, sex abuse from a young age and a belief that, whatever is asked for, a heavy price will be exacted. "Who are you?" she asks. "Did you grow up here?"

"I grew up around Scottsbluff," Sylvia replies. "I came here to work at the hospital, but they fired me."

"Congratulations," Karla says. "They fired me, too."

Out in the hall, they can hear the residents being mustered for the viewing of Turtle Lodge's high-school alumni. Karla thinks, *Good thing there's no alumni banquet for this place.* "All right," she says at last. "I'll go with you so long as there's no talk about a vision quest. My next question is, how do you plan to get me up there?"

"We have a mule," Kyle says, and explains his idea to make a travois, which sounds as half-baked as everything else he's said. He's really planning for Philip to figure it out, though Philip's name hasn't been brought into the conversation.

"Your idea is a crock of petunias," Karla says. "You can't even lift me."

"We can lift you," Kyle promises. "Sylvia, here, is stronger than she looks."

"Once we get up there, how do you plan to get me down?"

"That won't be hard," Kyle says. "Gravity will help us."

THE REASON THERE'S A BOBCAT ROAD to the top of the butte— the old trail the Lakota used has washed away—is that three steel towers have been raised there: one belongs to the state's public broadcasting system, one is for the Nebraska State Highway Patrol, and a square and sturdy microwave tower harks with its five ears in five directions. A metal shed inside a hurricane-fenced compound bears a KEEP OUT—HIGH VOLTAGE sign. There is also a concrete helipad for servicing the towers. The depression where young men once lay in terror is filled and covered over; the glacier-remnant forbs and grasses are all but extinguished. Nothing beautiful remains except the view, far and wide across the sandhills.

At two o'clock in the afternoon, Kyle, Sylvia, and Brownie emerge from below the rim, followed by Karla, papoosed in a pair of men's XXXL overalls that have been duct-taped to the travois. Being rattled up over the ruts has been awful, mattress or no mattress, and Karla would murder her benefactors if she could move. Now that she's here, she has no idea how she'll get down again; the descent promises to be far more dangerous than the coming-up. Of her three companions, the mule Brownie appears the most sensible. Kyle has already broken his promise not to talk about a vision quest.

Karla has never tolerated men who babble, except, it seems, now she has to put up with one. Kyle keeps going on with what he knows about Lakota culture, which he's gotten mixed with Omaha and Pawnee culture, along with buckskinner culture and *The Last of the Mohicans* as portrayed by Hollywood. He's built a sweat lodge in his father's back yard, which he heats with firebricks since no stones are available. He's acquired a pipe from some guy in Minnesota and intends to send it off to have it blessed by a medicine man he's found on the World Wide Web. He admires all things Indian but has never been to South Dakota, except to see Mount Rushmore and the Black Hills.

Brownie, now that the climb is over, stomps her hooves and shakes her furry ears. Karla can sense that something is bothering the mule; Brownie pisses, and her urine falls too close to Karla's head. "Can someone take me off of this contraption?" she asks her escorts. "I would like to look at the sky and sniff a breeze that doesn't carry the smell of a mule's ass."

"How was the ride up?" Kyle asks. "That's how the old people and babies used to travel, you know."

"It was horrible," Karla says. "Those poles scraping the ground set my teeth on edge, and my neck feels like I've been in a car accident."

"Well, if you're going to do nothing but project bad karma," Kyle says, "I'm sorry I went to all this trouble for you."

"And thanks so much for asking," Karla says. "Can you get me off this thing now?"

The two able young persons unhitch the poles from Brownie's packsaddle and lower Karla's mattress to the ground, so that Karla's head is even closer to Brownie's urine. Meanwhile the mule is watching the three towers undulate. From her height atop the butte, she can see the curvature of the earth; while she has no theory vis-à-vis the earth's roundness, the idea of having to balance on a rolling ball, however large, makes her queasy. Further, the sound of masking tape being pulled loose from the mattress is snakey, and now that she's thought about snakes, she can smell them.

Lying inches from a puddle of mule piss makes Karla want to sit up, but she cannot do it. For one thing, her belly muscles have atrophied; for another, the men's overalls they have slid her into are duct-taped to the mattress. She can look up at the perfect sky, or a little to one side or the other, but she can't see any ground below the butte. "I wish you would lift me up," she says. "The smell down here is nasty."

Kyle is thinking about something else, but Sylvia hears. "Oh, I bet it is," she says. "Kyle, help me move her. We can't just leave her on the ground like that."

"Move her yourself," Kyle says. "I'm looking for a place to set up my altar." Slung from Brownie's packsaddle is a buffalo skull painted blue on one side and yellow on the other; Kyle has also brought some sage and his pipe. The pipe carries the initials of its maker carved with a Dremel tool and is authentic in that it actually is a pipe, carved from pipestone stolen from a quarry on national parkland, in which tobacco or any combustible substance can be smoked. The stem is authentic too, carved in a flat shape as can be seen in cultural museums. This pipe cost Kyle forty dollars and a couple of old-fashioned pocket watches, themselves each worth forty dollars according to the biker he'd traded them from. Brownie, suspicious of any movement near her heels and with the smell of snakes in her nostrils, is thinking she should aim a kick at Karla's head, but before she can seize the opportunity, Kyle leads her away a little and busies himself with the packsaddle, removing his buffalo skull and a bag that contains a canteen and a block of cheese.

Sylvia can't drag the travois loaded down with the mattress and Karla, but she manages to rotate it and get Karla's head away from the puddle. "Let me help you sit up," she says to Karla. "The view is pretty from up here if you look past all the beer cans." She unpeels the tape that is holding Karla to the mattress and gets behind her to lift. "There's nothing to prop you up with," she says. "We should've brought a pillow or something."

Being boosted into a sitting position creates a painful pull at the backs of Karla's thighs. "I need to move my legs," she says. "If you kind of fold them in front of me, maybe I can sit up by myself."

"It would help if you could prop yourself up," Sylvia says.

"Forget it," Karla says. "I'll just lie back down and look at the puffy clouds."

Philip, breathing hard, emerges above the rim carrying a cooler of ice and beer. He glances at Karla, who wears nothing but a hospital gown and rodeo-clown-sized overalls. "Could've brought the beer on the travois," he grumbles, "and left the fat lady on the back of the truck."

"If a museum is on fire and there's a case of beer and an old fat lady, which are you going to save?" Karla asks him. She likes Philip. He doesn't talk as much as Kyle.

"Don't know," Philip says. "I'd have to sit and have a couple of beers while I thought it over."

They place the cooler behind Karla's back so she can sit up and look around. "Did you ever come up here with your husband?" Sylvia asks.

They know Karla was married to an Indian because of her married name, Horse Looking.

"I don't think Gerard ever came up here," Karla says. "There was no road at the time, and he weighed three hundred pounds. Plus, he didn't care for rattlesnakes."

"Are there snakes up here?" Sylvia asks. "Kyle never told me."

"There used to be tons of them," Karla says. "I think they got mostly hunted out." Philip goes behind Karla to get a beer from the cooler. "I'd drink a beer," Karla says. "If one of you will hold it for me."

"I didn't know you liked beer," Sylvia says.

"Oh, my God," Karla says, "I used to suck it down by the truckload."

The three of them drink beer and watch Kyle putz around, setting up his altar. "I don't deal with this vision quest bullshit," Philip says. "I get all the visions I need out of a beer bottle."

"Kyle needs to do this," Sylvia says. "He feels like his life has no direction."

Time passes. The sun is hot. The breeze is pleasant. "I need to pee," Karla says. "I don't know how that's going to work. You're going to have to get me out of these overalls."

"Fuck," Philip says. "You should've done that before you left the Sailors."

"How was I to know? This whole thing's crazy in the first place."

A rodent the size of a chunky squirrel barks at them from a safe distance; tolerated nowhere else in Dunlap County, prairie dogs have colonized the top of the butte. Philip and Sylvia pull Karla by the arms and drag her to a prairie dog mound, where they park her with her naked bottom above the hole. Karla relieves herself gratefully. "Never underestimate the simple pleasures," she says. "This has to be ugly for you."

"It's not so bad for us," Sylvia says. "I can't speak for the prairie dogs."

"If you're done, let's stand you up," Philip says. "I'll take one arm. Sylvia, you take the other."

"I can't," Karla says.

"Try," Philip says. "Help us with your legs." They manage to hold her in a standing position while Sylvia swipes at her bottom with a paper towel. "We have to put you on the mattress," Philip says. "My back is killing me."

BROWNIE THE MULE HAS BEEN WATCHING Kyle perform mumbo-jumbo with his pipe and his buffalo skull painted with house paint. Brownie is skeptical of the skull. She can identify it as the head of some animal; she's seen cows, and this looks similar, only dead. She can tell from the creature's horns that it's not a horse. Brownie has spent a good part of her life alone in a pasture, longing to be a horse. Her mother was a horse and beautiful, with a shapely head and a flowing mane and tail. She had a lovely way of running and a voice tender as a clarinet and loud as a trumpet. Brownie's own voice comes out a ludicrous, honking bellow. Her way of running, awkward but efficient, is nothing like her mother's, and no little girl has ever petted her and told her she was pretty. Her life has been one of boredom and disappointments, interspersed with abuse.

She feels light as air now that the travois with its fat lady has been removed; the rattle of the dry wood poles had made her want to buck, and she feels justified in refusing to move should they attach the rig again. She still wears the packsaddle and bridle, not without resentment, but just now something fascinating is happening to her. She is growing up and up to giant proportions, while the tiny ripples in the ground beneath her feet are taking on the contours of valleys and mountain ridges. An ant the size of a cattle truck is traversing one of the valleys, and she is glad that most of her is in the stratosphere where she can't be bitten. The three sugar cubes laced with LSD that Sylvia fed her have had two hours to dissolve and take effect, just enough time to get her to the top of the butte.

The man they call Kyle is far below her now. He has pulled up the grass in a circle in front of the painted skull and piled it all in the center, along with some twigs and dry wood he's brought (though of course it was Brownie herself who brought the wood), and he's trying to set fire to it. The grass doesn't want to burn. Ever since she was branded, Brownie hates the smell of fire, and something tells her that the smell of burning grass is especially bad. She tries to send him a message by hee-hawing, but he doesn't listen. She has shrunk back down to normal size, and now she is shrinking further. The buffalo skull has caverns she could crawl into.

A butterfly the size of a horse wants to land on Kyle's head, but he keeps brushing it away. It comes to land beside Brownie and turns into her mother, a white mare with beautiful wings. Brownie reaches to smell her and they touch noses. It's her mother all right, transformed wonderfully but still herself. They converse telepathically.

*You are beautiful. I love you. I wish I, too, had wings.*

*Be patient, my darling. All is known. Your thoughts have wings.*

*Where is your pasture? I want to graze beside you.*

*I am everywhere. I am always with you. Whenever you smell the sweetness of clover, that will be me.*

Her mother becomes a butterfly again and floats away, leaving Brownie devastated. What did she mean when she said she was everywhere? Did she mean she is dead and her body diffused into earth and air? If her body has disappeared, is her spirit then more free? Brownie feels her own body beginning to diffuse, but before she can separate into molecules and float away from herself, something catches her attention. The man they call Kyle is behaving strangely.

Kyle has brought charcoal lighter fluid to squirt on the pile. He has taken the cap off the can and shaken it (does it hurt the can to have its cap removed? Brownie thinks she hears a little cry of pain) and the liquid has splashed on his leg, darkening the fabric. Now it all catches fire with a poof that sends Brownie jerking back against her halter. Kyle, instead of squatting before the fire, has dropped his pipe and begun to dance. First he stomps his foot (Brownie stomps her foot too) and then he starts to jump and twirl, increasing the tempo and howling. The fire is dancing with him, clinging to his leg, and now the other man comes running to join the dance. He catches Kyle in his arms and throws him to the ground, and beats the fire that is holding onto Kyle's leg. He has sometimes treated Brownie in a similar way, and it frightens her to watch him slap and pound the little fire. Now the woman comes (not the great big old one, the other one, the one who moves) and they all make a lot of noise. Their noise appears to Brownie as colliding spheres that clash disagreeably, and she backs away, pulling at her halter rope. The rope is tied to a stake, but the stake pulls up easily, and Brownie is able to move away from the colliding spheres.

The old fat woman who can't move—the one who lies on the mattress that smells of cat urine—is not emitting noises, and Brownie drags the picket rope to stand beside her, while, many steps from them, the dance goes on. Brownie tries telepathy again, but the woman is neither a horse nor a mule and communication is poor.

*Why don't you grow wings and fly like my mother?*
*Help me—idiots—smoke—grass burning.*
*What does it mean if you and I are only clouds of molecules?*
*Mule—carry—away from fire.*

Brownie may be stoned out of her gourd, but she knows she doesn't want to carry anyone. A packsaddle is a packsaddle; it's not for people. Humans make her nervous because they're irritable and don't speak clearly. When you don't understand them, they get angry.

She is glad to see that the little fire has survived its beating. It seems cheerful now, its molecules bouncing happily and rising up as smoke to join the puffy clouds. Then she sees the three humans coming toward her, with the one they call Kyle hopping in the middle. A look in their eyes signals that they mean to catch her, and she sees their sharp white teeth and clutching hands. A shiver runs down her spine and she tries to move away from them, but the picket stake has caught on the fat lady's mattress.

Now they have caught her rope. She struggles to get away from them, kicking dirt on the fat lady, but it is useless because her molecules won't stick together. She tries to rearrange herself as a bird, then as a flower, but the humans are not fooled. The young woman holds her halter, while the man who's not Kyle, the one who attacked the fire, is trying to hoist the Kyle person onto her back. A horrible stink chokes her nostrils; she remembers this smell from the worst experience of her life, when a gang of men caught her and threw her to the ground and burned her with a red-hot iron. The memory floods her and she tries to run away, but the woman, the young one who can move, won't let go of her halter.

Now they have loaded the Kyle person onto her back and are leading her to the trail. She sees the world in its fullness far below; the horizon curves in the distance. A flock of flying horses wheels near the clouds above her, and suddenly she knows what she must do. Her molecules shift and come together, and, with her shining new wings spread wide, she shakes her head and loosens her halter and gallops toward the edge. No longer awkward but running beautifully, she soars, up, up, and up, through the rushing air.

ONCE THE COMMOTION DOWN BELOW HAS DIED AWAY—the mule screaming, the gunshot, the wail of the ambulance—Karla finds herself alone, left there to die. Trouble is, she doesn't feel like dying. She tries yelling, but even though she can hear sounds a mile off, nobody in town can hear her from the top of the butte. Kyle's fire is still burning in what's left of the shortgrass prairie, but nobody bothers to put out fires that start on top. Karla is a little concerned that it might get close to her, but the flames are small and the mattress would probably protect her. She's more afraid she will get too chilly once the sun goes down.

You would think somebody at the Sailors of Galilee would check her room. They must not have missed her yet, because nobody comes.

She is lying there helpless as a 300-pound salami when she hears crows. A light-colored owl comes and lands on a rung of the microwave tower, and a mob of crows follows, cawing and flurrying, trying to get near enough to peck their enemy. Unperturbed by the crows, the owl studies Karla for a while, then spreads its wings and flies down to alight beside her. It's a large bird and grows quickly larger, until it transforms into an ancient bright-eyed woman with walnut skin and chopped-off salt-and-pepper hair that bristles about her head like a halo of feathers. She wears a faded denim jacket and a necklace whose central ornament is a beaded scalp. She glances down and pokes Karla's leg with her toe.

189

"What you doing? Why don't you get up?" Her voice is harsh; she sounds like a crow herself, or a person whose vocal cords are ruined by tobacco and whiskey.

"I can't," Karla says. "I'm paralyzed. Who are you?"

"None of your business who the fuck I am," the woman says. "How come you got paralyzed?"

"I tried to drink a gallon of straight alcohol."

"You got to stay away from that," the woman says. "That shit will kill you."

"Do you think you could help me get down off this butte?"

"How I'm gonna do that? You weigh, like, fifty tons."

"But you were an owl a minute ago. Aren't you a medicine woman, or a witch, or something?"

The old woman glances back at the crows, now perched on the braces of the microwave tower. "Yeah, well, owl medicine got its limits. You don't know nothing about it. Where you gonna find a gallon of raw booze? All the bootleggers here been dead for fifty years."

"From the gasohol plant at Willow. You must be out of touch."

"I'm out of touch, all right." The woman coughs, a cough so long and powerful that it bends the tough little grasses and blows the smoke of the fire out over the town of Turtle Lodge.

"You got any money?"

"How would I carry money?" Karla asks. "You can see I'm practically naked."

"How about them overalls? Anything in the pockets?"

"I didn't look in the pockets," Karla says. "I told you, I'm paralyzed."

The old woman picks up the clown-sized overalls that the three kooks used as a bag to transport Karla. She turns the pockets inside out and finds a quarter, a piece of chalk, and a cat's-eye marble. "Riches beyond belief," the woman says. "You better put your arm over your face, or them crows gonna peck your eyes. They got no ideas about right and wrong, crows. They also got a type of humor you wouldn't like."

"I keep telling you, I've had a stroke," Karla says. "I'm paralyzed."

"Move your fuckin' arm," the woman says. "I ain't gonna tell you again."

Slowly and painfully, Karla lifts her right arm and plops her forearm down over her eyes. "Holy crap. I didn't know I could do that. Who are you, really?"

"I'm your baby's gramma. Really. Now sit up. I want to see you sittin' up."

Of its own will, Karla's arm drops down and props her in a sitting position. She watches the old woman go over to the fire and pick up something red. It's the bowl of Kyle's pipe. "Would you look at this shit?" the woman says. "This pipe got no history. It can't do nothing but get some fool in trouble." She turns toward the microwave tower and throws the pipe bowl at the crows; it hits an upright and shatters, and the dark birds fidget nervously. She turns back toward the painted skull. "I never seen such garbage," she says, and kicks the skull. One of its horns falls into the ashes. "Whoever done this got no respect. They friends of yours?"

"They're some of the local stupids. One of them works at the nursing home. That's where I'm supposed to be right now."

"I bet he don't work there no more," the woman says. "Not after what he done with you."

Karla hears a whirring sound above her. Evidently the woman hears it, too; she looks up and shades her eyes. "It's one of them tiny helicopter things," she said. "Drones, they call 'em. I got to go now. I don't want them to see me." She quickly reverts to owl form and opens her wings. "Say hello to my granddaughter."

"If it's Joy you mean, she's locked up in a minimum-security prison over in France."

"I been in jail. It ain't fun. I'll draw off them crows, but they're liable to come back. You best remember to use that arm to cover your face. If they do come back, you can tell them I plan to eat one of 'em tonight."

THE DEPUTY WHO OPERATES THE DRONE notifies the dispatcher that there's a 300-pound woman in a hospital gown up on the butte, answering the description of the resident who's gone missing from the Sailors of Galilee. Trouble is, there's no good way to get a 300-pound woman down from the butte. The deputy gets out of his car and climbs the trail and puts an emergency blanket on her, and they call in a maintenance helicopter from North Platte. It takes two hours to get there because the pilot has taken the weekend off and needs coffee to get sober. The deputy puts out what's left of the little grassfire and stays with Karla until the chopper comes. He's a home-grown man and says he remembers her from when she used to wax floors at the high school.

They leave the travois poles and the mattress on the butte to puzzle the next visitor.

The next morning, when the physical therapist enters Room Nineteen, she flips the switch for the overhead light and Karla puts her arm up to shield her eyes. "Hey!" says the therapist. She has considered her expensive college degree to be the key to a wasted life, but now here's a patient who is actually improving. "Do that again."

"Do what again?" Karla says. "And could you turn that light off, please?"

From that day, Karla starts a slow recovery. She develops gross movement of her limbs, and the therapist gives her two small weights to handle to build her strength and improve her coordination. Before long she can sit up and feed herself, and not long after that she can stand and walk to the bathroom. Her good friend Penny cheers her on and helps her, but once Karla gathers hope for recovery, she does the exercises willingly. The fogginess in her brain improves; she can speak more clearly, and they move her out of Room Nineteen to make way for a more helpless resident.

That resident is Kyle, whose neck was broken in his tumble from the butte. Kyle is a quadriplegic with nowhere to go and nothing to look forward to. His brother has taken over Sylvia, and the two of them talk of getting married. On one of their trips to visit Kyle, they encounter Karla pacing the hallway, and a wonderful thing happens. Karla and Sylvia fall in love, not as lovers do, but in the way that a puppy and her owner fall in love, or two old horses in a pasture. Sylvia devotes herself to Karla, and it is a rare day when Karla doesn't have a visitor. Her hair, gone white as cotton, takes on cheap dye beautifully, so that over the next brief span of years, she wears every color of the rainbow.

Karla walks with a limp, and her arm-wrestling hand remains weak, but her recovery is so remarkable that they try moving her to assisted living. It turns out, however, that her judgment remains clouded. The first thing she does with her independence is to go to the Silver Dollar and get drunk, and it becomes clear that she can't manage on her own. She returns to the Sailors, Room Five rather than Room Nineteen, and lives out her life there at Dunlap County's expense, with help from Sylvia and from Penny who supplies her necessities.

Before Karla's final cardiac arrest, she lives long enough to see her daughter and her grandchildren. Joy gets out of prison and takes a job in the Socialist government, and on her vacation she brings the kids over to see the town where she grew up. Of course they want to go to South Dakota to visit the reservation. They are young adults now, thinking of college and their futures, and, though they're kind, they show little interest in Karla. She would have liked to take them fishing, but it can't be done. It's been years since she's owned a boat.

When Joy takes her departure, they have a final chat. "Your grandmother was a witch and a pipe carrier," Karla says. "By rights, her pipe belongs to you, if you want to claim it."

"I suppose that means something," Joy says. "It's Indian stuff. I don't understand it."

"Just as well," Karla says. "There's no one to teach you. Better leave it alone."

They look at one another for a long time. Karla says, "I have nothing to leave you but a couple of old photographs. There is one thing. Look in that little box in the drawer beside the sink. There's some costume jewelry and a thimble."

Joy goes to the drawer by the sink and takes out the box. Rather than the steel thimble she's expecting, she finds one made of glass. It is decorated with miniature flowers and feels as light as the shell of a robin's egg. "Is this the one?"

"Please take it to Fanny and give it to her with my love," Karla says. "Maybe she'll bake some kolaches. I showed her how to do it."

"You should come with me to France," Joy says. "You can give it to her yourself."

"Not me," Karla says. "Too much water between here and there. You have a safe trip, now. I love you a bunch."

"I love you, too, mama," Joy says. "It's a strange world, isn't it?"

"It's a fast ride and a bumpy one," Karla says. "Don't break your neck. Enjoy it if you can."

"I'll do my best," Joy says. "Thanks, ma. Thank you for everything."

"What everything? I gave you nothing but bad memories," Karla says with tears in her eyes.

"You gave me all you had to give. You gave me my life."

"Well, you're welcome. I hope it's been mostly a good one. Or will be, from now on."

"It will, Ma. Truly, I can't thank you enough."

"Oh, honey. Please, don't. I named you Joy, but when I look at you, the joy is mine."

The doorbot closes the door with a little sigh, and the girl is gone. Karla looks out the window for her rental car, but the parking lot's on the opposite side of the building. Turtle Lodge Butte is ugly as ever with its radio towers, eroding but good to last another million years.

# ABOUT THE AUTHOR

BOB ROSS GREW UP IN AINSWORTH, NEBRASKA, during the 1950s and early 1960s. He remembers stifling car rides to "the ranch" as a small boy, when he rode backwards, kneeling on the front seat, to avoid getting carsick. Later, in the 1970s, that same small ranch became a refuge during a time of psychological re-orientation.

Besides eight years in the cattle business, which he was never good at, he has garnered a Master's in Fine Arts and taught at a number of universities, finishing with a 20-year stint teaching Freshman Composition in San Antonio, Texas. He has earned a fellowship at the Fine Arts Work Center in Province-town and has received an NEA grant, and has published a book of poems, a book of essays (with a collaborator), and a book of fiction, *Billy Above the Roofs*, published in 2021 by Stephen F. Austin State University Press. He is married to Janice Miller, a professional test developer, and lives half the year in San Antonio and half in northern Nebraska, near the town where he was born.